# The Deadly Dying

# The Deadly Dying

by

Hawthorne Vance

**Copyright:**

©2007 USA by Edward V. Smith III



**Published 2007 by:**
KiwE Publishing, Ltd.
Spokane, Washington
http://www.kiwepublishing.com

**Library of Congress Control Number:** 2007926745

**ISBN:** 978-1-933973-03-6

**Printed in the U.S.A.**

*To Nikki,
whose steadfast support
makes my life whole.*

# Preface

One hundred years ago Joseph Conrad wrote The Secret Agent. The book was about anarchists and terrorists in London around the turn of the past century. The book contains the following:

"On the other side of the fireplace, in the horse-hair armchair where Mrs. Verloc's mother was generally privileged to sit, Karl Yundt giggled grimly, with a faint grimace of a toothless mouth. The terrorist, as he called himself, was old and bald, with a narrow, snow-white wisp of a goatee hanging limply from his chin. An extraordinary expression of underhand malevolence survived in his extinguished eyes. When he arose painfully the thrusting forward of a skinny groping hand deformed by gouty swellings suggested the effort of a moribund murderer summoning the remaining strength for a last stab. He leaned on a thick stick, which trembled under his hand.

'I have always dreamed,' he mouthed, fiercely, 'of a band of men resolute in their resolve to discard all scruples in the choice of means, strong enough to give themselves the name of destroyers, and free from the taint of that resigned pessimism which rots the world. No pity for anything on earth, including themselves, and death enlisted for all good and service of humanity — that's what I would have liked to see.'"

One would think today that Karl Yundt's dream had come true. Society is currently engaged in a battle between men who disregard all scruples and those who seek goodness and service for humanity.

Those with no scruples are not limited to a few Middle Eastern men between eighteen and thirty. Included among those with no scruples are the stalkers, the rapists, the robbers, the murderers, and the identity thieves. Thank God, there are those who oppose the evil doers. Thank God, there are those who will lay down their lives for the sake of goodness and freedom.

There will always be a place in American literature for the hero who stands up against evil wherever he or she might encounter it. There will always be a place in American literature for the ordinary person, who in extraordinary times, finds the strength and will to rise to the occasion.

# Chapter One

*Conrad Dellifield IV brushed his silver hair until not one strand was out of place.* He checked his teeth in the mirror, and adjusted the Windsor knot on his tie. He straightened the vest on his tailor made blue pin striped suit. He carefully placed the American flag pin in the left lapel of his suit coat. Conrad Dellifield IV, at age sixty-two, had reached the pinnacle of his career as a probate and trust lawyer.

It had not been easy to get where he was today. He was born with a fancy name, but into a family with nothing else. His father had deserted his mother when he was seven years old. His mother had gone to work to support herself and her only son in an era when most women stayed at home. Conrad had compensated for his lonely existence as a child by making up grandiose tales for his classmates. He became so good at his story telling that his teachers in elementary school would go to the teacher's lounge while Conrad regaled the class with his made up stories. It was a given that Conrad would become a lawyer.

With the help his mother could give, he worked his way through undergraduate school, becoming president of his class. He managed to join a fraternity and earn enough money part-time to pay his dues. He was a good student and got a full scholarship to law school where he also excelled. It had been hard, but Conrad had it made. He had a beautiful wife and three children, each successful in his or her own right. If you had a tough trust or probate matter in Dallas, Texas, one man to call was Conrad. He respected other lawyers and they respected him.

This was how Conrad came to be appointed by Judge Radford Rice to be the administrator of the Estate of Helga Brandenberg, deceased. Helga Brandenberg had come to the United States from Germany shortly after World War II. She had built a highly successful cosmetics business, and had sold it when she was sixty-seven years old. She retired to a high-rise apartment in the Turtle Creek area of Dallas. Eight years after selling her business she was found dead in her apartment, an apparent suicide. She had left no will. Judge Rice had appointed Conrad as administrator of her estate to collect her assets, pay her debts, and determine her heirs for the purpose of receiving her estate.

Conrad had accepted the appointment believing it to be a routine probate matter. He was soon to learn that this would be anything but a routine matter. Before this case was resolved he would have to rely on everything he had learned in the last thirty-seven years of law practice. As much as it disturbed him, he would also have to depend upon one of his least favorite clients, Akard McCoy private eye.

# Chapter Two

*Helga Brandenberg was born in Munich, Germany in 1927.* She came from a prominent family and was well educated. The Second World War had not been hard on her family while Germany was winning. The family had done well financially during the war because of their interests in the chemical industry. Helga's father and her uncle owned a chemical company that developed synthetic fuel. When the German war machine was running low on petroleum products, Helga's family stepped in and prospered.

After the war was over the family suffered great hardship, but managed to gain back some of its fortune in later years. Helga left Munich in 1951 and against the wishes of her family came to the United States. She secured a job in New York City with a major cosmetic company working in research. Her educational background in chemistry suited her for the job.

Helga was good looking, a fact that did not go unnoticed by men at her place of employment. She was a slender blond with curves in all the right places. She advanced through the ranks in the research department at a rapid rate in spite of her less than flawless use of the English language. Some people said it was because she was smart. Others said that she could do things with her body that men could only dream about. She was a very private person and kept the secret to her advancement to herself.

Helga did not like the cold of Munich, and she didn't like the cold of New York City in the wintertime. She liked to ski in Vermont. As a child and young girl she had skied in Switzerland. Her summer vacations were spent in warm climates such as Florida. She liked to get a suntan. She liked the way men looked at her when she wore the early two -piece bathing suits.

A few years passed, and she got the opportunity to be the assistant director of research and product development of a new company plant opening in Dallas, Texas. In the early 1960's Dallas was growing, and the climate suited a young woman who liked to get a tan and show off her body. By this time Helga was in her mid-thirties. She was unmarried, but it was said that she did not lack male companionship.

A single woman with a good income could afford to travel. Yearly Helga would go back to Germany. When she visited her mother, Helga would go to Paris and buy herself a new wardrobe. Helga would leave her old clothes in Germany to be given to her cousins. She would bring the new clothes back with her after she had sewn the labels from the old clothes into the new ones. She had them cleaned before she came back and somehow was never bothered by U.S. Customs.

Helga liked Mont Blanc fountain pens. She would buy one or two every time she came to Munich. She never tired of seeing the Glockenspiel chime the hour at 11:00 am. The intricate figures circling in the tower at the Munich City Hall always amused her. She liked the Hofbrauhaus. The crowded beer garden appealed to her earthy side. Her cultured side preferred not to see over-served men urinating in the street outside the building, but that was the price she paid for this annual diversion.

She liked to stroll with her mother in the Englischer Garden. They both enjoyed the Japanese Tea House in the park. She loved Munich and Germany, but not enough to give up the warm climate of Texas. For two weeks every year she was a German. She spoke German, she ate and drank German and she looked German.

In Dallas, she resided in a high-rise on Turtle Creek. Turtle Creek winds through the old part of Highland Park, and then heads south toward downtown Dallas. On the west side of the creek, luxury high-rise apartments stand like rows of corn. They cry out to the average guy and gal, "You have to be rich to live here." In the summer hard bodied young women jog by the high rise monoliths wearing as little as the law allows. Dowagers wearing broad brimmed straw hats, long sleeved blouses and sunshades walk their small, well-groomed dogs. In the winter they do the same thing, they just wear more clothes. In the spring and fall they just enjoy the best weather Dallas has to offer.

Chauffeur-driven dark cars pull in and out of the driveways to the buildings. Doormen open car doors and help the dowagers unload the day's shopping haul. Just a short distance away is the Crescent Court with its shops and upscale restaurants. Further south, in the downtown area the flagship store of Neiman-Marcus caters to the denizens' every need.

This was the atmosphere in which Helga lived and died. She saved her money and invested wisely. She got venture capital that allowed her to start her own business. Her company had made her rich. How rich, no one knew for sure. Wealth did not buy her friends, nor did it buy her love. Sex did not equal love. Sometimes Helga would get the two confused. Most of the time, she was well aware that she had traded fortune for loving companionship.

Her only faithful companions were her wiener dogs Fritz and Helmut. They never left her side. They slept on her bed at night. The only time she was away from them was her annual trip to Germany. After she sold her business in the mid 1990's, the dogs helped fight the loneliness. There were people in the building she had a speaking acquaintance with, but she had no real, close friends. But for the barking of the dogs, Helga's body might not have been discovered until the weekly visit by her maid.

# Chapter Three

The barking dogs had alerted the neighbors on the twentieth floor that something was wrong. Security was called and a uniformed guard knocked at the door only to get no response. The guard called the maintenance man and he removed the door to the apartment. Inside the barking dogs gradually retreated to the bedroom where Helga lay at the foot of the bed. One arm was hanging off of the bed and several inches from her hand lay an empty pill canister. A half-empty quart bottle of vodka was sitting on the night stand. A short distance from the pill canister was a tube of lipstick. Written on the vanity mirror in a shaky, downward scrawl was the German word, "schlecht."

The rest of the apartment was neat except for the kitchen. Dirty dishes were in the sink. The remains of a meal were scattered around the floor of the kitchen table. It looked as though the dogs had helped themselves to what might have been a dinner or lunch. The closets were perfectly arranged. Garments were grouped according to color. The clothes were expensive. Several pieces of Cartier jewelry were in plain sight.

"Get the manager up here," the security man said.

Sherman Counts, the manager, arrived shortly. He was dressed in a natty double-breasted black suit, accompanied by a silver tie.

"Call the police," Sherman said to the security man.

"For God's sake, put that door back where it belongs," Sherman yelled at the maintenance man.

"See that the dogs are taken care of," Sherman said to no one in particular.

As an after thought he added, "Don't anybody touch anything until the police get here."

Several of the residents of the twentieth floor were peeking into the apartment. Sherman told them to go back to their apartments. He explained that Helga had passed away and that arrangements would be made for the removal of her body. Before they left he inquired of each if anybody knew anything about Helga's family. The other residents were of little help. One neighbor lady said that she had been told by Helga that Helga's mother had died several years before. She thought that Helga had some cousins who still lived in Germany.

Sherman wished to himself that someone would take this untidy mess off of his hands. After all, his job was to dress neatly and kiss old ladies' asses all day. A plain- clothes detective, a uniformed policeman and someone from the coroner's office showed up at Helga's apartment. The plain-clothes guy was named Patterson. He was near fifty, medium height and bald. His blue eyes were watery and without expression. He was sweating. This was not unusual because Texas is hot even in the springtime. He was still sweating in spite of the air conditioning, making his rumpled suit stick to his shirt, which in turn was stuck to his body.

"What's happened?" asked Patterson.

"We found her here when the neighbors complained of the dogs barking," Sherman dutifully replied.

Patterson stood over her body wiping the sweat from his face with his handkerchief. The handkerchief was no match for the perspiration, and it was becoming damper with each stroke across his forehead. "Looks to me like she took the last train to Drugville. Who is her next of kin?" Patterson asked to no one in particular.

"She had no one but the two dogs," Sherman said.

"When you're through here, take the body to the morgue," Patterson said to the medical examiner.

Patterson pulled a notebook out of his breast pocket and started making notes with his sweaty hand. He asked the neighbors about Helga's habits and friends. He kept drawing blanks. The neighbors had seen her around the pool in earlier years. She always wore fewer clothes at the pool than befitted her age. The women reluctantly admitted that Helga still had the body to wear the skimpy two-piece suits, at the time. In recent years, she had been almost a recluse. Most of her food was brought in. She did walk her dogs. When spoken to, she usually only nodded.

Patterson and his associates left. An ambulance took her body away. Sherman was told to lock the apartment until a representative could be appointed for her estate. One of the neighbors offered to care for the two dogs.

Sherman locked the apartment. It was very untidy having someone take her own life in his swanky digs. "Oh well, no one knew her anyway," Sherman said to himself. Someone would buy the apartment in due course. The courts would appoint someone to act on behalf of the estate if she did not have a will naming an executor.

People had died in the complex before. Those people had friends and relatives. There was someone there to take care of things. Rich people don't leave dangling participles like no will, no relatives and no friends. The whole situation was just damned inconvenient. Probably, before long, some smart-ass lawyer would be coming by trying to give orders. "He can just piss off," Sherman said under his breath.

# Chapter Four

Judge Radford Rice sat in his chambers. Across from him sat Conrad Dellifield IV. Judge Rice, short and gray-bearded, looked over his desk at Dellifield with his reading glasses perched at the end of his nose. Dellifield looked around the office that he had visited a hundred times before. Judge Rice was a loner and did not court the favor of lawyers, even in election years. He was eight years older than Dellifield. Both men had a mutual respect for each other, even though they did not socialize.

"I wanted to talk to you about the Brandenberg case," Judge Rice said to Dellifield.

"What about the case, your Honor?"

"I got a call from a lawyer in Germany yesterday. He spoke perfect English. He wanted to know when his clients would get their money."

"You just appointed me as administrator last week. I have not had a chance to get a handle on the assets. All the papers in her apartment are written in German."

Judge Rice nodded, "I gave him your name. His name is Hans Grueber. I told him to call you."

"Thanks a lot. I am going to have to spend some of the estate's money and get a translator to look at the papers in the apartment. I think I'll call the language department at S.M.U."

"Do what you have to. You're the administrator. If I didn't think you could handle the matter effectively, I would not have appointed you."

With that admonition, the silver-maned lawyer bid the judge good day and headed for the high rise on Turtle Creek to gather more information from Helga's apartment. The high rise was less than ten minutes from the Records Building that houses the Dallas County probate courts. It was the first of April and the azaleas were beginning to bloom along Turtle Creek. The bushes are large and flaming pink blooms mingled with white ones, giving the area a brilliant blast of color.

Conrad always enjoyed the drive. He went this route to his office because the drive from Highland Park to downtown Dallas via Turtle Creek was much more relaxing than the faster, but sterile Dallas Tollway. April and October make Dallas bearable. May through September can be sweltering. In April one can drive along some of the city freeways and see the wild flowers that Lady Bird Johnson was instrumental in getting planted. October brings the welcome cool air that summer had deprived the residents of enjoying.

Conrad pulled up to the door of the high rise. The valet parker met him and let him out of the silver Mercedes. Conrad checked in at the desk and headed for the twentieth floor. When he opened the door to the apartment, it seemed as if something was different from the last time he was there. He had stacked many of Helga's personal papers on the kitchen table, but now, somehow, the stacks did not look the same. In particular, her personal diary, which was written in German, seemed to be out of place. Conrad made a mental note that he was going to have the diary translated.

He walked into the bedroom where Helga had died. No one had touched anything. As the administrator of her estate, it was his job to look after things, and he should have seen that the place was cleaned up. "I must be getting old," he said to himself.

Conrad stared at the vanity mirror, which still bore the word "schlecht." He had bought a German-English dictionary because of the numerous papers in the apartment written in German, even though he knew that the task of translating was beyond his abilities. "Schlecht" in German means "bad." Perhaps, that was how things were going in Helga's life and that was why she ended it.

The more Conrad stared at the word written on the mirror, the more he looked at the word, the more something seemed wrong. He went back into the kitchen and got Helga's diary. He looked at the writing in the diary and then looked at the writing on the mirror. They did not look the same.

Conrad was a probate lawyer. In his almost forty years of practice he had tried many will contests. In some of them the authenticity of the decedent's handwriting had been in question. Although he was not a handwriting expert, he had examined and cross -examined enough experts in court to have a good understanding of the handwriting comparison. He looked at the diary and then looked at the mirror over and over again. His conclusion: Either Helga did not write "Schlecht" on the mirror or she did not write her diary.

The medical examiner had determined her death was a suicide. She had enough Ambien in her body to put an elephant to sleep. She was 80 years old. She was lonely. Besides that, who would want to kill her? The police were satisfied. Why should Conrad complicate this estate? He had her kinfolk in Germany to worry about. Still, there was plenty of money in the estate to spend a little on investigation. It might be nothing. On the other hand, if someone had killed Helga, he had the duty to pursue a wrongful death action to recover damages on behalf of her estate. The thought pained him, but he might just call Akard McCoy, private detective.

# Chapter Five

*Four doors from Helga's apartment, Jacob Franks drew deeply from* the oxygen canister that had become his constant companion. Somehow, there was irony in the fact that a doctor had smoked himself almost to death. He was barely mobile and he was tethered to a long tube that allowed him to walk around his apartment. He could get out, but only the assistance of the life-sustaining bottle that fit into the wheeled cradle that he pulled along after him.

"That damned lawyer is upstairs snooping around," he said to himself. "So what? Let him snoop all day. He's not going to find out what happened or why it happened." Jacob chuckled. Even if someone were to find out, what could they do? That was the beauty of the whole plan. All of them are in the same boat. That was the plan. Punish those the law would not. If they get caught, it's no matter. Each of them would, in all likelihood, be dead before he could be punished. None of them had a family that would be embarrassed by what they planned to do. Let the lawyer snoop. It will not stop them from carrying out their plan.

Jacob Franks had been born Karl Frankel. He changed his name when he came to the United States. Like Helga, he had been born in Munich. Like Helga he had been a young boy when World War II began. Unlike Helga, he had been born Jewish. His parents did not belong to the National Socialist Party, as did Helga's. Helga's parents survived the war. His did not. They perished in a place just outside of Munich called Dachau. He almost died himself. Only his youth and his spirit helped him survive.

After the war, as a displaced person, he ultimately immigrated to Canada where he became a doctor. All of his close relatives died in concentration camps. He married, but he and his wife had no children. When his wife died at age fifty-two, Karl moved from Vancouver to Seattle and changed his name. He taught in the medical school at the University of Washington. When he retired he moved to the warmer climate of Dallas, Texas.

Like many doctors his age, Jacob had been a smoker. He would tell his patients about the danger of smoking, but he could not kick the habit himself. Now in his late seventies, he had lung cancer, and it was terminal. Somehow now his condition did not matter. In fact, now it was working out perfectly, according to their plan, Jacob's and the two others who were dying. They all lived in the same high rise on Turtle Creek. Who can punish a person who is going to die anyway? That was the plan. They would be the judge, the jury, and the executioner.

The plan was very simple. They, meaning Jacob, Bernie and Bill, would simply see that justice was done where it had previously been denied. Someone had done a terrible act and gotten away without any punishment. The public would sigh and think that God would make things right in the end. Why not help God out a little and serve as his avenging angels?

Bernard "Bernie" Pittsfield had prostate cancer. He had licked the disease fifteen years before. Now it had returned and there was little hope of his recovery. Bernie had been a banker. He started out as a loan officer. He was smart and had convinced a group of friends to invest with him in a small bank in Addison, Texas. At that time, Addison was a tiny suburb of Dallas.

The small bank was situated on what would become a major intersection. Several outlying banks in bedroom communities were acquired. As Dallas exploded so did the small, surrounding communities. The banks prospered. The land at the intersection in Addison became as valuable as the bank itself. Large out-of-state banks became suitors. They bid against each other. First Superior Bank won and Bernie became rich.

William "Bill" Arrington had a weak heart. He had been in the insurance business and at one time owned a successful agency. He had sold the company when his heart began to fail.

Jacob, Bernie and Bill shared several things in common. They all ended up living in the same high rise on Turtle Creek. None of them had any close family. All were in some phase of dying. Each of them had a searing hate for people they believed had gotten away with some sort of evil that went unpunished.

The idea had come to them a few months earlier. They were sitting in Bill's apartment watching Court TV. A trial ended with a finding that the defendant was not guilty. As they discussed the verdict Bernie said, "Wouldn't it be nice if someone killed that guy? Someone who had nothing to lose."

The three men looked at each other for a moment. Bill broke the silence, "We have nothing to lose. We are all dead men anyway. We could do something like that."

"We could. We really could," Bernie replied.

"And I know just the person," Said Jacob.

Bill and Bernie stared at Jacob for some time. Neither said anything for what seemed an eternity. Finally, Bernie asked, "Who?"

"Helga Brandenberg," Jacob replied. His voice was deliberate and his gaze was like ice.

# Chapter Six

*Conrad Dellifield IV stared at his phone. The police had determined* that the death of Helga Brandenberg was a suicide. His job was to administer her estate, not solve a crime, if in fact a crime had even been committed. Still, "Schlecht" written on the mirror was not in Helga's writing. He was sure of that. He did have the duty to pursue a wrongful death claim.

He picked up the phone and dialed the number of Akard McCoy, private detective. Conrad had a love-hate relationship with Akard. Akard was a sometime client. Akard was also a huge pain in the ass. The preceding year Akard had received some acclaim by bringing a terrorist cell in Milan to justice. Akard's girl was the best looking woman that Conrad had ever seen. Her set of 37D's had not gone to waste on Conrad's eyes even though he was a distinguished lawyer in his sixties.

After three rings, Akard answered.

"Akard, Conrad Dellifield."

"What an honor to hear from the Barrister."

"Thanks for your kind words. I may have a job for you."

"You mean, like in a paying job?"

"Exactly."

"When do you want to see me?"

"Whenever you can leave that 'rat hole' you call an office and come to a civilized place like mine."

"No, you come to the rat hole."

"If you want the job, you will be in my office in thirty minutes."

"You win. I'll be there in fifteen minutes."

"Glad you understand the terms of working together."

It was only fifteen minutes from the office of Akard McCoy in Deep Ellum west on Elm Street to the First Superior Bank skyscraper. The fifteen minutes changed the scenery from Akard's office in an old electric motor rewind shop with a loft apartment upstairs to the sixty- story office of Dellifield, Lockout & Cash Attorneys and Counselors at law.

Akard's office consisted of a card table with two plastic chairs, a refrigerator filled with beer looked after by the twenty-two pound "One-Eyed Cat" and Clarence, the English bulldog. It had not been that long ago when the cat and dog had saved Akard's life from terrorist intruders. "One-Eyed Cat" had left his perch from atop the refrigerator to land on one man's head, firmly planting one of his huge paws in the man's eye, blinding him. Clarence had taken a part of the other man's calf away. But for the heroics of the two animals, Akard would be dead. He suitably rewarded them by affixing small hero metals to their respective collars.

The garage was at the rear of the old building. It housed Akard's vintage Taurus and the antique Jaguar XKE , which had been left to Akard by his grandfather. It was April. And not yet hot enough in Dallas to overheat the XKE. The drive was fifteen minutes. Akard opted to take the Jag.

The old Jag started on the first crank. The starter button was located on the dash. Akard had splurged on a new black leather interior and a new red lacquer paint job. Akard loved the smell of leather. Sometimes he went over to the Galleria to the Church's shoe store just to smell the new shoes. Akard's girlfriend Corrine, whom he called Zelda-Corrine, thought this was weird. She thought a lot of things that Akard did were weird.

It was ten-thirty in the morning. The rush hour traffic was over, but traffic in downtown Dallas was never light. The old Jag's 275 horses purred like its namesake, the jungle cat. In less than ten minutes Akard was parked at the fifth level of the underground parking lot of the First Superior Bank building. He remembered that the coffee in Dellifield's office, even though served by a white-coated waiter, tasted terrible. He stopped in the underground shopping area of the building at Starbuck's and purchased a grande butterscotch latte.

Akard took the elevator to the upper levels of the First Superior Bank building. The elevator opened to the offices of Dellifield, Lockout & Cash. It only took one glance to tell that unless you had a lot of money, there was no way you could be a client of this bunch. Akard was a client only because his grandfather had been a prominent Dallas attorney. The trust fund he had left for Akard allowed him to practice his profession of private investigator with marginal success. Akard was always trying to get Dellifield to break the terms of the trust. Akard wanted principal from the trust. To get it, he had to get a law degree. Akard having been kicked out of law school ten years before, getting to the principal of the trust seemed unlikely.

The receptionist was dressed in a tailored suit and spoke with an English accent. The top button of her silk blouse was unbuttoned revealing some nice cleavage.

"May I help you sir," the receptionist said in clipped tones.

"Akard McCoy, to see Mr. Dellifield."

"Excuse me, Sir, did you say, Akard? Like the street three blocks away?"

"Yes, spelled A K A R D, just like the street."

"I am from England and I haven't met anyone named after a street."

"My father lost his virginity at a whorehouse when Akard Street was the home of the red light district. If you had ever seen the family coat of arms, you would never forget it.'"

"I can well imagine. I am terribly sorry that I asked."

The conversation was interrupted by the appearance of Conrad Dellifield IV. Dellifield was wearing a three-piece blue, chalk-striped suit. The suit was accented by a white on white French cuffed shirt and patterned Hermes tie. In contrast, Akard was wearing a pair of wrinkled cargo pants and a Dallas Stars T-shirt he had purchased at Target.

"Akard, good to see you," Dellifield said in his usual condescending tone. "I see you brought your own coffee. Step down to my office. I have something to discuss with you that I think you will find interesting."

Akard followed Dellifield down the paneled hallway, noting that the prints of caricatures of English barristers and Judges had not changed since his last visit. The corner office was occupied by Dellifield. It was a large office containing a massive desk as well as a conference table surrounded by six overstuffed leather chairs. The walls were filled with certificates from the Texas State Bar, the American Bar Association and the American College of Trust and Estate Counsel. Various tables and shelves contained pictures of Dellifield with people of importance including the current President of the United States.

"Are you keeping busy?" Dellifield asked.

"I can always stand more business," Akard replied.

"Let me tell you about a situation involving an estate I am administering." Dellifield then told Akard about Helga Brandenberg; the circumstances surrounding her death and his concern over the difference between the writing on the mirror and on her personal papers.

"This sounds like a matter for the police," Akard said.

"The police have determined that it was a suicide and have no interest in pursuing the matter further," replied Dellifield.

"Maybe they're smarter than you think."

"That is not the issue. They have a suicide ruling. They have no suspects. They have more unsolved murders than they can handle. They have no motivation."

Akard considered what he had heard. This was a chance to make some money that did not involve window peeping in divorce actions. Dellifield would pay him whether he found anything or not. It was just as important to prove that there was no wrongful death as to prove there was foul play.

"You say that the stiff was German?" Akard asked.

"The deceased was of German descent — AKARD!"

"If her papers are in German, I will need to have them translated. I may find something that will indicate why someone would have wanted her dead. I can get someone from S.M.U. or the University of North Texas. You pick up the tab. I can go to work now."

"I want you to start now. Try to be a little more civilized when you are dealing with German speaking individuals."

"I can treat Krauts with the same respect I treat everyone."

"That is exactly what I am afraid of. Get to work before I change my mind."

As Akard left the office the receptionist purred "Goodbye." This time the second button on her blouse was unbuttoned.

# Chapter Seven

*Akard headed the Jag toward the Oak Lawn area of Dallas where* his girlfriend, Zelda-Corrine, owned a part interest in a fitness center. Akard was hoping that Zelda-Corrine would know a German professor from one of the area universities. Zelda-Corrine taught a women's self-defense course on Wednesday nights. Perhaps one of her students would have a connection with a person knowledgeable in German.

It was 11:30 in the morning when Akard pulled up to the fitness center. Zelda-Corrine was in her leotard, displaying the tickets that first caught Akard's attention. Akard suggested lunch. Zelda-Corrine would be ready after a shower and change of clothes. Within a short time she was ready. She emerged from the locker room wearing a blue light-weight sweater and navy slacks. Sweaters were made for Zelda-Corrine in the same way that they were made for Demi Moore.

"I hope you don't mind that I am not wearing any make-up," she said.

"I can stand to be around you when you are not wearing anything," Akard replied.

"You have a one track mind."

"I can't help it. You just do that to me."

Zelda-Corrine sighed. "I guess someday I will be arrested for contributing to the delinquency of a pervert."

Akard smiled. "As punishment for my behavior, I will take you to a soup and salad joint instead of heading to Mama's Daughter's place to get a chicken fried steak. Actually, I have something serious to talk to you about."

Zelda-Corrine reluctantly got into the old Jag. She had been in it on more than one occasion when it had quit. Usually it was at a time of day when it backed up traffic for blocks.

The fitness center in Oak Lawn was situated in the gay community. Thousands of gay men lived in that area. Akard felt that he would get more admiring glances than Zelda-Corrine at the soup and salad place known as the Wilde Oscar's. Nevertheless he wanted to show Zelda-Corrine that he could be as tolerant as the next guy.

On a warm sunny day, the guys were crowded together in front of the Wilde Oscar's eating in the open-air area. Akard got out of the Jag, and, like a gentleman, opened the door for Zelda-Corrine and helped her to her feet. He grabbed her hand. "I want the boys to know that I'm with you."

Much to Akard's surprise, the men in the restaurant paid no attention to him. Zelda-Corrine held back a smirk.

"Do you know anyone who speaks German?" Akard asked.

"There is a woman who teaches German at a local high school in one my fitness classes."

"Do you think she could do some translation for me? 'Smoothmouth' is paying"

"What are you doing for Mr. Dellifield? I didn't think he liked you."

"He tolerates me. He is involved in a case where he believes that an apparent suicide was murder. The D.B. was a German. She left behind some papers written in German and Smoothmouth wants me to check it out."

"I am not sure I want anyone I know to get involved with you. I accept the fact that you are a child in a linebacker's body. I don't like the idea of unleashing you on an innocent school teacher."

"Let me be the judge of her innocence."

"That is what I am afraid of."

"Call her, will you?"

"OK."

Akard and Zelda-Corrine finished their meal and Akard dropped her off at the fitness center. He headed south to the high-rise on Turtle Creek. When he arrived, he pulled the red Jag up to the front of the building. He dismissed the attendant at the door and said that he would park the car himself. The attendant gave Akard a look of disdain as he was being enveloped in a cloud of blue smoke from the ancient Jag.

Akard parked the car and presented himself at the security desk of the high-rise. He introduced himself and explained that he was in the employ of Mr. Dellifield. The security guard told Akard that he had been apprised of that fact by Mr. Dellifield. He handed Akard a key to Helga Brandenberg's apartment.

Akard took the elevator to the twentieth floor. As he walked to the Brandenberg apartment he sensed that a door down the hall was slightly ajar and that someone was looking at him. He walked directly to the door and it shut just before he got there. He knocked loudly on the door and an elderly man with an oxygen tube in his nose answered the knock.

"Excuse me, I am looking for Helga Brandenberg's apartment," Akard said.

"Who wants to know?" the elderly man wheezed.

"I work for the attorney who is taking care of her estate."

"What are you going to do in there?"

"Look, Pal, I'm here to do an inventory of the assets in the apartment, I'm not here to play twenty questions."

"2020," the old man said as he slammed his door.

Akard walked down the hall to apartment 2020, opened the door, and went inside. The sunny day had begun to turn dark. In Texas, a sunny April day can suddenly become dark and thunderstorms and hail can come on with great ferocity. This was going to be one of those days. Akard wondered if he had rolled up the windows on the Jag or if the hail would damage the red lacquer paint job. Then he remembered that he had parked the car in the garage beneath the building.

The wind began to howl and the rain started lashing against the windows that looked out at the skyline of downtown Dallas. The whole scene took on Gothic proportions. The screaming wind whipping around the building conjured an image of Helga Brandenberg crying out to find her murderer, if, indeed, one existed. Even for a brave man like Akard the situation caused him to shudder.

He shook off the uncomfortable feeling and went about his work. He sorted through papers and noted that they were in German. He looked at the clothes in her closet and saw that she wore a size six. He looked at the few photographs in various albums and noticed how Helga aged through the years. In her day, she had been a great looking woman. Akard could not help but wonder what it would have been like to have sex with her when she was young. He caught himself and remembered what Zelda-Corrine had said about him being a pervert. He started acting like the trained detective that he was and carefully studied the contents of the apartment. It became clear to him that he needed the translator to figure out the papers written in German. He would be back when he had one.

As Akard left he thought he saw the elderly man's door ajar again. Writing it off as just a curious old man with nothing to do, Akard left the building to go to his office.

The telephone rang in Bill's apartment. It was Jacob.

"Get Bernie and come up here now," the voice said.

"Why?"

"Just do it, its important."

"Well, alright"

Within five minutes Bill and Bernie had joined Jacob in his apartment.

"So, what is so important?" Bill asked.

"There was a guy snooping around Helga's place. He said he worked for the lawyer, but he looked like a cop to me," Jacob said.

"What does a cop look like?" Bernie asked.

"This one is in his thirties; he's about 6'3" and weighs close to two-forty, Jacob replied.

"What was he wearing?" Bill asked.

"He had on a Dallas Stars T-Shirt," Jacob said.

"Unless he had on a suit and showed you a badge, I for one am going to forget it," Bill said. "Besides that when I have more time, I would like to discuss our next project," Bill said as he walked toward the door.

# Chapter Eight

*T*he *telephone rang at six-thirty the next morning in Akard's* combination office-living quarters. It was Zelda-Corrine. Normally, she would not have to call because she would have been in the bed with him, either at her place or his. But last night she had a night class at the fitness center teaching women self-defense. She was tired and told Akard to amuse himself without her. This was one of the few nights that One-Eyed Cat and Clarence, the English bull dog, had gotten to sleep in bed with Akard because Zelda-Corrine was allergic to cat dander. As it was, he would have to change the sheets and put the boys downstairs if he expected Zelda-Corrine to enter his bedroom again.

"You don't have that damn dog and cat in bed with you, do you?"

"Of course not. They are just animals, not bed mates."

About that time, Clarence gave out a loud moan. "Busted," Akard said.

Zelda-Corrine, trying hard to control herself said, "Change the sheets and I will use my allergy medicine and MAYBE I will see you again."

Akard, choosing his words carefully, said, "I'm on my way to the washing machine, and the boys are on their way downstairs."

Zelda-Corrine continued, "The reason I called was to tell you that Nell Munson, the German teacher, can work for you after school today. She is good looking so I am coming too. We will meet you in the lobby of the high-rise. She said her fee will be twenty-five dollars per hour."

"In order of importance, two women are always better than one unless you get into an argument. I will meet you there at 5:30. Smoothmouth is probably getting at least $400 per hour so $25 per sounds pretty modest. Meet me at Mama's for breakfast."

"I will meet you in one hour. Take a shower and leave the cat hair at home."

Other than the facts that Zelda-Corrine was the most beautiful woman he had ever seen, was sensuous, a Black Belt in Karate and put up with his act, Akard wondered what he saw in her. When he was through pondering, Akard put the sheets in the washer, took the boys downstairs, showered, put on his jeans and Willie Nelson T-shirt and thought about what he wanted for breakfast. Before leaving, he looked in his filing cabinet at his Beretta Model 92 and decided that he would not need it today.

Akard decided against taking the old Jag and instead drove his 1997 Taurus. He headed to the Mama's Daughter's Diner on Irving Blvd. In route, Akard pondered his life and planned what he would have for breakfast. His professional life was hit and miss, ranging from contacts with the F.B.I. to photographing straying spouses in compromising situations. He had a beautiful girl friend and two devoted pets. He had a trust fund set up by his grandfather, which allowed him to continue his unsuccessful private investigation business. He thought he would have two eggs over medium, biscuits, ham and a side order of grits. He would ask for honey to go on the biscuits instead of the small packages of pseudo jelly.

The drive from Deep Ellum to Mama's was short, so his contemplation was likewise short-lived. When he got to the restaurant, Zelda Corrine was standing in front. She was wearing a salmon colored top with black pants. She greeted Akard with a peck on the cheek. He put his arm around her waist and they went in to dine.

"So why do you need someone to translate German?" Zelda-Corrine asked.

"Smoothmouth thinks someone may have knocked off this old lady because there is some handwriting in German in lipstick on a mirror that does not look like her regular handwriting."

"Don't talk with your mouth full."

"Yes, mother."

"If I am your mother you know what that makes you."

"I will not go there, thank you. Anyway I am going to make a few bucks chasing this rabbit. Smoothmouth is particularly interested in her diary which is written in German, hence my need for a translator."

"What is so important about the poor woman's diary?"

"I don't know. I suspect it may tell us something about her past or if she might have been afraid of someone."

"Why not leave this to the police?"

"The police have other things to do. Smoothmouth feels that he has an obligation to her estate and heirs to find out the truth for sure. I can always use employment, so I am not going to argue with him."

"Do you ever call Mr. Dellifield 'Smoothmouth' to his face?"

"Only when I'm intoxicated."

"Better stay sober for a while. I need to get to work."

"I will see you at 5:30 at the high-rise. Does Nell know how the get there?"

"Yes, she does. You can call her Miss Munson. Bye."

Zelda-Corrine gave Akard a peck on the forehead and left. Akard noticed two things as she left. The first was that every man in the restaurant was staring at her. The second was that he was stuck with the check again.

# Chapter Nine

*A*t *five-thirty, Akard arrived at the high-rise. The same doorman* gave him the same look of contempt, particularly this time since he was driving the vintage Taurus instead of the red Jag. He parked the car himself and went inside. Waiting in the lobby were Zelda-Corrine and a pretty blond about the same age as Zelda-Corrine. Akard reminded himself that this was business, not of the monkey variety. Zelda-Corrine introduced Nell to Akard and they exchanged inanities.

Akard led the ladies to the twentieth floor. When he was unlocking the door, it again seemed that the elderly gentleman down the hall was spying on them. Akard ignored the old man and ushered the women into the apartment. He showed Nell where the various stacks of papers were and began his own quest for liquor. He found that the bar was well stocked.

"How about a toddy for the body?" Akard asked.

"Water for me," Nell said.

"Same here," said Zelda -Corrine.

"Fitness freaks," Akard said under his breath.

Akard produced three glasses, which he filled with bottled water from the refrigerator in the bar. His water was mixed with Scotch.

Nell proposed a plan. First, she would look through each stack of paper. She would separate the important looking papers from the trivial. Zelda-Corrine would make a list of the important papers. Akard would drink his Scotch and keep his hands to himself. Akard was about to take the remark personally when he reminded himself of the fact that he could watch two beautiful women work while he drank and earned a hundred bucks an hour. After all, he was a college graduate with almost one year of law school. That was before he had been dismissed from law school ten years previously.

About two hours into the project, Akard ordered pizza. He went down to the security desk and picked it up. When he got off the elevator, he thought he saw the old man dragging his oxygen canister behind him. It looked as if he had a stethoscope hanging out of his pants' pocket. The thought crossed his mind that the old man may have been listening at the door.

As Akard entered the apartment the women said in unison, "Guess what?"

"What?" Akard replied.

"There is a lock box at the Deutsche-Bayern Bank in Munich," Zelda-Corrine said excitedly. "Nell found the papers."

"Is there an inventory that will tell us what is in the box?" Akard asked.

"No. I can only tell you that the lock box is in Munich and that she would go to the box when she visited Germany," Nell said.

"This information will be helpful to the lawyer, but I don't know that it will shed any light on the circumstances of her death," Akard replied.

Akard suggested that they eat the pizza before if got cold and continue the conversation while they ate. The women were also agreeable to the opening of a bottle of red wine.

"I guess Smoothmouth won't care about wasting some of the Estate's assets in a good cause," Akard said.

"Who is Smoothmouth?" Nell asked.

"Just ignore him," Zelda-Corrine said. "Smoothmouth happens to be Akard's name for the lawyer who is paying for us to be here tonight. Well, paying for you guys anyway."

"I found some other things as well," Nell said. "There is a picture of a small girl with a man and a woman. They may be the deceased woman's parents. They are all well dressed. The man is in a suit. Around one of the sleeves on his suit coat is an armband with a swastika on it. There are also multiple photocopies of the front page of a Munich newspaper dated in March of 1944. There is a photograph of a tank and in the background is a shell pocked building. There was also an article from an old English newspaper that said that on November 27, 1944 the British R.A.F. dropped 12,000 pound bombs on Munich. It was the first time that these block-buster bombs had been used against a German city."

"Sounds to me like she may have had a little hostility in her craw about the war, but that was sixty-years ago," Akard said.

"Just because she kept these things doesn't mean that she was mad," replied Nell.

"You may be right," Akard said. "What about the diary?"

"That will take me a while to translate. I will have to get back with you in a few days," Nell replied.

"Let's see what else we can find," Zelda-Corrine said.

The apartment had two bedrooms. Nell was looking through one and Zelda-Corrine was looking through the other. Akard stayed with his drink and finished off the pizza. After about thirty minutes, Zelda-Corrine appeared wearing a low-cut, back dress, a diamond necklace and an expensive ring on four fingers of each hand.

"This dress is old and out of style, but it came from Paris," Zelda-Corrine gushed. "Look at these rocks."

"I assume that you are talking about the jewelry," Akard said.

"Wow," Nell said as she entered the room. "Where did you find that jewelry?"

"It was wrapped up in a towel at the bottom of her underwear drawer. Do we have to tell Mr. Dellifield?" Zelda-Corrine said.

Akard replied, "I do have some professional ethics."

"Let her have her fun, Akard. She is just kidding," Nell said. She continued, "I have an early day tomorrow. I'll take the diary with me and let you know what I find in a couple of days. I can find my way out." Nell picked up the diary and left.

When Nell had left, Akard approached Zelda-Corrine. She filled out every thread of the black dress. She looked like a woman who could wear that kind of jewelry well. He wished he could afford to give those kinds of trinkets to her. He kissed her and said, "Let's spend the night here."

"NO!" she replied. "The security people know we are here."

"Screw them," Akard said.

"I had rather not, but if that is what you want to do to me it is going to be at my place," she said tossing her auburn hair.

"You win. Change clothes and let me have the jewelry. I will take it to Smoothmouth in the morning."

They left the building arm and arm.

Shortly after they left, Jacob called Bill on the phone.

"Some people were in Helga's apartment. It was the same guy who was here yesterday. He had two women with him. I listened at the door as long as I could. One of the women is a German translator. I am sure that it is just a matter of time until they find out about Munich," Jacob gasped into the phone between draws of oxygen.

"Relax. Someone was bound to find out about Munich. That does not lead them to us. Maybe they can finish the job we can't do. Go to bed." Bill hung up the phone.

# Chapter Ten

*Life was always better when Akard awoke with Zelda-Corrine nestled* on his shoulder. She looked good asleep, her hair almost covering one eye, and her face shiny and clear of make up. Akard would marry her in a second. Zelda-Corrine, though thirty-three, felt no biological clock ticking. She had reservations about spending the rest of her life with a man who occasionally had a gun pointed at him. She had willingly faced death with him in the past when she went with him to Italy on a case that occurred a year before, but she was not sure she wanted to do that again. In the meantime she was content to drift with this hulk of a man who had once aspired to become a lawyer and now was a private eye.

Akard brushed her hair away from her eye and gently kissed her on the forehead. He reached under her pillow and removed the towel containing Helga Brandenberg's jewelry. Zelda-Corrine opened her eyes and looked at Akard. "Do we have to give it back?" she asked.

"Conrad Dellifield IV, Esquire, would not have it any other way," Akard said.

"You are certainly being formal this morning. What happened to Smoothmouth?"

"I'm afraid that I will call him that to his face and lose this great paying job."

Zelda-Corrine got out of bed and stretched. She touched her toes several times. Akard liked the show because Zelda-Corrine was buck-naked. She went into her closet and came out wearing her jogging suit.

"I am going to run four miles, come back, have some yogurt, and then go to work. Care to join me?" she asked.

"No, I am going home and feed the boys, shower and get some saturated fat in my diet. Then, I am going to call Dellifield and give him a report. I may even go to see him in person."

"Zelda-Corrine hugged him and nibbled his ear. "Call me this afternoon. Let's go to a movie tonight," she purred.

"It's a date," Akard lightly brushed her breast on his way out.

Akard stopped off at a McDonald's drive through and got two egg and cheese biscuits and a large coffee. He waited until he got back to his office in Deep Ellum so that he could share breakfast with his dog and cat. One-Eyed Cat and Clarence met him with a great showing of affection. Akard pondered if this was real or an attempt to get his egg biscuits. He ate his breakfast after pouring dry pet food topped with part of a biscuit into the boys' respective bowls.

"Gentlemen, let us ponder the situation," Akard said. Neither the dog nor the cat looked up from their bowls.

"Alright, let me ponder the situation. I have a case that probably should be left as is. On the other hand there are things that just do not add up. Consider, this gentlemen, I have a lock box in Munich. I have a photograph of a man wearing the symbol of Nazi Germany on his sleeve. There is a diary that is yet to be translated. Certainly enough to bring to the attention of the barrister, wouldn't you think so?"

The bulldog looked up from his food and belched. The cat, whom had finished eating, yawned.

"Thanks for your sage advice. I always appreciate the way you help to solidify my thoughts," Akard said to his inattentive audience.

The bulldog whined indicating he needed to go into the alley to heed the call of nature.

Akard called the office of Dellifield, the lawyer. He explained in detail (at least as much detail as Akard was capable of) about what he had found in Helga's apartment. Dellifield seemed mildly interested.

"When will you know what is in the diary?" The lawyer inquired.

"Probably, in a couple of days."

"If you find something more, let me know."

"Would you like to know about the diamond necklace and assorted diamond rings, of the Cartier variety?"

"What are you talking about?"

"The stuff that was wrapped in a towel. The stuff that you and your high priced staff missed in her underwear drawer. I could have pawned it and you would have never known about it."

"That's where you are wrong. I happen to know that your girl friend has integrity. Just bring the jewelry to my office today."

"Yes, your worship."

Akard hung up and decided to take his pets for a walk. The sight of a large man walking an English bulldog and a twenty-two pound cat on leashes through downtown Dallas amused Akard. It did not amuse some of the bar owners and shop owners in Deep Ellum. Akard was good about picking up after the dog. No one ever tried to pet the cat. It not was a good thing to do. No one wanted to pull back a scratched up nub.

# Chapter Eleven

*At ten o'clock the same morning, Jacob, Bernie and Bill were* having coffee in Bill's apartment.

"What do we need to do about the situation?" Bill asked.

"If you are asking about the people who were in Helga's apartment last night, we need do nothing. So they go to Munich. Maybe they will find the reason we killed Helga and do something about the situation there." Jacob replied

"I am not going to lose sleep over Helga." Bernie said. He continued, "I have another candidate for a peaceful rest, anyway. After all, Bill said he wanted another project."

"Tell us about it, Bernie," Jacob said.

"There is a man originally from El Salvador who owns the landscape company that keeps the grounds here. He does not know that I speak Spanish. I overheard him talking with another man who drove up in the parkway. Apparently Armando, our man, and the other guy have a scam working on older Hispanics. What they do is approach an older person and tell them that they have a winning lottery ticket. They cannot collect the proceeds because they are in the country illegally.

They will share the proceeds if the mark will take the winning ticket to Austin and collect the prize. One of them will go with the mark to Austin, but in the mean time he needs some good faith money to see that the mark does not keep the lottery proceeds. The con guy will buy the tickets to Austin, etc. with the money from the mark. They were laughing that they took one old lady for $9,000."

"Just tell the police what you heard," Jacob said.

Bernie replied, "We will all be dead when either of them is brought to justice. These are rats that need to be exterminated."

"Then you tell us how to do it. You can barely go outside. Wherever I go, it's dragging or pulling oxygen. Bill is not in that great a shape," Jacob said.

"I have it all worked out. I can still drive a car. I will not be able to do so much longer. I have watched Armando's habits. I know when he is bossing the loading of equipment in the trailer. He stands in the same spot. This time of year the grass doesn't grow that fast. He still comes once a week. I will come gunning down the hill and fake a black out. By the time I come to, he will be history."

"Pretty clever, Bernie," Bill said. "The paper and the television news are always showing some old guy that loses control of his car and kills somebody or damages property. What about being sued?"

"I got that covered. His heirs will have to sue my estate. I will not have an estate other than my car, furniture and clothes. All of my liquid assets are in a charitable remainder trust. When I die, which will not be long, the money goes to my University. In the meantime I live off the income the trust produces."

Bill said, "So, you knock off this piece of crap. He may not deserve this much punishment. Helga did. Maybe we should wait a while until the Helga mess dies down."

"We don't have much 'while' left," Jacob said.

# Chapter Twelve

*Akard had finished his stroll with the boys down Main Street and returned* by way of Elm Street. His walk with the bulldog and the huge cat had, as usual, drew curious and pissed-off glances. One woman had stooped to pet One-Eyed Cat, but withdrew when Akard had told her that he was a small bobcat, which he had raised since a kitten.

To sharpen his mind for the day, he worked the commuter crossword puzzle and the word games in *The Dallas Morning News.* When he completed reading the paper he decided to take the Brandenberg jewelry to the counselor and ask for an advance on his pay. Today, he decided to dress in business casual. This meant he would wear a sport coat with his jeans and T-shirt. He wore a T-shirt that was green and plain in front. On the back were printed the words: "*You learn more about a person in one hour of play than you do in a day of conversation — Plato.*"

No one would see the back of the shirt because he would be wearing a jacket. Akard had gotten the shirt as part of the package for playing in a charity golf tournament. It had been washed a number of times and the shirt was fading. Akard liked the shirt. It made him feel cultured.

It was a cool morning, so Akard drove the old Jag to Dellifield's office. He could have walked, because the office was a straight shot down Elm Street from his place. He had already caused enough attention with his pet walk, so he decided to drive. He would make the lawyer reimburse him for the parking. He found a vacant parking meter, but he would tell the attorney that he parked beneath the building at a cost of $10.00.

When he got to Dellifield's office, the English receptionist straightened her hair and arched her back to let Akard know of her endowment.

"Good morning, Mr. McCoy. Mr. Dellifield is with a client. May I take a message for him?" She purred.

Akard still had the jewelry wrapped in the same towel in which it had been found. He unrolled the towel on her desk and lay bare the expensive jewelry.

"You can model these for him when he comes out of conference," Akard said.

"I could never do that. Mr. Dellifield would fire me."

"Do the next best thing. Tell him that I brought this towel by and he should look inside." With that Akard wrapped the jewelry back in the towel.

"I had prepared this receipt. Please sign it," Akard said.

"I could never do that. That is too much responsibility for me."

"Who can sign?"

"His legal assistant, Mrs. Arnold could sign."

"Go get her."

"I can't do that. She is in the conference with Mr. Dellifield."

"Are they in the front conference room?"

At her nod, Akard walked into the conference room. He put the towel down on the table. Three startled people looked at him. He said, "Excuse me, sir, but you left your towel in the washroom." With that he left the room.

"You should not have done that," the comely receptionist said.

"That's what he should expect from his bastard son."

"You are kidding, of course."

"Of course."

With that, Akard left. Dellifield would forgive him someday. Perhaps this was not the time to ask for an advance.

Akard went back to his office and called Nell about the diary. She told him that she should be finished by the next day. Having nothing else to do, Akard went to a book store and bought a paper back book entitled *Say It In German.* He studied the first few pages and came up with a sentence. He called Zelda-Corrine at her fitness center. When she answered the phone he said. "Ich gehe ins Theater."

"German with a Texas accent," she said.

"So what did I say smarty-pants?"

"Without getting into my pants, I think you were trying to tell me that you are going to the theater."

"I am trying to learn some German so that I won't be so ignorant on this case."

"Your ignorance transcends this case, but you are not going to the movies without me. There is a midnight movie at the Arts Theater that I want to see. You will have to stay up tonight."

"That is not the best part of town to be up late in."

"You are a big, tough guy. I am not worried. I have a women's self-defense class tonight. Pick me up after nine. We can have a late dinner and see the show."

Akard did as he was told. He picked Zelda-Corrine up at 9:15 after she closed the fitness center. They had dinner and then saw *Casa Blanca* for the fifteenth time. The show was over at 1:30 in the morning. Akard had parked his car about a block away on a dark side street. As they walked to the car, four young men fell in behind them.

"We may have trouble," Akard said.

"Let's just get in the car and get out of here," Zelda-Corrine replied.

It was too late. They were surrounded by four surly youths. They were a mixed bag, two Anglos, a Black and a Hispanic.

"Hey, man, I like your girl," one of the white guys said.

"Yea, man, we all like her," the Hispanic said.

"Why don't you guys grow up an' go home to mama," Zelda-Corrine interjected.

"Watch your mouth, bitch," one of the white guys said.

"Watch you mouth, moron," Akard said.

The Hispanic guy pulled a .25 caliber automatic from his pants pocket.

"Eat this…," he tried to say. He never finished because Zelda-Corrine had delivered a perfectly timed kick to his throat. He grabbed his throat and Akard put his lights out with a right cross to his chin.

One of the white guys had a motorcycle chain around his waist and tried to swing it at Akard. Zelda-Corrine tripped him and Akard kicked him in the groin on the way down. The black guy was reaching for the gun on the ground when Akard wrapped the motorcycle chain across his forearm. You could hear the bone in his arm snap when the chain hit him with full force. The one remaining assailant was coming at Akard with a knife when Zelda-Corrine delivered a kick to his kidney. As he put his hand behind his back in pain, Akard slugged him in the stomach with a vicious blow.

Zelda-Corrine picked the small automatic off the ground and then picked up the knife. Akard held the chain in his left hand as he looked at the skinned knuckles on his right hand. The four young men were lying in the street.

"You fine, clean-cut, young men have anything else you would like to say to us tonight," Akard asked to no one in particular.

About that time, a blue and white Dallas police car came around the corner. The car pulled up and two officers got out with guns drawn. One officer was in his late forties and had black hair graying at the temples. The other officer was younger and about four inches taller. The taller of the two appeared to be in his early thirties. The headlights from the police car illuminated the area where the four thugs lay on the pavement in various states of agony.

"Hello, McCoy," the older cop said. "What's happened to these lovely children?"

Akard recognized the cop from having worked with the police during his ten years as a private detective. He replied, "Well, Roy, these boys were tying to play with knives and guns, and it turns out that they hurt themselves."

One of the thugs groaned and said, "Get us some help, man. These two beat us up for no reason."

The younger cop responded. "You're telling me that this woman beat the crap out of you for no reason?"

The black kid got up holding his arm. "That asshole hit me with a chain," he said pointing to Akard.

"You carry a chain with you?" Roy asked Akard.

Zelda-Corrine spoke up, "He doesn't. I try to keep a chain in my purse at all times, just in case I run into some vermin like these punks."

"If you want these, you can have them too," Akard said as he handed the pistol and knife to the older cop.

"You carry these in you purse too?" The younger cop asked.

"Only when I carry a large enough purse. Since Akard was buying tonight, I only had room for the chain in this clutch bag," Zelda-Corrine said.

Roy took out a small notebook, and said, "Let's cut the crap and you tell me what happened. I am going to trust the lady to set the facts straight."

"These young gentlemen made some offensive remarks to me. Akard, in his own way, scolded them for their behavior. When one pulled a gun, I used my skill in Karate to disarm him. Akard just used his foot and fists. He did use the chain he took away from one of the goons to keep another one from picking up the gun. Other than possibly trying to rape me and shoot Akard, they were model citizens. We just made the mistake of going to a late movie in the wrong neighborhood."

"She's lying, man," one of the white guys said. "They jumped us for no reason."

"Tell that to the judge," Roy said. "I'll call the meat wagon and take these young hoods to Parkland Hospital. When they have patched them up, they will be the guests of Dallas County for a while."

The younger cop said, "Mr. McCoy, do you have a card in case we need to reach you?"

"No, but there is only one Akard McCoy in the phone book and I am it. You can always find me through my friend, Lieutenant Charles Raines," Akard said.

Akard and Zelda-Corrine waited until an ambulance and another police car arrived, and the would-be assailants were carted away.

When Akard and Zelda-Corrine got into Akard's car she said, "It's late and I have had my exercise for today so don't get amorous." Akard replied, "In the words of Scarlet O'Hara, 'Tomorrow is another day.' "

# Chapter Thirteen

*Z*elda-Corrine *woke up the next morning wheezing. After the early* morning adventure, she went to Akard's place. Neither had shut the bedroom door and One-Eyed Cat and Clarence had joined them in bed. Jacob woke up wheezing because he was dying of lung cancer. Nell Munson woke up eager to tell Akard about what her translations revealed. Conrad Dellifield woke up second guessing himself about turning Akard McCoy loose on an important case. Akard woke up knowing he was going to catch hell for letting the pets get on the bed. Other than that, a cloudless, blue spring sky greeted the players in this drama.

Akard ran into the bathroom and got two allergy pills. He gave them to Zelda-Corrine with a glass of water. One-Eyed Cat yawned and went back to sleep. Clarence licked Zelda-Corrine on the face.

"It will be several tomorrows, Scarlet, before you have another day," she said to Akard.

"Drat."

"Take your menagerie downstairs. I am going to get ready and then you can take me to a nice breakfast."

"Thank you for your understanding nature."

"Just do it, Nike boy."

Obeying that admonition, Akard took the animals downstairs. Clarence went out into the alley to do his thing while One-Eyed Cat used the litter box. Akard looked at himself in the mirror on the wall downstairs. No scratches or bruises from the night before were evident. Still, unshaven, he looked like hell. He pondered how Zelda-Corrine could look so good in the morning. She had no makeup on and her hair was not combed. She probably took a lot better care of herself than he did. To make his pondering easier, he reached into the office refrigerator and got himself a cold beer.

Akard was not a big drinker. He did not smoke. He worked out some. That was how he met Zelda-Corrine at her fitness center. He looked at his watch. It was eight-thirty. Thank goodness Zelda-Corrine had employees who were there to open the fitness center for the early morning crowd. Thank goodness he did not have a nine-to-five job. The cold beer tasted good. The telephone rang. Akard answered. It was Nell Munson.

"Hello," Akard said.

"Is this Akard?" the voice replied.

"The one and only."

"This is Nell Munson."

"Hi, Nell. What's up?"

"I think I have found some very interesting information in Helga's diary and other papers."

"When can we meet?"

"I am going to teach my classes now. Why don't you take Corrine and me to dinner tonight?"

"Where?"

"The best place Mr. Dellifield will spring for."

"That would be Burger King."

"Try harder."

"The Green Room, near my place, at seven o'clock."

"Perfect. Say hello to Corrine. Bye."

Akard realized again that he was the only one who added a Zelda before Corrine's name.

"Is it alright if we have dinner with Nell at the Green Room tonight," Akard yelled.

"Why, hell yes, it is alright." She yelled back.

Moments later Zelda-Corrine came walking down the stairs wearing a pink warm up suit. She kept a supply of them in Akard's closet. She also kept a supply of makeup and other items to keep her beautiful on the nights she stayed over. Akard could smell the sweetness of the soap she had used. As usual, he lusted for her, but knew he was wasting his time for the present.

"I need to get to work. You take a quick shower. We can eat in Oak Lawn. You can shave at the fitness center. It would not hurt you to work out a little. So eat light." Akard could not tell if this was an order or request.

Akard and Zelda-Corrine ate breakfast at a small, fast-order place in downtown Dallas. Akard, for one of the few times in his life, had oatmeal and wheat toast without butter. Zelda-Corrine had yogurt and fruit with herbal tea. Akard knew that he could eat what he wanted for lunch and was already thinking about the barbecue he was going to have.

After breakfast, Akard dropped Zelda-Corrine off at the fitness center. He balked at working out, claiming his hand hurt from the blows he had delivered the night before, but he did shave.

He went back to his office. When he checked his call notes, he had a call from Lieutenant Charles Baines of the Dallas Police department. Lieutenant Baines was a college man assigned to the intelligence division of the police department. Akard had known Baines since Akard's early days as a Pinkerton. Baines had bailed Akard out of more than one jam after Akard became a private eye.

Akard dialed the familiar number. A voice on the other end answered, Lieutenant Baines, may I help you?

"Yea, go screw yourself."

"And a pleasant good morning to you, too, Akard."

"What do you want, 'Dead-eye'?"

"I hear you and the woman who is dumb enough to hang around with you beat up some of our finer young citizens."

"Young citizens, my ass."

"You guys are lucky. All these guys have a long rap sheet. You could have been shot."

"Have they been bonded out?"

"I think we will keep them a while. You and Corrine will have to testify at some point, unless they cop a plea."

"Say the word."

"That's not why I called. I hear you are nosing around a suicide case over on Turtle Creek. What do you know that I should know?"

"Meet me at Sonny's for lunch. I will tell you what I am at liberty to discuss."

"Deal, see you at noon."

Akard spent the rest of the morning cleaning his Beretta 92 and reading his German book. At noon he met Baines at Sonny's. He made up for his meager breakfast with a rib plate, potato salad and cole slaw.

"So, what's the skinny on the German dame?" Baines asked.

"'Smoothmouth' Dellifield fancies himself a detective. He thinks maybe she was knocked off because the lipstick writing is not in her handwriting."

"That reminds me of the old joke about the father who accused a young man of making improper advances to his daughter. When asked by the young man why her father felt that way," the father replied, 'Someone wrote my daughter's name in urine in the snow last night, and it was in her handwriting.'"

"Pretty close to Smoothmouth's analysis."

"So, what do you know?"

"Very little at this time, but I do know that there is a lock box in Munich. I don't know what's in it. I am going to find out tonight what her diary says. There is probably nothing to this. If I find out more I will let you know."

Akard and Baines finished their meal. Akard washed his down with a cold beer. Baines was on duty, so he settled for iced tea.

Akard went back to his office and took a nap in his chair. He woke up at 6:00 and realized that he was meeting the women at 7:00. The Green Room is a fancy place. Akard showered and shaved. He put on a freshly pressed pair of gray slacks, an open collared blue shirt and a blue blazer. He looked at himself in the mirror. He was not a bad looking guy when he cleaned up. His short-cropped blond hair had no hint of gray. His steel-blue eyes were accented by the blue shirt. As he brushed his teeth, the thought occurred to him, *"Zelda-Corrine could do a hell of a lot worse."* On the other hand, she could do a hell of a lot better.

Akard strolled down the street to meet the two beautiful women at The Green Room. The food was much too healthy for Akard's tastes. A person could order a dinner from a choice of options, but the chef would choose most of what accompanied the entree. Akard preferred chicken fried steak and cream gray. This was an item not to be found on the menu of the Green Room.

When he walked into the bar area, he saw Zelda-Corrine and Nell sitting at the bar. Nell was wearing a low cut, black velvet top and black leather pants. Zelda-Corrine was wearing a peach colored cashmere sweater with matching wool pants. All of the men in the bar, whether accompanied by a woman or not, were glancing in the direction of the two women.

Akard swaggered over to the two distinctive women. He spoke, "Hey, ladies, here's your candy man."

"He isn't even a breath mint," Zelda-Corrine said.

"He's not so bad," Nell said.

"Thank you for that," Akard acknowledged.

The two women were drinking white wine. Akard ordered a beer. After exchanging some small talk the three were ushered into the dark dining room by the hostess. The waiter advised letting the chef choose. The women each chose fish to be accompanied by what the chef would choose. Akard chose the beef tenderloin.

"What do you have for me?" Akard asked Nell.

"I am not sure I am smart enough to know. I read the diary. This is what I discovered. She has money in a lock box in Munich. Every month or so, she notes a payment by Herman in Munich. She hates Jews."

"I follow you on the first two, but what is the indication that she hates Jews?" Akard said.

Nell replied, "This diary goes back a number of years. She wrote in a small delicate hand. She used a fountain pen. Apparently her father had a chemical business. After World War II he was accused of supplying chemicals used to exterminate Jews in the Nazi concentration camps.

Her father denied this and he was never charged or prosecuted for a crime. Before he died, a Jewish activist group tried to seek reparations from him and his company. Nothing came of it, but Helga believed that the notoriety hastened her parents' death."

"Do you think that she was sending money to some neo-Nazi or hate group based in Munich that was targeting Jews?" Zelda-Corrine asked.

"Could be," Akard said. "That might be a reason for some one to take her out and that could be the reason the German word for 'bad' was written on the mirror. Could be is a long way from proving that she was murdered. Whatever, I need to brief Dellifield on what you have found out."

"Do you need me to meet with you and Mr. Dellifield?" Nell asked.

"No need for you to take off work, yet," Akard replied. "I think I can handle the initial report. You keep looking through her papers. Look at any correspondence she might have with this Herman. See if she has an address for him. Dellifield is not a young man. If the Judge sends him to Munich, I am not sure he should go alone."

"I can see the wheels turning," Zelda-Corrine said. "Don't think that you can go to Munich without taking me."

"What about me?" Nell asked. "You are going to need a translator."

"Wait a minute, wait a minute," Akard exclaimed. "No one has even said that Dellifield was going to Munich, let alone our happy throng."

"You will find a way," Zelda-Corrine said.

The idea of Akard being in a foreign country with two beautiful women certainly had its appeal to Akard. He had devious thoughts about how he might get in bed with both of them. Akard was not dumb. He did not use his male organ as a compass. As a practical matter, it would be asking a lot to get Dellifield to allow him to go, Dellifield might let Zelda-Corrine go, if Akard paid her way. Nell would be out of the question. A translator would be available in Germany. He closed the conversation with the words of wisdom his mother used often when he was a child. "We'll see."

The rest of the evening was spent in pleasant chatter, mainly between the two women. This was alright with Akard. He liked to watch women talk. He liked their hand gestures. He liked the giggles.

He liked to see their polished nails as they flashed before his eyes when the women's dialogue got animated. Akard just liked women, period. He liked well-dressed, sweet-smelling women. He liked them to be intelligent. He liked them to be built like Venus, but with arms. Most of all, he liked them to like him.

The evening ended with Nell and Zelda-Corrine leaving in Nell's car. Akard walked to his abode several blocks away. "*What a waste. Two goddesses leaving him alone to* sleep *with a one-eyed cat and an English bulldog,*" Akard thought to himself.

The next morning, Akard awoke lacking human companionship. One-Eyed Cat had positioned himself under Akard's arm and his tail was brushing Akard's nose. Akard blew the cat hairs out of his face and said, "Cat, you test me, really test me. One of the best looking women around this town is notably absent. Some of it is your fault." One-Eyed Cat blinked his remaining eye and yawned.

"It's damn hard to talk to you, cat. I have a number of things I would like your opinion about. For example, what do you think about the proposition that somebody killed Helga Brandenberg?"

One-Eyed Cat closed his only eye and went back to sleep.

"If I am bothering you with my questions, please do not hesitate to tell me." Addressing the bulldog that had been sleeping at the foot of the bed, Akard said, "Clarence feel free to chime in at anytime, if you have an opinion." Clarence turned over on his back with his feet in the air in anticipation of a belly rub.

"You guys are totally worthless. I have serious issues to discuss here, and you are no help to me at all."

After that remark, both animals headed downstairs to be fed. Akard followed them. He realized that most pets are only companion animals for the food and shelter. It had taken the cats about 4,000 years longer than dogs to get the message, but after all, in the past, they had saved his life. So he would just have to rely on humankind for issue solving.

He took the pets for their daily downtown Dallas walk with the usual reaction. When he returned he decided that he could skip breakfast. Instead, he read the morning paper and tried to guess when Conrad Dellifield might show up at his office. He knew Dellifield got to work early. At nine o'clock he called. He told Dellifield that he had some important news to tell him. Dellifield told Akard that he had a ten-thirty appointment and to get to his office as soon as possible.

Akard arrived at Dellifield's office two minutes early.

"Good morning, Mr. McCoooy," the English receptionist purred.

"I am here to see Mr. Dellifield," Akard replied.

"He is expecting you, please go back."

As Akard entered Dellifield's office he was met with a barrage. "Do not ever interrupt me again when I have clients," Dellifield roared.

"Yes sir," an out of character response from a seemly contrite Akard.

"What do you have to tell me?" inquired Dellifield.

Akard told him about what Nell had discovered in Helga's diary. He talked about the money that might be in a lock box in Munich. He told about her apparent hatred for Jews.

"I think someone found about her financing some radical group in Germany and had her knocked off," Akard explained.

"It is a vast difference between thinking and proving a proposition which now is at best a surmise."

"You are going to have to go to Munich anyway to find the money so you might as well check out if you have a wrongful death action."

"The probate court here has no jurisdiction over someone in Germany."

"The Germans did not come over here. They got someone else to do it for them."

"I will talk with Judge Rice and see what he thinks."

"While you are at it, ask him if the estate can spring to take me along."

"Why on earth would I even consider such proposition?"

"Because, if you won't take offense, you are no longer in your physical prime and you may need a body guard."

"I suppose that you want to take that girl friend of yours as well."

"Here's the deal: We use airline miles to get there and back; you pay my per diem only when I'm on the job. You may find that someone else has his eyes on the money and tries to take it away from you."

"Perhaps, for once, you might be talking sense. My wife and I have been to Munich before. She would not enjoy a trip like this with me. Obviously, I will have to clear this with the Judge."

"If he says yes, when would we go?"

"It will take some time. The Judge might want to hear some evidence. If not, there are still mechanical things to be done. The German bankers will require an Apostille."

"A what-the-hell?"

"An Apostille, it is obvious that the year you spent in law school is of little use to you. The German bankers are not interested in seeing our court documents in English. The papers which show my authority to act issued by the court in Dallas must be translated into German. Once they are translated into German the documents must be presented to the German Consul here. The Consul will compare the documents written in English with the German version. He will then stamp each page with an official stamp. When finished, the document will then be fastened together at the top with a cord and the ends will be sealed with a sealing wax on which the Consul's seal will be impressed. The German bankers will then have a document to rely upon. The same document can be presented to a German court, if a probate proceeding in Munich is deemed to be necessary."

"Well, isn't that a kick in the ass?"

"Get out of here, Akard, before I regain my sanity and forget I ever considered taking you to Munich."

"Just remember that I can protect you. Zelda-Corrine ain't bad to look at either."

"Goodbye, Akard. Come back when you cannot stay so long."

Akard left with a smile on his face. "*He is going to take me with him,*" Akard thought to himself.

As Akard was leaving the premises the English receptionist spoke, "I am not doing anything for lunch."

"Sorry, but you would be too much of a good thing."

"I beg your pardon."

"Don't try and figure me out. Nobody else can."

"Oh."

With the verbal exchange over, Akard left the office of Conrad Dellifield. "*She might be a very good thing, but so is Zelda-Corrine. Too much of a good thing can get me hurt by Zelda-Corrine,*" Akard mused as he rode the elevator to the ground floor.

# Chapter Fourteen

Armando Zavalla arrived with his crew of landscape workers at the high rise on Turtle Creek at about 8:30 am. The members of the landscape crew were all Hispanic. The workers for the most part wore worn out blue jeans and T-shirts. The T-shirts had long since lost their shape and color. Some bore the logo of a Mexican soccer team. Others probably came from a resale shop in a neighborhood where they lived. None of the workers were smiling. This, for most, was just another day in an existence not a life. Much of their meager wages would be sent back to relatives in Mexico or Central America. Many of them were in the country illegally.

Armando Zavalla did not look like the rest of his crew. He was clean-shaven except for a hair line mustache above his upper lip. His hair was coal black and combed back across his head. His eyes were as black as his hair and had a detached look that suggested his mind was somewhere other than on the job at hand. His whole persona was that of a cruel and ruthless taskmaster.

Armando Zavalla walked toward the entrance of the high-rise apartment house. He greeted the doorman with a smile that appeared to have been painted on his face. He strutted over to the office manager of the building and entered the manager's office without being announced by the secretary seated in the outer foyer.

"Buenas dias, Senor," he said to the manager, Sherman Counts, who was engaged in looking at a stack of papers.

"Don't you believe in knocking?" the manager said in a disgusted voice.

Armando Zavalla shut the door to the manager's office and said, "I think we need to talk about a raise for my services."

"Why?"

"Because, Senor, some of my people are related to some of your help here. They tell me that perhaps some of your people are undocumented. It would be a shame for your Federales to learn of this fact."

"It would seem to me that you have the same problem."

"Senor, I am but a humble man who knows nothing of these things. But you, Senor, are a man of great learning who must know of these things."

"You want me to pay you hush money?"

"No, no, Senor. I simply want a higher wage so that my poor workers can rise above the state of peons."

"Your peons, as you call them, would never see a penny of any extra money that I might pay."

"Senor, you greatly misjudge me. I want nothing more than to pay my men more."

"I will think about your proposal. For now get the hell out of here."

"I will be back when the mowing is done. Have an answer."

Bernie Pittsfield had been in the outer foyer asking the secretary about assisted living, if and when he became totally incapacitated. He had overheard the loud voices in the manager's office, but could not determine what was being said. Armando Zavalla's eyes were flashing when he walked out of the office. He changed his demeanor when he saw the secretary and Bernie. As he passed he said in an oily voice, "Buenas Dias."

"*Buenas Dias yourself, asshole! Today is the day you die,*" Bernie thought to himself.

Bernie had to make a split second decision as to whether today was the day he killed Armando or not. Should he talk to the others? No, they knew what he was going to do. They just did not know when.

Armando Zavalla strutted out the door. Bernie Pittsfield shuffled after him. Armando Zavalla walked toward his crew barking orders to no one in particular.

"May I have your car sent up?" the doorman said to Bernie.

"No, I need the exercise. I will walk down and get the car myself," Bernie replied.

Every step for Bernie was difficult. At the most he was only weeks away from having to give up driving altogether. His back hurt from the activity of the cancer near his spine. The pain was almost unbearable. He reached his car in the underground garage and paused for a moment to catch his breath. He slowly opened the door and eased himself into the seat.

His car was an older Buick Roadmaster. Some of the less kind residents of the high rise referred to the car as a pregnant elephant. The car was suitable for the purpose at hand. It was large and had a powerful engine. It would withstand a crash and Bernie would escape unharmed.

Bernie put the key in the ignition and started the car. He pulled slowly out of the garage. The exit from the garage led to the driveway of the building, which in turn exited on Turtle Creek. He slowly headed to the street. Armando Zavalla was berating a worker. The worker was on his knees working on a flowerbed near the drive way. Armando Zavalla was standing in the driveway with his back to Bernie's car.

It was a perfect situation for Bernie. He slammed his foot on the gas and aimed at Zavalla. He hit Zavalla in the back and his body hurled across the hood leaving a shattered windshield and lots of blood. A smile crossed Bernie's face. It was to be his last smile. He lost control of the car and crashed into a large tree at the entryway to the driveway. Zavalla lay dead in the driveway. Bernie was dead in his car.

The worker who had been talking to Zavalla ran over to Zavalla's body. He then ran toward the doorman who was running toward Zavalla's body. The workman spewed forth, in rapid succession, a flood of Spanish words. The doorman left the worker standing over the body and headed for the office of Sherman Counts. A crowd was gathering outside the building when Sherman Counts approached the bloody scene. He was yelling over his shoulder for security and for someone to call the police.

"Jesus H. Christ," Sherman Counts muttered to himself. "First the old Brandenberg dame, and now this guy."

The good news was that Zavalla was no longer a problem to him. The bad news was that if people did not stop dying in his place some of the residents might move out. On the other hand, the residents did not lease their apartments. They owned them. They were rich and they would be looking for someone to blame.

As Counts sorted out his plight, a police car arrived. The policeman called for ambulances to take the bodies away and for a crime scene investigation unit. In a short while, both groups arrived. Yellow crime scene tapes cordoned off the drive way and tree. Startled residents discussed the situation among themselves in hushed tones. Sherman Counts was everywhere talking with everyone from the police department and trying to calm down the rattled residents.

"As I see it, a sick old guy who should not have been driving probably had some kind of seizure and lost control of his car," Sherman opined to one of the investigators.

"Could be," the investigator replied. "We will know more when the M.E. takes a look at the bodies. Who were these people?"

"The old guy was a retired banker. He had cancer. He should not have been driving. The other guy ran the crew that does our landscape work."

"Did they ever have any run-ins?"

"To the best of my knowledge they never met each other."

"We will call you if we need you. Thanks for the information."

"You are entirely welcome."

The crime scene investigators measured distances with tape measures. They took photographs of Zavalla's body. They took photographs of Bernie's body and his car. They took photographs of everything in sight.

From his balcony Jacob gasped for air and wept. Helga had deserved to die, he was convinced of that. Zavalla's murder was a marginal call. But Bernie, poor Bernie, he was not supposed to die. He made the decision on his own. He did not tell him or Bill about his plans. Maybe Bernie was better off. He was in such pain. He died thinking himself a hero.

Jacob was agonizing. He should be down there showing his concern. Everyone knew Jacob was Bernie's friend. Everyone also knew that he was chained to his oxygen. It was a matter of time, maybe weeks, before he would have to go to an assisted living facility. It was either assisted living or having caregivers come to his apartment. Neither was a pleasant thought. It had seemed so right to avenge the wrongs that society would probably not correct. Now there was the reality of the consequences of elderly, sick men trying to pull it off.

Jacob's mental scourging was interrupted by a knock at the door. It was Bill.

"My God, Bernie is dead," Bill exclaimed.

"I know, I know. It is terrible," Jacob answered.

"There was blood everywhere. Zavalla was mangled. Bernie had blood coming out of his mouth. People were asking me what got into Bernie. I told them he must have had a heart attack or stroke. What in the hell are we going to do?" Bill asked as tears ran down his face.

"We are going to bury our friend. You will have to make the arrangements. I can't leave the building. Maybe you can get some help from that idiot, Sherman Counts. He ought to be good for something besides being a pompous ass," Jacob said.

"Counts is very busy right now. He is running everywhere trying to calm the residents and assure them that it was just an unfortunate accident. The landscape workers are in a panic. Most of them do not speak English. They are afraid of the police. They think someone will call Immigration. Counts has the help here who speak Spanish calming them down. The police are asking Counts about Bernie's next of kin. Nobody knows. Even we don't know," Bill said.

"Did Bernie have a will?" Jacob asked.

"He said he had a charitable trust. Someone is going to have to hire a lawyer," Bill said.

"I just had a great idea. Let's ask Sherman Counts to tell us the name of the lawyer who is handling Helga's estate. We will hire him to look after Bernie's affairs and at the same time try to find out what he knows about Helga's death," Jacob said.

"That may be risky, but what in the hell do we have to lose?" Bill answered.

"Only each other, Bill. Only each other," Jacob sighed.

While the Zavalla incident was taking place at the Turtle Creek apartment house, Conrad Dellifield IV, was in the chambers of Judge Radford Rice.

"As your honor knows, I have been investigating the circumstances of the death of Helga Brandenberg. I have been utilizing the talents of one of Dallas' finest private investigators. (Conrad could hardly contain himself with that description of Akard.) The investigator, in turn, has used the services of a translator who has come up with some very interesting facts. There is a lock box in Munich. Ms. Brandenberg may have been funding subversive activity in Germany. Her death might not have been a suicide. All of which suggests that I need go to Munich," the lawyer said.

"Conrad, I trust your judgment or I would not have appointed you as administrator of this estate. That German lawyer, Hans Grueber keeps calling here. His clients keep bugging him about the case. I, of course, have no jurisdiction in Germany, but I can certainly send you over there at the expense of the estate. I am concerned about your safety. Neither one of us is a kid anymore," the jurist said.

"I was hoping you would allow me to take the investigator with me. He would use his reward miles on the airline to get there. I would pay him his per diem out of the estate."

"Who is this investigator?"

"Akard McCoy."

"Akard McCoy! My God, he could cause us to go to war with Germany if you turn him loose. I have friends in the Dallas police department and they tell me he caused quite a stir in Italy on a case he was involved in."

The lawyer knew it was time to turn on his glibness. "Your honor and I have known each other for over thirty years. During that period of time I have developed a great deal of respect for your honor's wisdom and profound respect for the law and the citizens of Dallas County. I would not have suggested McCoy if I did not think he would be an asset in this case. The man does have one year of law school."

"You can cut the crap, Conrad. I am not on the bench right now. I am going to let you take McCoy with you. He will probably do a good job of protecting you. If he starts an international incident, it is your ass that is going to be in a sling."

"I took the liberty of preparing a court order which allows me to go to Munich and conduct an investigation as to the assets of Helga Brandenberg. It also allows me to take an investigator with me to assist in the location of assets. I have left the name of the investigator blank so that you can fill in the name."

"Not only no, but hell no. You present me with an order that has Mr. McCoy's name already typed in. I am not about to be accused of thinking about him myself."

"As your honor wishes, I will have someone from my office bring an order down later today."

"Good enough, as you are leaving, check with my clerk, Martha, she will give you the address and telephone number of Herr Grueber. He does not call himself a lawyer. He calls himself Dr. Grueber. It is my understanding that he holds the same position as our lawyers when it comes to handling estates. When you get to Munich expect to be called Dr. Dellifield. Some lawyers are referred to by the title of Doctor."

Dellifield left the judge's chambers and got the information he needed to contact Hans Grueber. He liked the idea of being called Dr. Dellifield. What was even better he might even make Akard call him Dr. Dellifield while they were in Germany. That would serve the smartass right. Conrad chuckled to himself.

The lawyer went back to his office and looked through his phone messages. He checked his email. He then decided to call Akard. He checked his palm pilot and got Akard's number. It was not on his auto-dialer of frequently called numbers. The auto-dialer was reserved for well paying clients of which, Akard was not one. He dialed Akard's number. The phone was answered by someone speaking in a falsetto voice. "McCoy Investigations," the voice said.

"Akard McCoy, please," the lawyer replied.

"May I say who is calling and the nature of the call?" the voice answered.

"For God's sake Akard, quit trying to pretend that you have a secretary. Everyone in town knows you have no help," the lawyer said in a put out tone of voice.

"Let me see if Mr. McCoy is available to speak with you," the voice said, totally unperturbed. "Oh, you are quite fortunate; Mr. McCoy can take a minute from his busy schedule to visit with you."

The deep voice of Akard then took over the conversation.

"Good morning, Mr. Dellifield, or is it afternoon already?"

"Akard, you would try the patience of a monk."

"How can I help you today?"

"First of all, you can stop acting like a moron. Secondly, I have committed a huge error by getting Judge Rice to allow you to go to Munich with me."

"Goody. May I take Zelda-Corrine?"

"Only if you pay all her expenses and she stays out of our way."

"That's a deal. When do we go?"

"It will take a week or so, probably before the end of the month. I will need Nell to translate the court documents. Then I will have to make an appointment with the German Consul to get the Apostille. Then, of course, there will be the travel arrangements."

"Don't worry about the travel arrangements; I will call my friend, Brad Hawthorne, the travel agent."

"Frankly speaking, Akard, I am afraid our tastes in accommodations are too different to allow you to make that decision on my behalf. I have been to Munich a number of times and I have my favorites."

"Get me a date to leave, so that Zelda-Corrine and I can use our miles to get the tickets."

"Judge Rice will not let me fly first class on the estate so I will be using my miles to upgrade to business class."

"Figures, would you like to hear my theory about why Helga was sending the money to Munich?"

"You mean you have actually been working on the case?"

"Damn straight. I have been to the library and searching the Internet. Did you know the German government has been fighting the rise of the neo-Nazis?"

"I have heard something to that effect. Tell me more."

"The neo-Nazis have Web sites where they advocate violence. About one third of the Web sites are in the U.S. where they are protected by First Amendment rights. The Web sites in the U.S. offer to sell merchandise, such as Nazi flags, which are outlawed in Germany. Some of the Web sites provide bomb-making instructions.

"Violence toward foreigners, particularly people with black faces, has increased in recent years. Eastern Germany is noted for its xenophobic crimes. Recent statistics show that it has twenty percent of the country's population, but more than half of the anti-foreigner crime.

"The skinheads talk about 'nationally liberated zones' which means foreigner free neighborhoods. There is a wide spread belief that foreigners are taking jobs from German citizens.

"My take on all of this is that Helga could have supported one of these neo-Nazi groups and helped pay for their Web site. Someone could have found out about what she was doing and knocked her off. On the other hand, she may have become aware of the violence she was helping to promote and had conscience pangs. Then, she knocked herself off."

"Akard, you astound me. Do you have any facts to support your theory?"

"I have no facts, yet. While you are doing your legal thing in Germany, I can check my theory out."

"I am not sure I want you to check out your theory. Doing so could place us in harms way."

"Suit yourself. I thought I was hired to see if there was a wrongful death claim."

"You were and you are, but pursuing the investigation in Germany may be going too far. I will give it some thought. I think we can leave for Germany in about two weeks. I will call you in a day or two with definite plans. Have Nell Munson call me. I need her to start the translation of the court papers as quickly as possible."

"Right."

The lawyer hung up the telephone.

Akard looked at his watch and decided it was time to eat lunch. He thought he could accomplish two things at the same time. First and foremost, he wanted to see Zelda-Corrine. Taking her to lunch always got him strokes he could call upon when he screwed up, which was frequently. He would have lunch somewhere close to the high rise. He thought it would be a good idea to look around Helga's apartment, in case he found other papers that needed to be looked at by Nell Munson.

Akard called Zelda-Corrine and she agreed to have lunch with him around 1:00 pm. It was about 11:15 am and that would give him time to go by the apartment before meeting Zelda-Corrine for lunch. When he arrived at the high rise the drive way was partially blocked by a police car and yellow police line tape was draped around a tree and over some saw horses. A wrecker was pulling a Buick Roadmaster out of the driveway. Two ambulances were also leaving.

"*What in the hell is going on at this place?*" Akard thought to himself. He pulled his car up to be valet parked. He left the car and walked down the driveway to where two uniformed policemen were talking to a man in a suit.

"What's going on here?" Akard asked no one in particular.

The guy in the suit said, "Who wants to know?"

Akard reached in his wallet and produced a card. It read: "Akard McCoy, Private Investigator, Notary Public and watermelons in season."

"So, you are McCoy. You are Lieutenant Baines' buddy," the Suit said.

"I'm McCoy. You can ask Baines if I'm his buddy," Akard replied.

"What we have here, Mr. McCoy is a case of an old fart in a Buick creaming a Greaser. Creamed himself in the process," the Suit answered.

"Well you certainly covered the situation nicely. I hope no one from the ACLU was listening," Akard said.

"Cut the crap, McCoy. Why are you here?"

"Certainly not to see you. I'm here on a case. By the way, was the old guy on oxygen?"

"No, he was not. Why do you want to know?"

"Just curious, see ya."

Akard left the company of the police and made his way to the twentieth floor of the high rise. He went into the apartment and started looking through papers. He paused a moment and took a glass from one of the kitchen cabinets. He cupped the glass in his hand and walked down the hall to Jacob's door. He put the glass very carefully to the door and listened. He heard a sound coming from the room. Along with the labored breathing, someone was definitely crying. *"Could it be that Helga's neighbor and the other old man knew each other? Were his death and Helga's death in any way connected?"* These thoughts crossed his mind, but he blew them off for the time being.

Akard returned to the apartment and looked again through papers and her personal belongings. He looked behind pictures on the wall. He took out drawers in the kitchen and in the bedroom and looked at the bottom of each drawer. He found nothing. He took the mattress off of the bed and looked at the frame and turned over each bed slat. He found nothing He picked up a flashlight from a nightstand in the bedroom to look at the top shelves of the closet. He pushed the switch and nothing happened. He shook the flashlight. It did not come on. He unscrewed the base and dropped the batteries into his hand. Between the two batteries was a small piece of paper. Written on the piece of paper were the words "autobahnkreuz 12."

Akard took the small piece of paper and placed it in his wallet. He would either call Nell Munson or look the word up in his German Quick and Easy book.

Akard looked at his watch and realized it was time to meet Zelda-Corrine for lunch. He was overcome with the two great H's in a man's life. He had hunger and he was horny. Normally he could control both urges. After all, it was just a little before noon. He could have lunch soon. The other depended on Zelda-Corrine's mood. She did have a business to run. It had been a few days since he had been intimate with her. He stopped at the grocery store on the way to pick her up and bought a ten-dollar bunch of flowers.

Zelda-Corrine was waiting for him at the front of the fitness center. When she got in, he handed her the flowers. She leaned over and kissed him softly on the cheek.

"No," she said.

"No what?"

"No nooner. I have a class to teach this afternoon."

"Drat."

"You could have saved ten bucks on the flowers."

"Do you really think I am that cheap?"

"Yes, but if you are nice and attentive to me at lunch, I will make it worth your while tonight. There is one condition."

"Only one?"

"No dog or cat in bed with us."

"Good deal! I will spend the night at your place."

"Bring some clean clothes. I hate it when you put your dirty clothes back on in the morning."

"Yes, MA'AM."

Akard then devoted his attention to the other H. She looked so good that he would forego a chicken fried steak or Mexican platter. He drove over to a little Italian place on Lovers Lane. Zelda-Corrine ordered the chicken lemone with a small house salad. Akard ordered pasta and a shrimp cocktail.

"There was some more excitement at the high rise this morning," Akard said.

"What happened?"

"An old guy in a Buick killed a Mexican. Ran over him and then hit a tree and killed himself."

"Was it the old man who lives down the hall from Helga's apartment?"

"No, but a funny thing, I listened at his door and I thought I heard someone crying."

"You listened at his door? Why on earth did you do that?"

"Because, sweet buns, I am a detective. A detective detects things."

"Do you think that he knew the man who was killed?"

"Which one?"

"The old man, dummy."

"They lived in the same place. They probably knew each other."

"Are you trying to connect this to Helga's death?"

"I just don't know."

"Let's talk about something pleasant."

"You mean like tonight in bed?"

"No, like going to Munich. Can I go for sure?"

"Smoothmouth has bought into that proposition as long as I pay your way and you don't get in the way."

"Listen, I can pay my own freight. As for getting in the way, try doing without sex for the entire trip."

"He did not mean it that way. He was referring only to the time we are dealing with the bankers."

"I see. I keep you satisfied at night while you two play mouthpiece and body guard in the day time."

"No, you play co-body guard, and we both put up with the stuffed shirt. He will find a museum to go to or find an elegant place to dine and then go to the symphony."

"So, what are we going to see when we are not body guarding?'

"I'll bring the guide book with me tonight."

"Think you will have time for it?"

"Depends."

"On what?"

"Eat your food and then take me back to work."

"Roger."

Akard did as he was told. He ate his food and took Zelda-Corrine back to work. He made sure that she took the flowers with her. After all, ten bucks is ten bucks.

# Chapter Fifteen

*Akard went back to his Deep Ellum office. He looked in his German book and found out that "autobahnkreuz" meant* highway junction.

*"What in the hell does highway junction 12 mean? Why would the note be hidden in a flashlight?"* Akard pondered these thoughts. He was still thinking when the phone rang. It was Lieutenant Baines of the Dallas Police Department.

"Akard, I just wanted to let you know that two of the guys you and Zelda had a run-in with the other night have bonded out. One of the officers at the jail overheard them say that they were going to even the score with you and Corrine. I doubt that they would come after her in broad daylight, but they might come after you at your run down office. They might get tanked up on booze or high on something. Look out."

"Thanks for the heads up. I will keep an eye out. While I have you on the phone, have you heard about the double death at the Turtle Creek high rise this morning?"

"I was over there taking another look at the Brandenberg apartment. I walked right into the crime scene."

"Yeah, I heard you wised off to one of our detectives."

"You mean the Neanderthal bigot in a suit?"

"Please keep your opinions to yourself. You're not trying to connect the Brandenberg suicide to what happened this morning?"

"I don't know anything about this morning, except what your guys told me. On the other hand, I never rule anything out. That's what makes me so good."

"Yeah, you're so good. That's why there is always a line of clients outside of the shitter you call an office. Anyway, I warned you about the punks."

"How do they know who I am?"

"My guess is that they caught your license number on you car as you drove away, and got one of their buddies to look it up on a computer."

"They would not have Zelda-Corrine's address, so they will come after me, if they are that dumb."

"Keep your pistol handy. See ya."

Akard took his Beretta out of the file cabinet and slid a shell into the chamber of the gun. He put the pistol into the middle drawer of the desk. One-Eyed Cat was in his usual place on top of the refrigerator and Clarence the bull dog was napping at Akard's feet.

"Boys, we may have visitors later today. I am not in the mood to shoot anyone, so I will let you handle the situation. I know you can handle the matter because you have done it before," Akard made his pronouncement to two totally disinterested animals.

Akard spent the afternoon going over two divorce cases he was keeping an eye on. In one matter, he had been all over town following an airline executive who was supposedly having an affair with a woman highly placed in the fashion industry. They would meet in various cities across the country and sometimes in Europe. The wife's lawyer had hired Akard to follow them around Dallas and Akard had associated colleagues in other cities to do the same.

Akard had put together a thirty-page report that listed everything that he and the others had done to try and catch the husband and the girlfriend in the act. Unfortunately, a careful reading of the report would show that the two lovers had been too circumspect to be caught.

Akard came up with an idea that might save the day. He told the wife that he would send a bill to the husband by mistake. The bill would list all the places that he and the other detectives had been following the couple. The husband would not know what was in the report. He could only speculate what was in the report. At the very least, it would really piss him off.

In the other case, he just needed to type the report. The wife was having an affair with her boss. About once a week they would go to a hotel or motel near the airport. It was unlikely that they would be seen by anyone they knew. Akard followed them for weeks. They followed about the same pattern and had recently gone to a hotel just west of the airport. Akard took a chance and went to the hotel the day of the week the couple usually showed up. He sat down near the registration desk and waited. The man and woman came in at different times. Akard heard the room number when the man checked in. The man made a call on his cell phone and, a short time later, the woman went to the room.

Akard followed the woman into the elevator and punched in a different floor. He exchanged pleasantries with the woman, although she never looked him in the face. The woman got off the elevator first. Akard got off at the next floor. He waited a few minutes and went to the floor below. He checked out the room location. It was his lucky day. The room overlooked the parking lot. He knew the make and model of both of their cars from having followed them for weeks. On the other hand, he could not pick the lock to the room because it used a computerized plastic card. There was no way to put a recorder behind the headboard.

Akard went down to the parking lot and checked out both cars. The red light on the top of the dashboard indicated that both cars had theft alarms. He went to his car and got his camera with the telescopic lens. He then went to the couple's cars. He crouched down beside each car and pulled at the doors setting off the alarm on each car. He then walked nonchalantly back into the hotel. He went back to the floor the couple were occupying and hid in the stairwell.

As he expected, the couple panicked and headed for the parking lot. The man was zipping up his pants on the way out of the room. Akard caught the scene on film. He waited in the bar and the couple returned to the room. After two hours they left. He caught them on film again as they kissed beside her car. Sometimes Akard hated his job.

Akard busied himself writing his report on the couple's activity at the hotel. He skipped the part about thinking of breaking into the room. He simply said that he had seen them come out of a hotel room in a hurry and that the man was zipping up his pants. He had the photographs to prove it.

It was nearing time to get ready to see Zelda-Corrine when he noticed that the two punks he had the altercation with several nights before were trying to see through the Venetian blinds that kept the public from staring into his office. He took the Beretta out of the desk drawer and placed it in the back of his waistband. He swung the front door open rapidly, and pulled the punks into his office. They were semi-conscious from either drink or drugs.

"We're going to whip your ass," one of them said, swinging wildly and almost falling down in the process.

"Damn right," the other one said pulling a blackjack out of his jeans' pocket. He lunged at Akard. Akard took the blackjack away from him and put it in his desk.

The two punks continued to thrash wildly at Akard, though they had yet to land a blow.

"Tell you what," Akard said. "A woman has whipped your asses. Now I'm going to let a dog and cat do the same."

Akard pushed one of the punks against the refrigerator disturbing One-Eyed Cat. The giant feline jumped from his perch onto the chest of the startled punk. He slid down the man's chest digging his claws in on the way down. The man was screaming in pain when Akard picked up the huge cat and dropped it on the man's shoulders. One-Eyed Cat repeated the process on the man's backside.

Meanwhile, Clarence had lunged at the other man's crotch and had taken a firm bulldog grasp of the situation. Akard called Clarence off and as the man placed his hands on his throbbing scrotum, Akard delivered a punch to his chin. He then picked One-Eyed Cat up and placed him back on top of the refrigerator.

Clarence's prey lay on the floor dazed. The other punk was sitting on the floor in agony. Akard removed the Beretta from his waistband and stuck it in the sitting man's mouth.

"Listen, you simple bastard," Akard said. "If I ever see you again I am going to blow your fucking head off. Comprende?"

The punk nodded his head.

"You are going to have some time to think about it," Akard said as he dialed 911.

It was only a few minutes before the police arrived. The officers knew Akard.

"What happened, McCoy?" One of the officers asked.

"The men are pet abusers. The pets fought back," Akard replied.

"We had heard there might be trouble," The other officer said.

"I'm going to sue his ass," the punk who had the run in with One-Eyed Cat said.

"What for?" the first officer asked.

"He turned that damn cat loose on me for no reason," the punk said.

"Well, you can tell that to the jury who will be sending you to jail," the second officer said as he handcuffed the punk.

As they were led away, the two punks both yelled, "We are going to sue your ass."

"Sue the animals," Akard said. "I don't have insurance."

After the punks had been carted away, Akard realized he was running behind schedule. The pets would have to be fed. After all, asking a cat to wake up long enough to get in a brawl requires a substantial reward. The English bulldog was only slightly less lazy. He gave each of them a treat and filled their respective bowls with dry food. He had to wait until they finished before he could take Clarence to the alley for his bathroom break. All this took time, so he called Zelda-Corrine to tell her he would be a little late. Even though he had hardly broken a sweat in the fight with the punks he felt he needed to clean up. He did so, and just in case the other two punks came calling, he put the Beretta into a shoulder holster as he slipped on a corduroy sport jacket.

Akard made his way to Zelda-Corrine's condo and offered his apology for being late.

"What kept you?" Zelda-Corrine asked.

"I had a run in at the office with two of the four punks we had the rumble with the other night."

"You don't look any worse for wear."

"I let the boys handle the situation."

"That is just like you to let your pets fight your battles. You should be ashamed of yourself. One of them is visually impaired."

"The combatants were equally matched. The two punks were higher than a kite. Besides that, One-Eyed Cat is simply a small bobcat posing as a domestic companion animal."

"I should call the SPCA."

"Please don't. I would make the newspapers."

"I'll let you off this time. Where are you taking me to eat?"

"Because you are special, I am taking you to a fish place in the West End."

"Perfect. I want to share a bottle of wine."

"Of course, my dear."

It is only a short drive from the Oak Lawn area of Dallas to the West End district. The West End is a major tourist attraction for Dallas. An old warehouse district was turned into upscale restaurants and shops. The weekends get a little crazy and Akard tried to avoid the crowds. This was a weeknight and one could usually get in a place to eat without a reservation.

Akard valet parked the car and the two of them were seated in the restaurant without waiting. Zelda-Corrine ordered sea bass and Akard ordered grouper. Akard had developed a taste for grouper several years before when he was investigating an off shore insurance company in the Cayman Islands. The wine of choice for the evening was a Pinot Grigio.

"I want to talk about Munich," Zelda-Corrine said.

"Talk away," Akard replied.

"I have been reading books, and there are so many places I want to see. I want to go to the Nymphenberg Palace and see the gardens."

"I saw a picture of those gardens. They are so long that if you had a one-hole golf course it would be a par ten. You would have to watch out for the fountains because they would be a water hazard."

"Akard, would you please give me a moment to be romantic outside of the bedroom?"

"Continue."

"I want to go to the Marienplatz and see the Glockenspiel. We should be there at eleven o'clock in the morning. The show lasts for seven minutes."

"That's almost as long as I can last in bed."

"Akard, behave."

"Continue."

"I want to go to the Hofbrauhaus to drink beer and eat German food."

"I'm with you there babe. What else?"

"Oh, I can think of a thousand wonderful things. What about you?"

"Some guy things like the BMW factory, The Olympic Village. Things like that."

"Where do you think we will stay?"

"The Veir Jahreszeiten is probably the swankiest hotel. Smoothmouth will probably want to stay there. He can afford it. I am not sure that we can."

"We are using airline miles to get there. You have money from the Italian case, and I have some savings. We may never go again."

"You're right as usual. It has been a major victory to get Smoothmouth to let us go in the first place. We can afford it. Besides I am getting my usual $750 per diem. Smoothmouth probably gets that per hour."

"Don't bemoan what Mr. Dellifield makes. If you had finished law school, you could probably charge the same."

"Don't get personal. I like my job. Smoothmouth can't carry a gun."

"Akard, this has been a lovely evening. You gave me flowers today. Cheap, but the thought was sweet. The wine has made me mellow. I don't suppose that you would take me home and make mad, passionate love to me?"

"Akard McCoy, at your service ma'am, I can and I will."

So Akard took Zelda-Corrine back to her condo and did exactly what he was asked to do. It is very seldom that Akard McCoy gets things 100 percent right the first time. This time he excelled. You could tell he had excelled by the smile on Zelda-Corrine's face the next morning. She rolled over and stroked his hair and said, "Play it again, Sam." He did with great pleasure. The smile on her face continued through breakfast, which Zelda-Corrine fixed herself.

The smiles that had adorned the faces of Akard and Zelda-Corrine were not present in Jacob's apartment. Jacob sat staring into his cup of coffee that was getting colder by the minute. His friend, Bill, sat motionless, staring at the floor. The two old men, already doomed to death, seemed to be approaching the inevitable more quickly since the death of Bernie. Both of their faces bore the look of death. Their skin had taken on the color of candle wax. Jacob's breaths were more labored and had a deep rasping sound.

Finally, Bill broke the silence. "It seemed like such a good idea at the time," Bill said.

"Not all good ideas stand the test of history. The Germans must have thought that Hitler had some good ideas and look at the legacy that he left," Jacob replied.

"Do we stop this killing now?" Bill asked of Jacob.

"We should bury our friend and then make that decision," Jacob replied.

"His body is at Restland. No relatives have come forward to make arrangements. Neither of us is in a condition to go out there and do anything. I have asked that worthless Sherman help out. He says he will help make the arrangements if we will pay the funeral costs," Bill said.

"It's ironic that we are taking about killing worthless trash when it will be a effort for either of us to get to the cemetery. We will be residents there soon enough ourselves," Jacob said.

"I told Sherman to make arrangements for Bernie to be cremated. I hope that was the thing to do," Bill said.

"Who really cares? Bernie was just another old man that society forgot. We are the only family he has. Some third cousin may show up in a few months and raise hell about what we did. Screw him. We will not be here to catch the flack. Let's keep his ashes. We should leave instructions that we both want to be cremated. When the last of us dies, our ashes can be released on a windy day in Dallas and blown to who knows where," Jacob said.

"We have become two, old, cynical bastards. Someone once told me that life was a shit sandwich. That the more bread that you have, the less shit you have to eat. Where we are, the amount of money we have makes no difference. More bread will not help us. Let's get out of this funk and eat our shit like men," Bill said.

"Well spoken. What do you suggest that we do?" Jacob asked.

"We get Bernie cremated. We gather our wits. We see if, in the few days we have left, anyone else gets in our cross hairs," Bill replied.

Akard had his breakfast that Zelda-Corrine had fixed for him. He was surprised that she had bacon and eggs. She ate far too healthy to keep what he considered staples in her apartment. Most of the time, she had her yogurt and he ate at Mama's Daughter's Restaurant.

He had kissed Zelda-Corrine passionately when he left. His hands ran over her incredible breasts the whole time he was kissing her.

"Don't start something that you can't finish," Zelda-Corrine purred.

"I can damn well finish as I proved last night. Sometimes affairs of state loom larger than my animal attraction for you. Those are difficult words for me to say at a time like this. Call it self-sacrifice, like Bogart letting Bergman leave in *Casablanca*." Akard emoted.

"Yeah, sure, your 'affairs of state' consist of taking your dog and cat for their morning walk down the streets of downtown Dallas. I often wonder how you keep from being arrested."

"I'll have you know that One-Eyed Cat always uses his litter box. Cats are that way you know. Clarence does crap on the sidewalk, but I always clean it up."

"Get out of here before I forget that I love you."

Akard left, but not before he kissed Zelda-Corrine again. He kissed her in a way that she would not forget.

It was later than the usual time that Akard took the pets for their morning walk. Clarence had managed to hold things in, but he barely made the alley before he found relief. One-Eyed Cat looked with disdain at an animal that did not have the sense to use a litter box. The cat resented being restrained by a leash. He was also scared of the traffic that was speeding down Elm Street.

More people were on the street at this time of morning and their attitude about a dog and cat in their way ranged from mild curiosity to annoyance. No one was willing to rebuke Akard. So, Akard and the animals finished the morning walk without incident. Akard rewarded them with their morning treats.

Akard looked at his calendar. It was blank. He had some window peeping matters in the works, but he was not motivated to follow errant spouses this day. On the other hand, he did need to make a living. The Brandenberg matter would not withstand too strict a scrutiny when it came to billing on a time basis. He hoped that lawyer Dellifield was about ready to go to Germany.

Akard looked in his desk to check his passport. It was current. He had some time to kill so he once again searched Web sites for any reports of Neo-Nazi activity. He came across a report that stated an incident that occurred the past fall. According to the report, police in Munich prevented a planned bomb attack. The police seized a bag with 1.7 kilograms of TNT. Six suspects had been arrested.

*"Smoothmouth is damn lucky to have me going with him. He is no match for these guys,"* Akard thought to himself. This reinforced his belief that having Dellifield take him and Zelda-Corrine to Munich was worth while. *"You know, terrorists come in all ages, colors and political beliefs. You don't have to be a young man or young woman with middle-eastern ties to be a terrorist,"* Akard mused.

In spite of his rough exterior and devil may care attitude, Akard loved history. He studied it at the Dallas Public Library. The downtown branch of the library was within easy walking distance of his Deep Ellum office-home.

Because of his young age, Akard had no personal knowledge of World War II. Nevertheless, he was fascinated with the subject. He had made a particular study of Adolph Hitler. He knew that the early Nazi party meetings were held at the Hofbrauhaus in Munich. He certainly planned to go there while in Munich, if not for the historical standpoint, then to be there to drink the beer and eat the food.

Hitler had begun his famous march on Berlin in Munich, on November 9, 1923 from a beer hall named the Burgerbraukeller. Hitler was a painter and one of his water colors was called "Of Old Vienna." There were photographs in books Akard had read showing Hitler on the streets of Munich in the company of Julius Streicher, a virulent anti-Semite. Akard had studied this one man, Hitler, whose views resulted in the conquest of Europe and the elimination of millions of Jews, and, in one way or another, had affected on the population of the world.

*"How strange it is that history repeats itself. Why do subsequent generations fail to learn the lessons of the past? Oh hell, I guess that is why society allows lawyers to live and prosper,"* Akard thought to himself.

Hitler loved Bavaria. From everything that Akard had read about Bavaria, he knew that he would love it, too, in spite of Hitler. Hitler's failed putsch in Munich had resulted in him and his followers receiving only light sentences with Hitler, himself, serving only eight months in prison. In January of 1933, when Hitler seized power, he stripped Bavaria of its autonomy.

Munich became the cultural center of the Reich. The first concentration camp was built outside of town at Dachau. There is a memorial there today to those who perished in the camp.

Akard felt that he had mused on the past long enough. He went to his computer and typed in "Munich." In spite of his wishes to the contrary, one of the first Web sites to come up dealt with the killing of the Israeli Olympic athletes in 1972. This was not what he wanted to see. This event had happened when he was only a toddler. He had seen old news clips through the years. He remembered the tributes to Jim McKay, the sports announcer, who had covered the event for ABC Sports.

Akard was ready to leave these unhappy thoughts. He did not like to think about death. It was not like he had never seen someone die. He had been at the bedside of his grandfather, Robert "Big Bob" McCoy when he had died. "Big Bob" was six-feet five inches tall. He weighed three hundred pounds. He was a titan in his lifetime. He had been one of the most successful trial lawyers in the history of the Dallas bar.

At the end of "Big Bob's" life, his body had wasted away. His skin had the ashen color that slow death brings to a person's face. Akard was holding his hand when "Big Bob" closed his eyes and stopped breathing. Akard had loved his grandfather and he would never forget his death.

He would never forget the one man he had ever killed either. Sure, the man was trying to kill him. Sure, it was a kill or be killed situation. Nevertheless, he would never forget the look on that man's face as he died. The look was a combination of hate and fear and hopelessness.

When you cut yourself, you wash off the blood and don't pay much attention to the details. When it's the blood of a man you just killed, it's different. In his case he had never met the man before. He could not understand why a man he never met could hate him enough to kill him. Akard had noticed the dead man's blood on his own hands. The blood was under his fingernails. It had dried around the cuticles on his fingers. It was in the lines of his knuckles. It was on his clothes.

When he finally got an opportunity to wash his hands, the blood had dried and changed to rust color. As he washed his hands, it seemed as though they would never get clean. He had spent ten years as a detective without killing anyone. He did not want to ever kill anyone again. Yet he knew if he stayed in the profession he was in, it was just a matter of time before he was faced with the situation again. If it happened, he knew he would kill again.

Akard felt he had enough morbid thoughts for the day and decided to take the old Jag for a spin. This time of year, it was cool enough for the car to run. Neither he nor the car could stand the Texas summer heat. It would be nice if the car was a roadster, but it wasn't. He had never turned on the heater because the engine and transmission heat were enough to keep him warm, even on the coldest day. He had never turned on the air conditioner because the car did not have one.

It wasn't easy to find a place in the country to drive, anymore. The countryside around Dallas was rapidly going the way of development. He decided to drive east to clear his mind of unhappy thoughts. As usual, he placed his Beretta on the seat beside him.

Akard pulled out of his garage and headed east. Even the land east of Dallas was being developed. Akard headed the Jag out highway 175. One of Akard's ancestors had been a peace officer in East Texas at the turn of the last century. He would go there on occasion to look in county's records to find references to his kin-folk. No one in the small towns he had visited had ever forgotten the name "McCoy."

The old Jag purred sweetly as it roared down the highway. Akard kept a keen eye on the speedometer. A bright red sports car draws the attention of the highway patrol. The day was cool and Akard had the windows down. The fresh air blowing in his face and the smell of the leather seats took his mind off the thoughts he had earlier.

Akard took a side road. He liked the country lanes with the hairpin turns. Out here, away from the city, life was simple. He could down shift and power into turns. These were things that could not be done in the city. In places, the trees on either side of the road met above the road and the sunlight barely shone through. It was pastoral. He wished that Zelda-Corrine were with him to enjoy the pleasure he was having. This was what the Jag had been built for. It had been modeled after the D Jag race cars. It did not have the class of the XK 120s, 140s and 150s, but it did get attention everywhere he went. He glanced in his rear view mirror and realized he was getting some attention he did not want. Riding his rear bumper was a large black pick-up truck. In the truck were two rednecks and they were giving him the finger.

"*I don't need this,*" Akard thought to himself. He stuck his arm out the window and motioned for the truck to pass. The rednecks behind him, instead of passing, bumped his rear bumper. The rear bumper on an XKE will not take much bumping. Akard down shifted to third gear and let the hammer down. The Jag lurched forward and pulled away from the truck. The truck increased its speed. Akard knew he could out drive the guys in the truck, but they had the advantage of knowing the road.

One of the problems of carrying a gun in your car is that there are occasions when you feel like using it. Akard had come out to the country to get away from unpleasant thoughts. The last thing he wanted to do was use his gun. He had a carry permit. He was a licensed private investigator. He was excellent with a handgun. None of this mattered to him now. He just wanted peace and quiet.

The driver of the truck was no match for Akard in taking the curves. Akard sped past a farmhouse and chickens were near the road. One flew up and hit the top of his windshield. Chicken blood was running down the windshield in front of him. One thing he had not restored was the windshield washer. He had slowed down enough for the truck to be on top of him again. Akard was having a hard time seeing the road, but he was not going to let these guys beat up his car, even if he had to shoot them. They had ruined his day. He would be damned if he would let them ruin his car.

Through the bloody smear of his windshield he saw a crossroad. He made a quick turn, and to his delight, he saw a sign that would direct him to Interstate 20. If he could make the Interstate, these guys would give up. For the most part, he was guessing about the road in front of him. The truck was bearing down on him again. He saw a sharp left turn to the Interstate and barely kept the car upright in making the turn. The truck fish tailed, but made the turn as well.

Up ahead was a truck stop. Akard pulled up to a gas pump. He got out, saw a paper towel and wet it in the container next to the pump. He cleaned off the windshield. The guys in the truck had parked beside the store at the station. Akard started putting gas in the Jag. The boys walked over and stood next to him.

"What kind of pussy would drive a car like that?" one of them said.

Akard sized them up. They were big and they looked strong. One of them was wearing a hat that said, "Goat Ropers Need Love Too."

"I guess that losers like you can only screw goats," Akard said.

The guy with the hat made a move for Akard and Akard caught him across the nose with his left hand. He then pulled him next to the Jag. He took the hose out of the gas tank, put it down the front of the man's jeans and filled his pants with gasoline.

"I guess even the goats won't have you now," Akard said.

The other man took a step toward Akard. Akard reached in the car and got his Beretta and put it in his waistband.

"Don't be a hero," Akard said. "You boys have had your fun. Now hit the road."

The man with the pants full of gasoline was wiping his bloody nose. He had barely started wiping his nose when the gasoline soaked through his underwear and hit his private parts.

"Yeoow," he screamed and made a dash toward the restroom.

"You had no call to done that," the other man said. "We was just havin' a little fun. I got a good mind to call the cops."

"I dispute the fact that you have a good mind to do anything, but if you want a cop, one is walking this way," Akard said.

"Oh, shit, man. Let's just forget the whole thang," the man said.

The peace officer approached and looked at Akard. "You got a concealed weapon permit for that gun in your pants?" the officer asked.

"I sure do," Akard said. With that, he got his carry permit, his driver's license and his private investigators license out of his wallet and handed them to the officer.

"Well, Mr. McCoy, I see you met the Johnson brothers. This one here is Monroe. The one in the men's room putting out the fire you started in his pants is Ricky. Most people call him Goose."

"We ain't done nothing," Monroe said.

"Monroe, where did you get the truck that you and Goose have been driving?" the officer asked.

"It belongs to a friend," Monroe replied.

"Did your friend steal it?"

"I don't know nothing about no stealing," Monroe answered.

"That's strange, Monroe, because my computer says it was stolen yesterday in Tyler," the officer said.

About that time, Goose emerged from the men's room. The entire front of his pants was wet. He took one look at the officer and took off running.

"You want me to shoot him?" Akard asked.

"The place is too crowded. You might miss. We know where to find him," the officer said.

"We ain't done nothing wrong," Monroe repeated himself.

"Monroe, you and I will take a ride to the station. You can tell me about your friend who lent you the truck. That looks like a shotgun in the truck. You boys know, as part of your probation, you can't have a firearm," the officer said.

"It ain't our gun," Monroe answered.

"I guess it belongs to the man who let you borrow the truck," the officer said.

"Damn straight," Monroe said.

"Monroe, why don't you put your hands behind your back and let me fit you with bracelets?" the officer said.

"I ain't done nothing wrong. We was just havin' fun. This asshole here is the one who should be cuffed for doing what he done to Ricky," Monroe said.

"I am sorry you had to meet the Johnson boys this way, Mr. McCoy. Their idea of fun is a little different from other folks. You are lucky they didn't shoot at you. I was parked behind a bush looking for speeders when you came past. I followed all of you here. I was looking up the license plate on the truck when you filled up Goose's pants. Have a nice day." The officer handcuffed Monroe and took him away.

*"I am ready to get out of Dodge. Nothing in Munich can be any worse than the locals I have had to deal with in the past two days. What happened to the serenity of the rural countryside?"* Akard thought to himself. He put the gas cap back on the Jag and headed back to the relative calm of Dallas.

Akard thought about a lot of things on the drive back to Dallas. In 1703, Jonathan Swift wrote, "Instead of dirt and poison, we have chosen to fill our hives with honey and wax, thus furnishing mankind with two noblest of things, which are sweetness and light."

Not that Akard would have thought of Jonathan Swift, but he would think of the contrast between leaving the loving arms of Zelda-Corrine and pumping high octane down the pants of a redneck. He would again ponder that not all terrorists are middle-eastern men between the ages of eighteen and thirty-four. Monroe and Goose were a brand of terrorists in their own way. They abused people and generally got away with it.

Sometimes a guy like Akard would come along and stand up to them. The police could not watch them every minute. They had both been in and out of jail many times. In the city, someone who was bigger and meaner would have taken care of them in one manner or another. In the country, they could bully just about everyone.

Still, Akard wondered if he had acted any better than they had when he gassed up Goose. No one had knighted him as an avenging angel, but they had pissed him off. Still, could he have handled the situation in a different way? "Oh, to hell with it," he said

Akard was late having his lunch. A man can't ponder the imponderables on an empty stomach. He saw a roadside diner that advertised chicken fried steak and pulled in. He had fried chicken fingers and fries. He poured cream gravy over the chicken fingers and covered the fries with half a bottle of ketchup. He washed it down with a root beer. He felt much better after lunch.

As he finished his drive back to Dallas, it occurred to him that he had never really checked Helga's telephone bills. He noticed that the heat gauge showed that the engine on the Jag was heating up a little. He could make it to his office before anything too serious happened. It would give him the opportunity to check his messages on his answering machine.

When he got to his office, he had three messages. The first was from Nell Munson who had more information concerning Helga's diary. The second message was from Conrad Dellifield. He had left word that the needed paper work was almost complete. He had made plane reservations for himself, Akard and Miss Paige. They needed to call the airline and give the reservationists their respective airline flyer's numbers to claim the mileage awards. The third message was from Zelda-Corrine saying she was having a girl's night out and for him to find some way to amuse himself.

Akard left his office for the high rise, driving the Taurus. Much in the same manner as Conrad Dellifield, he enjoyed the drive along Turtle Creek when the azaleas were in full bloom. When Akard was a boy, his mother loved to drive past the flowers on Turtle Creek in the springtime. She lives in California, now, with her second husband. She lived in the San Diego area where almost every day was like Texas in April. Akard's father had died young from too much booze and smoking. Akard's dad had not been sober enough to enjoy the azaleas, so, now, Akard would do it for him.

Akard pulled into the underground garage adjacent to the apartment building. The doorman gave him the usual condescending look. Probably had something to do with the cloud of blue smoke the Taurus left behind in the driveway. Akard had enough of confrontation for one day, so he simply gave the doorman a snappy salute as he walked past.

Once in the building, Akard checked in at the security desk. He no longer needed a key since Dellifield had provided him with one. He proceeded to the twentieth floor and let himself into the apartment. He wondered to himself if he was slipping. He normally would have checked the telephone bills as one of the first things he did in an investigation. It did not matter because he could not find any phone bills. "*This is odd, no phone bill,*" Akard thought to himself. He made a note on his note pad to have Dellifield, as administrator of the estate, secure copies of the bills.

The next thing he tried to find was a computer. If he found one, he would get a computer wizard to find a way to get to the email. He had not noticed a computer on prior visits. It was possible that Helga was one of the few people he had encountered that did not own a computer.

Even Dellifield used a computer and he had secretaries and legal assistants to do his work for him. Akard looked in every nook and cranny and could not find a computer, either desktop or laptop. What he did find plugged into one socket was a surge protector. "*Why would you need a surge protector if you didn't have a computer?*" Akard asked himself.

Akard decided to make a visit to the elderly gentleman down the hall. The one that he thought had been spying on him at an earlier visit. He walked down the hall and knocked on the door.

A gasping voice from within said, "Who's there?"

"Akard McCoy," Akard replied.

"Who are you?" The voice inside gasped again.

"I am a private detective working with the attorney who is the administrator of the estate of Helga Brandenberg."

Jacob paused. Was it better to send the man away or to find out what he was up to? After considering the options, he felt the more intelligent thing to do was let the man come into his apartment.

Akard could hear the man wheezing as he opened the door. Standing in front of him was a stooped over elderly gentleman. He was nearly bald. He was slight of build. His glasses were large and had thick lenses. He was wearing a pair of corduroy pants that had not been pressed in the memory of man. He had on a dress shirt that, at one time, had been white, but now the years had turned it a shade of yellow. Over the shirt, he was wearing a cardigan sweater, even though it seemed warm in the apartment to Akard. Both the sweater and the pants were brown. His shoes were brown with thick cushioned soles.

"*This man could be the poster boy for an old fart's club,*" Akard thought to himself.

"Please come in," the old man said graciously.

"Thank you," Akard replied as he entered the apartment.

The apartment had a medicinal smell. There were newspapers and magazines in stacks all over the room. There were small trays situated on either side of a reclining chair. The chair was positioned in front of a television set. Both of the small trays were covered with plastic prescription bottles. A humidifier was pumping mist into the room. The old man had an oxygen tube clamped to his nostrils. A long plastic tube was attached to oxygen bottles that sat in a wheeled cradle.

"My name is Jacob Franks," the old man said, extending his hand. His grip was weak and his hands were clammy. "How may I help you?"

Akard reintroduced himself. Then, he addressed the question he was asked.

"I am working with Conrad Dellifield. Mr. Dellifield is the court appointed administrator of the estate of Helga Brandenberg. Mr. Dellifield has asked me to assist him in the probate of her estate."

"Please have a seat," the old man said. Akard sat down on a couch that sagged under his weight. The old man sat down in his recliner, being careful not to step on the oxygen hose.

"Why does a lawyer need a detective to help in estate work? That seems odd to me," the old man said.

"The Brandenberg dame was from Germany, and I am trying to find out who gets her dough," Akard said, trying to sound like a movie detective he had seen on the screen as a child.

"I really don't see how I can be of any help in that regard. I barely knew the woman. True, we were neighbors, but I have been largely confined to my room in recent months," the old man replied.

"Were you ever in her apartment?" Akard asked.

"I may have been on one or two occasions," the old man answered.

"When you were in her apartment, did you notice if she had a computer?" Akard asked.

"I would have hardly noticed a detail like that. The few occasions I saw Ms. Brandenberg was when our mail got mixed up," the old man replied.

"You speak with an accent. It sounds like it might be German. You pronounced your 'W's' like 'V's," Akard observed.

"Yes, I lived in Germany many years ago, but I came to this country shortly after World War II," the old man replied.

"Where in Germany did you come from?" Akard asked.

"I came from Munich," the old man answered.

"I understand that Helga Brandenberg came from Munich. Did the two of you never compare notes about the old home town?" Akard inquired.

"I told you, I barely knew the woman. She once asked about my accent, but neither of us ever pursued that conversation. We had little in common. I am very tired now. Perhaps you could call again when I am feeling better," the old man said.

As the old man stood up from his chair, he reached for his oxygen tube. As he reached down the sleeves on his shirt and sweater pulled up enough for Akard to notice a scar on his under arm. It was the type of scar that Akard had observed when someone had a tattoo removed.

"Thank you for your time. I hope that I have not imposed too much on you. If you can remember anything about Ms. Brandenberg that might help in the settlement of her estate, please give me a call," Akard said as he handed the old man one of his cards.

"I am afraid that I have already told you everything that I know," the old man said as he ushered Akard out of the door.

"*That old buzzard knows one hell of a lot more than he is telling me. I can't believe that he and Helga did not talk about old home days in Munich,*" Akard thought to himself.

Akard left the building with more questions than he had answers. The unctuous doorman opened the door for Akard as he left the building.

"Good day, sir," the doorman said.

"Thank you," Akard replied. "How's your hammer hanging?" Akard's parting shot did nothing to endear him to the doorman. Akard didn't give a damn.

During the drive back to his office, Akard tried to sort things out. As usual, he had more questions than answers. Where were the telephone bills? Why was there a surge protector and why no computer? What, if anything, was the old man trying to hide? How many people in Dallas lived on the same floor in an apartment house that originally came from Munich? Was Jacob Franks Jewish? If so, had he found out something dark about Helga and done her in?

Akard knew it was easier to think up allegations than to prove them. He had been a detective from the time he was bounced from law school. He had also watched the O.J. Simpson trial.

When Akard got back to his office, he had a message on his telephone. It was from Nell Munson. She had left word that she had some more information for him. He looked at his watch. It was 6:30 p.m. The day had been eventful. He had left the arms of Zelda-Corrine only to have a confrontation with the rednecks. He believed that he had probably been lied to by Jacob Franks. Talking to a babe like Nell Munson would be a pleasant diversion.

He dialed Nell's number. After three rings, the voice on the other end of the line answered.

"Hello, Akard, thanks for calling," Nell said.

"I assume you have caller ID?" Akard answered.

"Yes, but I was hoping you would call. Corrine asked me to go to dinner with the girls, but I just didn't feel like going."

"You called and said you had some information for me."

"I do, but it would be so nice if you would come over and let me tell you in person. I could fix us both a little dinner. We could share a bottle of wine and get to know each other better."

*"This beautiful gal is coming on to me. Instead of a peanut butter sandwich here, I can have a dinner fixed for me. In the course of the evening I might even get laid. No. I am not stupid. I'm horny, but not that horny. Zelda-Corrine would kill me. Worse than that, she would cut me off,"* Akard had pondered the situation and made his decision. "Thanks for the offer, but I have a lot of paper work to catch up on."

"Are you going to be a good boy?"

"No, I'm going to be a smart boy."

"Rats."

"What did you have to tell me?"

"Since you have so much PAPER WORK, I would not want to add to your burdens this evening."

"I'll find a way to work it in"

"OK. Toward the end of Helga's diary she wrote that she thought someone had been in her apartment. She was also afraid that someone was going to harm her. She was worried about her work in Munich. I don't know if that means anything important, but it seems to fit with your questions about the circumstances of her death."

"That is very interesting. Did she mention anyone by name that she expressed these concerns to?"

"Yes. She said that she was going to let Herman know about her fears."

"This must be the same Herman that she was sending money to in Munich."

"You are probably right."

"Thanks, Nell, you are a dear."

"I'm a lonely dear and you don't know what you are missing".

"I am afraid I do, most of the time I weigh the consequences of my acts. At a different time and a different place, I would jump at the chance."

"Your mama raised you right. Good night, Akard."

"Good night, Nell."

"I must have lost my friggin' mind," Akard said to himself as he fixed his peanut butter sandwich. He took Clarence out for an evening walk. The crowds of people coming into Deep Ellum for food and entertainment were mildly amused at the sight of Akard walking his English bulldog through the throngs of young men and women. Many were holding hands. He missed Zelda-Corrine, even if it was only for one night. As Napoleon Bonaparte purportedly said in a letter to Josephine, "My soul aches with sorrow, and there can be no rest for your lover, but there is still more in store for me, when yielding to the profound feelings which overwhelm me, I draw from your lips, from your heart a love that consumes me with fire." On the other hand, the fire that was consuming his heart may have been from the peanut butter, avocado, pickle and mayo sandwich he had eaten.

He took Clarence back into his abode. He fed the pets and watched them wolf down their food as he munched on his second peanut butter sandwich. He called Zelda-Corrine and left word on her answering machine, "Luv you, babe."

Akard fell asleep in his bed with the television set in his bedroom still playing. Clarence and One-Eyed Cat joined him in bed in spite of the noise from the television.

# Chapter Sixteen

*Corrine Paige awoke with a slight headache from drinking too much wine the night before while laughing with her girl friends.* Jacob Franks awoke with the feeling that his death was not far off. As usual, he had spent a restless night hoping that his lungs would not fill with fluid, which would require a trip to the emergency room at Baylor Hospital. Akard McCoy awoke with a cat's tail across his face and a dog sleeping on its back next to Akard's left arm.

Akard was soaked with sweat. His sheets were in disarray. The fitted bottom sheet had been pulled away from the mattress. His pillow was wet, as was his T-shirt. He had dreamed wildly. The last dream he remembered was particularly weird.

He put on a pair of jeans and took the animals for their morning walk. He became obsessed with his dream and wondered how he could have one so weird. Akard had a good friend who was a psychiatrist. His name was Mark Mahoney. Akard had sent him plenty of patients arising out of his divorce investigations. It was early enough in the morning that he felt he could call him at home.

When he got back from his walk, he called the doctor's home telephone number.

"Hello," the voice answered.

"Mark, this is Akard."

"Good to hear from you, Akard. What do you need?"

"This may sound crazy."

"Most of the people I talk to are crazy. What's this about?"

"A dream I had last night."

"Akard, I don't have time for this."

"Help me out."

"OK, but make it quick."

"Alright, I am in a hotel room. I need to go to the bathroom. I am in the bathroom doing my thing when someone throws back the shower curtain. It's a woman wearing a name tag that says 'Macy's Supervisor.' The lady says, 'Must you?' I say, 'Lady, you are in my bathroom.' The lady says, 'No, you are in the ladies dressing room at Macy's.' I say, 'Lady get the hell out of my bathroom.' She says, 'over my dead body.' So I kill her."

"That's it?"

"That's it. What does it mean?"

"You're not making this up just to ruin my day?"

"Damn it, what does it mean?"

"First of all, were you having a bowel movement or urinating."

"I was whizzing. What difference does it make?"

"You asked for it. If you dream about a bowel movement, it goes back to your potty training. Your dream shows you are trying to please someone such as your parents. To dream of urination means that you are experiencing some burdens or feelings that you need to relieve yourself of. On the other hand, it may symbolize self-renewal. You may need to cleanse yourself emotionally and psychologically.

"The fact that you are in a restroom when someone else joins you indicates that you have difficulties getting enough privacy. The woman represented your feeling of insecurity.

"Your wanting to close the shower curtain shows that you are repressing thoughts. You don't want to share your thoughts.

"The fact that you killed the woman shows that you can only solve confrontation with violence. You could have told the woman she was right and that you were sorry. You could have suggested that Macy's and the hotel work the matter out between them and leave you two out of the equation. In other words, Akard, you are more fucked up than I thought.

"If you want to pursue this violent attitude of yours, call my office and make an appointment."

"Thanks Mark. You have been a great comfort to me in my hour of need."

"Seriously, Akard, a lot of your problems relate to your profession. You have told me in the past that you had wished that you had finished law school?"

"We have gone over this before. My grandfather set up a trust for my benefit. He was the famous lawyer, Robert 'Big Bob' McCoy. At six-feet-five inches and weighing three hundred pounds, few people messed with him in the court room or outside the court room. The trust provides that I can't get the principal until I finish law school. I think I am too damned old to start over."

"That's a problem, alright. Can't you go to court and do something about it?"

"I have asked Conrad Dellifield to do something. He is supposed to be the best there is. He tells me that it may be a reasonable restriction."

"Good luck, Akard. Come see me. We will discuss your situation in more depth."

"Thanks."

Akard did not know whether he felt better after the conversation or not. Munich had to be better. He needed to call Dellifield and tell him what Nell Munson had said. He needed to talk with Zelda-Corrine about getting ready to go to Munich. He decided that he would not tell her about the invitation from Nell Munson the evening before or about his dream. No reason to let her think he was weird. Although… she had long since figured that out herself.

He needed to see what the weather was like in Munich in April. The Internet, as usual, was helpful. The average temperature was in the 40's. The average rainfall was about four inches. It could snow in the mountains. Akard would need to go shopping. He was one of the few detectives without a good trench coat. He had sweaters and slacks, but he had no really nice wool slacks. Most of all, he needed a new suit that was heavier than the ones he seldom wore. He needed a hat to cover his crew cut. He decided to wait until he got to Germany and buy a Tyrolean hat, a green one.

He called Zelda-Corrine at home because he knew that after a night out with the girls she would be having a slow start.

"Hello, Akard."

"Caller ID?"

"Yes. Thanks for being a good boy last night."

"What do you mean?"

"Nell Munson said you turned her down last night."

"Did you put her up to it?"

"No, she just called to tell me that you resisted her charms, and that I should be proud of you."

"Would she have called if I had taken her up on the offer?"

"I guess that is something neither of us will ever know."

"Moving right along, we will be leaving for Munich in less than a week. I checked the temperatures and you will need winter clothes."

"I did the same thing myself. My wardrobe is considerably better than yours. I am going to pick up a new winter scarf over there. That is about all I need. You, on the other hand are a fashion disaster."

"I am going to get a new coat, some wool slacks and a new suit."

"Thank God for small favors."

"You can go with me to shop if you want to."

"Thanks for the invitation. I have too much to do to get ready to leave the country. You don't pick out my clothes, and I trust you to pick out your own. I do expect to see you tonight. By the way, I appreciate you telling me on my voice mail that you love me. A woman never gets tired of hearing those words."

"Deal, I love you."

"See you tonight."

"You can count on it."

Talking to Zelda-Corrine was a breath of fresh air. Akard almost forgot about his dream. Zelda-Corrine seemed to be able to live with his first name. If someone came down too hard on her about his name, she could whip his ass, although she was not as likely as he was to resort to violence.

Akard called the office of Conrad Dellifield. The English receptionist answered the telephone. He asked to speak to Dellifield.

"Why, Mr. McCoy," she purred, "How pleasant to hear from you. I will put you right through to Mr. Dellifield."

"Akard, how are you?"

"I have some more information for you."

"Pleased to hear that, what have you got?"

"Nell Munson has finished reading Helga's diary. Helga wrote in her diary that she thought someone was out to get her. Also, don't you think it is strange that there were no telephone bills in her apartment? I could not find a computer either."

"Not everyone has a computer. I hate the damn things. I have to delete unwanted emails every day. The computer makes you too accessible. Maybe Helga was old fashioned like me."

"I doubt that there is anyone else like you. I don't know why she would have a surge protector if she had no computer."

"Good work, Akard. You have brought me some interesting news. I will have you look into the matter more when we get back from Munich. Munich will probably be very boring. I feel confident that there is no connection between what you have discovered and what we will find in Munich."

"Don't be too sure of that. Anyway, that is why you have me."

"We will be leaving in four days. Do you have your passport and clothing ready to go?"

"I need to pick up a few things. Zelda-Corrine and I will be ready when you are."

"Go by American Express and pick up a few Euros. You can charge most everything, but it is always handy to have some cash."

"Roger, I will talk with you later."

Three and a half miles away, Jacob Franks was calling his friend Bill. He asked Bill to come to his apartment because he had important matters to discuss with him. Bill arrived at Jacob's apartment within a few minutes.

"What's up?" Bill asked.

"Come in and I will tell you all about it," Jacob replied.

"All about it? What is *it?*"

"I had a visit from the detective yesterday."

"What detective?"

"The big guy. The one who has been snooping around Helga's apartment."

"Is he a policeman?"

"No, he is a private detective who is working with the lawyer."

"What did he want? Why did you wait so long to tell me?"

"I knew you were having a bad day yesterday and I did not want to make things worse."

"Hell, man, I am about to die. How can things get any worse?"

"I am about to die, too. Let's not bicker."

"Fine, just tell me what the guy wanted."

"He wanted to know if I knew Helga, if I had ever been in her apartment or if I had noticed if she had a computer. He wanted to know if we had any connection because of Munich."

"What did you tell him?"

"I told him that I knew very little. I felt sure he did not believe me."

"What happened to her computer?"

"She only had the laptop. I still have it."

"Maybe we should have left it in the apartment. At least, that way the police could have gotten her email and seen what she was doing in Germany."

"If the police knew, they would investigate her death more deeply. If I had not drugged her lightly when we were having a social drink in her apartment, I would never have seen her computer screen."

"Maybe it would have been better if you had not seen her screen."

"I lived through the Holocaust. There are people today who say it did not exist. I stood in the snow in freezing weather in my bare feet. I saw people run into electric fences and die rather than endure any more deprivation. I had to stop her. I had to stop her."

"We did what we did. We knew the consequences. We cannot stop the people in Munich, but at least we cut off their funds."

"Let's change the subject. You look like hell."

"Thanks, so do you."

Jacob looked at his friend. His skin color seemed to yellow more with each passing day. In contrast, Jacob's own pale skin seemed to become more translucent each day. Each of them was walking death. Their bodies were wasting away. Their hands had veins almost protruding through the skin. As a doctor, he had seen many people die. Watching his friend die, as well as seeing himself, was depressing.

"Want a cup of coffee?" Jacob asked.

"I had better just have a glass of water," Bill replied.

"I will get you one. You know, if the lawyer and the detective go to Munich, perhaps they can finish what we started," Jacob said.

"They will have to find out for themselves. I cannot bear the thought of spending my last days in jail."

"You are right. The whole matter is out of our hands."

Bill began to feel weak, so he left for his own apartment. He was bowed over and shaking his head.

# Chapter Seventeen

*S**hopping for clothes was something of a personal nightmare for* Akard. Most of the time, he looked like a poster boy for Goodwill Industries. He knew that Dellifield would expect him to create a good impression on the German bankers. Zelda-Corrine would always look good and she would receive most of the admiring glances. He never bought anything in the way of clothing unless it was on sale. Neiman-Marcus was not an option, although it was the closest department store to his abode. He opted to go to a discount clothier.

Although something of a slob, Akard read *GQ* and understood style. He knew that fake buttoned cuffs on a suit or sport coat gave a bespoke look to a garment. The bespoke look was more evident in Europe than in his part of Dallas. He went to a clothing warehouse store that has hundreds of men's suits, sport coats, slacks and accessories.

Akard wore a 48 long jacket. This made it a problem buying a suit because he was 35" in the waist. He could solve some of the problem by buying an athletic cut suit. He looked at winter weight suits until he found a charcoal gray suit with fake buttoned cuffs. The pants were too big in the waist and the salesman said that they could not be altered within his time frame. "Forget it," Akard said. The salesman winced and told Akard he would see that the alterations were made.

Akard then went to the sport coats and settled on a double breasted blue blazer in heavier wool. It was a well-known brand discounted sharply. He matched the blazer with two pairs of slacks in light and dark gray colors. He bought two shirts with straight collars rather than button down collars. He found a pair of black capped toe shoes in a size thirteen. His final purchase was a navy blue cashmere sweater.

Akard had the pants to the suit taken up in the waist and had all of the pants cuffed. He felt smug and self-satisfied. Dellifield would not be ashamed to be seen with him and Zelda-Corrine would be proud of his appearance.

The salesman told him that he had made a wise choice. Akard wondered how wise a choice it was to buy heavy wool clothing to wear in Dallas. It got cold some days in the winter, but those days were few. Akard did not dress up that often. It would not have been the wise thing to be wearing good clothes when he had poured gasoline down the pants of Goose a few days earlier.

He was about to leave the store when he realized that he had not purchased an all-weather coat. He went back in the store and settled for a trench coat with a zip out lining. He passed up on the overcoats knowing that he would have very little use for an overcoat in Dallas. Akard took the shoes, coat and shirts with him, and left the rest of his purchases to be altered.

Akard knew that he had a few matters to wrap up before he could leave town. One of these was to get the goods on a man who had been injured in a fall at a supermarket. Akard had checked the court records and found that he had been injured several times before and had filed suit to recover for his injuries. Akard's insurance company client had asked him to check up on the man and he had put off making an investigation. He knew he had to do something. He had been given the man's address several weeks before.

Akard went to the man's house and parked under a tree. He always carried several cameras of both the still and video types. The digital camera had made his work easier. He could email the pictures to his client without having to worry about the development process.

After about an hour's wait, the man came out of his house walking with a cane. He looked around to see if anyone was looking. Akard had slipped down in his seat when the man came out of his house. One thing about owning a 1997 Taurus is that, for the most part, both the car and its occupant go unnoticed.

The man started down the street and Akard followed at a safe distance. Akard tailed him to a bar in a seedy part of East Dallas. The man went inside. Akard parked across the street from the bar and waited a half hour before he got out of his car. He carried the smallest camera he had. It could easily be concealed in his pocket.

Akard walked into the bar and looked around. He looked at his watch and noticed that he had missed lunch. His stomach told him the same thing. There were only about four patrons in the bar. They were the type of men that one would expect to find in a seedy bar in a bad part of town. They were men whom society had forgotten. They were unshaven and bleary eyed. Most would be unemployed or under-employed. Some of them lived on handouts. Others worked just enough to keep themselves in booze. Akard wondered how he would stand out if he were wearing the clothing he had just purchased.

The man was sitting at the bar talking to the bartender. Akard sat down at the bar two seats down from the man.

"Do you have any food here?" Akard asked the bartender.

"We got sandwiches," the bartender replied.

"I will have a ham and cheese and a bottle of Bud," Akard said.

"You want chips with the sandwich?" the bartender asked.

Akard nodded yes. The bartender opened a bottle of cold beer and handed it to Akard. Akard noticed that the man he was following had an empty bottle in front of him and was mostly finished with the second. Akard took a swig of his beer and turned to the man two seats down.

"How's it going?" he asked the man.

The man did not look up. "Who wants to know?" the man replied.

"Oh, just a guy who is new in town looking for a job and a place to live," Akard said.

"Sorry, buddy, but I can't help you in either case," the man said.

"Just trying to make conversation," Akard said.

"Ain't interested," the man said.

"Sorry I bothered you," Akard said.

The bartender brought Akard his sandwich and Akard concentrated on his food. The man ordered another beer. Akard realized that if the man kept drinking, at some point he would have to relieve himself. He would watch and see if he walked with his cane. His report had said that the man needed a back operation and that he could not bend over.

Akard finished his sandwich and went to the restroom. He took a five dollar bill out of his pocket and dropped it on the restroom floor next to the urinal. He could only hope that no one would use the restroom before the man at the bar did.

When he returned to his seat, the man was almost finished with his third beer. Akard thought that the man must have a well-trained bladder to hold that much beer without a pit stop. Another man got up from his seat and headed toward the bar.

"*On shit, don't let him go to the restroom,*" Akard thought. He would not only lose his five dollars to an unworthy cause, but he also knew that the ruse would not work twice. The other man walked to the bar and patted the one he was watching on the shoulder.

"See you around," the other man said to the man at the bar. The man at the bar nodded and the other man left the bar. The man at the bar ordered his fourth beer. Akard was afraid if he nursed the beer he was drinking any longer the man would become suspicious. He ordered another beer. Half way through his fourth beer, the man got up and headed toward the restroom. He had left his cane leaning against the bar.

Akard waited a second and followed the man. The man was unzipping his pants when he noticed the bill on the floor next to the urinal. As he reached down to pick up the bill Akard pushed open the door and took pictures of the man bending over as rapidly as he could.

"You rotten bastard," the man said to Akard.

"Tell that to the judge," Akard replied.

The man straightened up and was holding a switch blade knife. Akard took one picture before the man lunged at him. The man was no match for Akard. Akard simply pushed him aside and took the knife away. The man fell to the floor

"You dirty rotten bastard," the man repeated himself as he lay next to the urinal.

"You won't need this," Akard said to the man, as he slipped the man's knife into his own pocket. "By the way, you can keep the five dollars. You may need it in the future."

Akard went to the bar and paid his tab. He took the man's knife out of his pocket and handed it to the bartender.

"The guy in the restroom pulled this on the wrong man. Keep it for him or give back," Akard said to the bartender.

The bartender looked at the knife and put it under the bar. The bartender said nothing. Akard took a picture of the cane leaning against the bar and left.

"*Another day, another confrontation,*" Akard thought to himself. Perhaps he would have another weird dream tonight. Maybe he should sell clothes like the guy he had met earlier. "*No, where else can I get paid for drinking beer and beating up drunks?*" Akard answered his own thoughts.

Akard went back to his office. He looked at the shots on the digital camera he had taken at the bar. He got three good pictures of the man bending over and one shot of him with the knife. He loaded the pictures in his computer and prepared a memo to email to the insurance company. He sent the email to the insurance adjuster he was working with. He explained the situation and what the pictures represented.

In a short while he got a reply to the email. It said:

"Good work, Akard. I think you shot his case down. I particularly liked the shot of him with the knife. I will recommend to the company that they pay you hazardous duty pay. Thanks, Ben"

Akard felt good. He would probably get a bonus for his work. There had been some danger. He would not tell Zelda-Corrine about the knife part. This assignment was better than waiting outside of motel rooms, waiting and hoping to catch someone with his pants down. Akard wondered why the penalties for sex outside of marriage were so severe. A man could lose everything he had if he got caught with the wrong person at the wrong time. For that matter, the same thing could happen to a woman. He thought about the offer from Nell Munson the evening before and the consequences of taking her up on the offer. He was better off declining. "*Let someone else screw her,*" Akard thought to himself.

Akard's thoughts drifted back to the Brandenberg matter. He felt like he ought to call his friend, Lt. Baines, and let him know of his conversation with the old man. He dialed the number and Lt. Baines answered.

"This is Baines."

"'Deadeye,' this is Akard."

"What do you want, Akard? I am real busy right now."

"I am just trying to be a good citizen. I have some more information on the Brandenberg case."

"There is no Brandenberg case. She committed suicide.

"Have it your way. I might change your mind."

"Alright, let's have it."

Akard told Baines about his conversation with the old man who lived down the hall from the Brandenberg apartment. He told him about the Munich connection. He told him that his instincts made him feel like there was something odd about the old man.

"Akard, I can't arrest a man for being odd. If I could, you would have been put in the slammer years ago. If it will make you happy, I will have the investigating officers look into the case again."

"I have done my duty. Have a nice day."

"It is always good to talk with you, Akard. Give Corrine my regards."

Akard hung up the telephone wondering why he had wasted his time. "*Let the old fool get away with murder. Who gives a crap?*" Akard thought to himself.

The dog and the cat were at his feet. Clarence was crying to get out and One-Eyed Cat was hungry as usual. He looked at his watch and saw that it was about time to see Zelda-Corrine. He took Clarence into the alley and let him do his thing. He then fed them both.

"Listen boys, I may spend the night elsewhere. Clarence, try to hold it until I get back."

He stroked both of them fondly and wondered if he really devoted enough time to his pets. A cat can get by on its own. A dog needs attention. He scratched both animals behind the ears and went upstairs to dress.

Even though he would probably be late, it seemed to Akard that he ought to take a shower. He took off his shirt and sniffed under his arms.

"Damn, who died?" he said to no one in particular. The whiff had convinced him of the need for hygiene. He took the shower, not for the preservation of health, but for the preservation of his relationship with Zelda-Corrine.

He dressed and bade the boys goodbye. He called Zelda-Corrine on his cell phone and told her he was on his way. He was driving the Jag, because it was cool outside, and he thought he looked cool driving it.

He picked Zelda-Corrine up outside of the fitness center. This was a sign that he was spending the night, because she was leaving her car parked in the garage next to the fitness center. He would take her to work in the morning and her car would be there.

She was wearing yellow pants with a white satin blouse and a yellow cardigan sweater that matched her pants. The sweater was unbuttoned. As she got into the Jag her sweater pulled away just enough for Akard to see her nipples pressing against the satin blouse.

She leaned over and pecked him on the cheek.

"You smell good. Did you shower just for me?" Zelda-Corrine said.

"Just for you, sweetheart."

"Thanks. What did you do today?"

"I went shopping and bought some new clothes. Then I beat up a drunk who was trying to cheat an insurance company."

"Akard, be serious."

Akard realized he almost told her about the incident with the knife. He decided to blow the whole incident off and talk about his clothes purchase.

"You would be proud of me. I have got some impressive rags for the trip. 'Smoothmouth' will not be embarrassed about taking me along."

"Tell me what you bought."

"Well I got a new suit. I got a blue blazer and two pairs of slacks. I got two new shirts and a new pair of dress shoes."

"I can't wait to see you wearing your new outfits."

"I can't wait to see you with your clothes off."

"Later. Take me somewhere nice for dinner. Somewhere that is romantic. Somewhere that is dark and candle lit with soft music in the background."

"How about Sam's hamburgers?"

"How about sleeping alone tonight?"

"Excellent point, you would have made a good lawyer."

"So would you if you had not gotten kicked out of law school."

"Ouch, that hurt, how about the French Room?"

"Neither one of us is dressed well enough to go there. Let's go to the City Café."

Akard headed the Jag to the City Café. He would not let the attendant park the Jag. He let Zelda-Corrine out of the car and parked in the retail parking next door.

The two of them were warmly greeted when they entered. They were seated at a small table in the back. Zelda-Corrine reached over and got Akard's hand.

"I missed not seeing you last night," she said.

"I missed not seeing you, too," he answered.

They looked deeply into each other's eyes.

"God, you're beautiful," Akard said.

"You don't look so bad yourself, fella," she replied.

The two of them ordered dinner. Zelda-Corrine ordered a house salad, veal Marsala and a side order of creamed spinach. Akard ordered a crab cakes appetizer, trout and a baked potato. A bottle of Merlot accompanied the meal.

The two of them talked about the trip to Munich and how much they should pack. Each, again, went over what he or she would like to see and do while they were there. There was a lot of hand-holding. Akard forgot the cares of the day. He forgot about how he made a living and the low lives he had to deal with. His thoughts were about the beautiful woman sitting across from him at the table. He looked into her eyes and glanced repeatedly at her perfectly formed breasts that were trying their best to break out of the satin blouse that was holding them in.

"See something you like?" Zelda-Corrine asked.

"I could not help but notice."

"Pay the check and let's go to my place. When we get there you can make an up close and personal examination of what you have been staring at."

"You mean, you want me to get closer to your face and look at your eyes."

"You know very well what I am talking about. I would not mind you looking into my eyes either."

Akard did as he was told and took Zelda-Corrine to her apartment. When they got inside, she wrapped her arms around him and kissed him passionately.

"You want to unwrap the package?" she asked.

Akard slowly unbuttoned her blouse. He unhooked her bra and let it fall to the floor. Staring him in the face was what he had been looking at all evening. Her breasts were perfect. He caressed each one slowly and gently. Zelda-Corrine let out a small moan. She put her arms around him again and pressed herself against his chest.

He led her into the bedroom where they made love until both were exhausted. They lay in bed on their backs, breathing deeply. Zelda-Corrine reached over and gently touched his chest, curling the hairs between her fingers. He pulled her next to him and they fell asleep in each other's arms.

# Chapter Eighteen

*Akard awoke the next morning feeling totally relaxed. Zelda-Corrine* could do more for his damaged psyche that all the shrinks he knew. He reached over to touch her and she was not in bed. He looked at his watch and it was 9:00 am. He did not want to think about what Clarence might have done to the floor of his place. Fortunately, the downstairs floor was still the same concrete floor that had been in the original motor rewind shop.

A note was pinned to Zelda-Corrine's pillow. It said:

"Akard. You do good work. I would love to share the after glow with you, but I have an early appointment at the fitness center. I am walking to work. There is cereal on the kitchen table. It will be good for you. Get the details of the trip settled. See you tonight. Love, Corrine."

The thought of cold cereal was somewhat repugnant to Akard. However, if Zelda-Corrine put it out for him, he was going to by God eat it. He wolfed the cereal down and got back to his place as soon as possible. Clarence and One-Eyed Cat met him at the door. Both were hungry. Clarence had held it as long as he could, but he had been asked too much. Akard muttered to himself, "It was worth it" as he cleaned up after Clarence. He took the boys for their morning constitutional. Both seemed happy to get outside.

Akard finished the walk and showered. His charge was to see that everything about the trip went smoothly. Zelda-Corrine had a regular job and the least he could do was to take the responsibility for getting the two of them to Munich.

He checked the emailed ticket confirmations. They would leave DFW airport around three in the afternoon. They would fly directly to Zurich. The flight would arrive in Zurich early in the morning. There would be about a three hour lay over in the Zurich airport. They would arrive in Munich after one o'clock in the afternoon.

*"This is good planning,"* he thought to himself. The trick to beat jet lag is to get to the destination in the morning and stay up as late as you can the day of arrival. That will allow you to go to bed on schedule and wake up almost refreshed the next morning. Zelda-Corrine had some magic pills that would knock you out on the way over so that you could sleep on the plane. You should also to eat light and stay away from too much booze and caffeine. He had learned this trick on another trip overseas. It worked, but it sure took the fun out of travel. He also admitted to himself that Dellifield's secretary had made all the air travel arrangements.

He started making a checklist of things to do. He needed to take the pets to the vet. He had to pick up his clothes from the tailors. He had to go by the bank and get some Euros. He had to pack. He had to leave his gun at home. That was a disturbing thought. Having a concealed weapon permit in Texas would not buy you any peace in Germany. He could not get a weapon there, anyway.

When you expect trouble, you want an even playing field with the bad guys. He would be on their turf. The bad guys would not bother to get a permit for their weapons. Whatever they might have could out-gun anything he could come up with. Maybe he was worrying about nothing. There may not be any bad guys and this trip could be a cake walk. All his instincts told him to expect trouble. He would see what he could find in the way of protection when he got to Germany. Whatever it might be, the other guys would have something deadlier.

Akard decided to defer trying to solve the problem until he could determine what the problem was. Instead, he called the vet and made arrangements for the care of the animals while he was gone. Taking

One-Eyed Cat to the vet in a car was a two-person job. Clarence loved to ride in a car. One-Eyed Cat, on the other hand, moaned in a low growl the entire way. The bottom of his paws would sweat. He could do some serious damage if he got spooked. Akard had the remains of a leather jacket that the cat had destroyed by climbing up its front while objecting to a ride in the car.

Taking the cat in a cage was a problem simply because someone had to get him in the cage. The best way was to let someone else drive while he carried the cat in a pillow case. Only the cat's head could stick out while Akard held a firm grip on his paws. The whole time, he would have to speak softly to the cat with words of encouragement. He would hope like hell that Clarence would not jump in the middle of them during the ride.

Conrad Dellifield IV took an entirely different approach to traveling. He had been to Europe, either for pleasure or business, over thirty times. He had established off-shore trusts in the Bahamas and in the Cayman Islands. He had been to Asia, but it was not his favorite place to go.

His clothes looked bespoke because they were bespoke. He did not have a large wardrobe, but what he had was either tailored in London or Milan. His shirts were made in London. He and Akard had one thing in common. Both men were six feet, three inches tall. That was where the similarity ended. At one time, Dellifield had been thin. When he graduated from law school he weighed one hundred and eighty pounds. He now weighed two hundred pounds. His frame could handle the weight and often people asked him how he stayed so trim.

Good tailoring will cover a multitude of body flaws. Dellifield's waist had gone from 35" to 38". His suit jackets were cut to conceal the bulge at the middle. If he removed his coat at all, he would try to hold his stomach in as long as he could. Sooner or later, he would have to take a deep breath and his chest would fall to his waist again.

He had packing for trips down to an art form. He would take two suits and a blue cashmere sport coat. One of the suits would be dark gray and he could wear the pants to the dark gray suit with the blue jacket. This would give him an extra outfit without the need for another pair of slacks. His socks and underwear came from a travel outfitter's catalogue. He would take three pair of each and that would easily last him for a week's trip. His one extravagance was that he insisted on having a fresh, starched shirt for each day of the trip. He carried a small steamer to remove any wrinkles that might form in his coats and pants.

He also packed an electrical current converter to adjust the current in Europe for the steamer and his electric razor. All of his clothes would fit into one garment bag with large pockets. His hand luggage would carry his files, a small notebook computer, an overseas cell phone and, most importantly, his medicine.

A few years ago, Dellifield had developed an irregular heart beat. It was controlled by medication known as Norpace. Because an irregular heart beat increased the risk of a stroke, he had to take a blood thinning medication. Once a month, he had to go to the doctor's office to be sure that the medicine that thinned his blood had not made it too difficult to clot. Getting this out of balance could cause internal bleeding, if too thin, and offer no protection against his heart throwing off a clot if his blood was not thin enough. He always took more medicine than he needed on a trip, in case he was unexpectedly delayed in getting back home.

This particular morning, he had followed his usual routine of getting up at six o'clock am. He took a brisk two-mile walk. On his return, he took a hot bath in his seven-foot bathtub with a whirlpool. His wife, Nettie, accompanied him on his walk. She would shower while he was in the bathtub.

The bathtub faced the shower. The shower stall was clear glass. Dellifield could watch his wife as she showered. He marveled every day at how she had maintained her size four figure. Unlike him, she had not gained a pound since they were married almost forty years ago. He loved to watch her soap her body and toss her wet hair under the flow of the shower head.

When his wife would step out of the shower, she would dry her head with a towel and slip into her bathrobe. As he got out of the tub, she would playfully slap him in the gut and say, "when are you going to do something about that?" Dellifield would always answer the same way, "I am working on it."

After the bath and shower, the Dellifields would have their breakfast consisting of cereal, a banana, one piece of toast and a cup of coffee for each of them. They would discuss the day's events as they read the newspaper. This particular morning, they discussed the trip to Munich.

"I wish you were going with me, my dear," Dellifield said.

"You know I would love to, Connie, but I have the Garden Club thing. I am the president, you know. Our big spring show is going to be the week you are gone," his wife answered.

"I know. It was very poor timing on my part."

"I will be very busy, so this is a good time for you to go, EXCEPT for the Ball at the end of the show. YOU WILL BE HERE, WILL YOU NOT?"

"Of course, I will be back in time for the Ball. It is black tie, is it not?"

"Yes, it is. It is my big night. I would just die of embarrassment if you did not show up."

"They will have to shoot me to keep me away."

"Thank you, Connie. You are so sweet to me. I knew I could count on you."

"Yes, my dear, you can."

Dellifield turned his attention to making a list of things to do before he left.

Zelda-Corrine went to work feeling great. Akard had the same effect on her as she had on him. She was singing as she came in the door of the fitness center.

"Good morning, everyone," she chirped as she came in the door.

"It was that good?" her assistant manager said.

"I can't deny it," Zelda-Corrine said as she swung her hips from side to side.

Zelda-Corrine looked at her schedule and then made a list of things she had to do before the trip.

Jacob Franks awoke to find he was still alive. "*I made it another night,*" he thought to himself. How many more mornings he would wake up was anyone's guess. He made a list of things to do that day. It contained only one notation. "Try to live through the day."

Jacob Franks had possession of the cremated remains of his friend, Bernie. No one else had come forward to make arrangements for a funeral. Jacob and Bill had paid for cremation of Bernie's body. There was no service, because there was no one to attend a service. Bernie's remains now rested in a polished wooden box sitting on a end table in Jacob's apartment.

"It is not turning out the way we planned, old friend," Jacob said to the box.

"The world is better off without Helga Brandenberg, but the world is not better off without you. Our plans seemed like such a good idea at the time. Perhaps, we're just too old and too frail. There is so much bad in the world and so little time. Were we any less evil than those from whom we sought retribution, based upon our own standards of guilt? I don't know, Bernie. I am sorry it ended this way for you. Please forgive me."

No response came from the box. Jacob continued his discourse with the box.

"There is this guy, Bernie, who is a detective. He works for the lawyer who is handling Helga's estate. The guy was up here the other day asking me questions. He wanted to know what I knew about Helga. He asked me about Munich. He asked about her computer. I think the lawyer may go to Munich. He may take the other guy with him. The detective looks tough. Maybe they can stop what Helga was financing. Maybe I will join you soon, Bernie. Maybe God will take me. That would be ironic. The last bad guy that I take out is me."

# Chapter Nineteen

*And it came to pass that the unlikely trio made their plans and the day had come to go to Munich.* Conrad Dellifield was driven to the DFW airport by his wife, Hattie. She drove her silver 400 series Lexus to the international gate of Amalgamated Airlines. Dellifield had packed his clothes in a way to insure that they would arrive unwrinkled, in spite of the best efforts of the airline to do otherwise. His wife, Hattie was dressed to the nines, just in case someone might see her dropping her husband off at the gate.

Dellifield gave his bag to a skycap to take to the first class check-in counter at Amalgamated Airlines. Hattie got out of the car and hugged Dellifield tightly.

"I am going to miss you," she said.

"I am going to miss you, too," he replied.

"Please be sure you take your medicine," she said.

"I will," he answered.

"And remember to be back in time for the Garden Club Ball."

"I will, my dear."

"Promise?"

"Promise."

Akard and Zelda-Corrine arrived at the same gate by vehicle in a far different manner from the Dellifields. They arrived by taxi. They would not part at the airport, as the Dellifields had done. They would be making the trip together and they could not be happier about the prospect.

Akard had packed in his own way, to insure that his clothes would also arrive unwrinkled. His luggage was not as sturdy as that of Conrad Dellifield. It was an even bet as to whether the luggage or the airline would win.

Zelda-Corrine was dressed in light purple pants, a dark purple blouse and a light purple cardigan sweater that matched the pants. As usual, every male in sight was looking her way. Akard, on the other hand, was noticed only because of his size. He had left his new clothes in his bag and was wearing his more familiar outfit of blue jeans with a corduroy coat. Both of them carried their all weather coats over their arms. Akard felt naked in one respect. There was no Beretta under his coat.

Akard looked around for Dellifield. He was nowhere in sight. Then, it occurred to Akard that Dellifield was probably in the Commander's Club of the airline. Akard and Zelda-Corrine would have to be content with spending their time waiting at Starbucks.

Shortly before boarding, Dellifield caught up with Akard and Zelda-Corrine. He had emerged from the Commander's Club looking dapper, as usual. He was wearing a blue sport coat with gray slacks. He had a burgundy turtleneck on under his jacket. Dellifield looked every ounce a first class passenger. Akard looked every ounce someone who belonged in steerage. Dellifield greeted them warmly, as only a man like him could greet people. They exchanged pleasantries while waiting to board the plane.

They boarded the plane in groups. The first class and business passengers boarded first, followed by the economy class passengers. Akard and Zelda-Corrine walked past Dellifield on their way back to steerage. He nodded as they passed, giving them a hint of recognition. The two of them made their way back to their seats, which were toward the rear of the plane. When they reached their seats and sat down, Zelda-Corrine reached over and held Akard's hand.

"I can't believe that we are really on our way to Munich," she said.

"Believe it, Babe. We are on our way to Munich. We are going to have a great time, in spite of Dellifield," Akard replied.

"Don't be so hard on the man. He really seems quite nice. He is the reason that we are going. Try not to forget that."

"I know, it's just that he is such a stuffed shirt."

"Don't confuse being a stuffed shirt with being a gentleman. You could learn a lot about how to dress and behave in public by just watching the man."

"Yeah, I could, but then I would not be nearly as much fun."

"You can have fun and still have manners."

"Let's change the subject."

"Alright, what are we going to do when we get to Munich?" Zelda-Corrine had changed the subject.

"As soon as we can, I want to go to The Hofbrauhaus, the big beer joint."

"It is a little more than a beer joint. I read that it is Munich's number one attraction. You would be pleased to know that 17,000 pints of beer are consumed there every day."

"Now, you are talking about my kind of place."

Zelda-Corrine had done her homework on things to see, but her tastes ran a little differently.

"I want to see the magnificent museums. There are so many wonderful things to see. How much time are you going to have to spend with Mr. Dellifield?"

"I wish I knew. Whatever he wants, I'll have to do. He has been our ticket to ride."

At the front of the plane, Conrad Dellifield was planning his agenda. The afternoon of the first day, he would orient himself to Munich. The next morning, he would meet with Hans Grueber, the German lawyer who represented the heirs of Helga Brandenberg. The two of them would go over the Apostille to be sure that it complied with the German law. Herr Grueber would have arranged a meeting with the probate judge in Munich. The judge was purportedly a woman, a very bright woman. She would examine the papers that Dellifield brought with him. She would hear argument from Grueber. If satisfied, she would issue authority for Dellifield to act on behalf of Helga's estate in Germany.

Depending upon how long the meeting with Grueber and the appearance before the judge took, Dellifield would next go to the bank. He would want Akard to go with him to the bank. There would be two reasons for taking Akard. The first reason would be that there was an American witness to what he discovered at the bank. This would be useful if any question ever arose in the Dallas Probate Court. The second reason was to let the German bankers become aware that two people were aware of what was in the lock box. Dellifield had no reason to mistrust the bankers, but there had to be a justification for bringing Akard. He would stress to Akard the importance of making a good impression. Herr Grueber would also be there as an observer for the heirs.

The trip from Dallas to Zurich was routine. Dellifield settled himself in business class, and continued his planning for his business in Munich. He had learned to have his meal brought to him all at once. He did not drink coffee and had one glass of red wine. After the meal, he would take a sleeping pill. He would put on eye shades and place his personal head phones over his ears to drown out the drone of the plane's engines.

Meanwhile, back in steerage, Akard and Zelda-Corrine did not have the same option on eating that Dellifield had. They did, however, follow the same routine, except Akard didn't stop with one glass of wine. Neither of them had eye shades or their own personal head sets. Zelda-Corrine had the same brand of sleeping pills. The trio slept peacefully until the flight attendants came by with the hot towels in what seemed like, and was, the middle of the night.

The plane landed in Zurich in the early morning hours. The duty free shops were open. Dellifield headed off to find the Commander's Club. Akard and Zelda-Corrine found a small coffee bar open where they could get a cup of coffee. It would serve as a morning jolt to help restore their senses, which were dulled from sleep or lack thereof. The layover in Zurich was long enough that all the shops began to open. Every luxury that one could imagine was for sale in the various shops.

Zelda-Corrine went through each shop and picked up and felt everything she could. Akard always thought that women have the thrill of shopping without having to buy anything if they could just feel all the material. He had to admit that feeling the cashmere sweaters wasn't all that bad. When all was said and done, the damage amounted to only a plaid Burberry scarf for Zelda-Corrine and a bottle of single malt scotch for Akard. She had looked at the jewelry and the expensive fragrances, but she was not a jewelry person and Akard was allergic to perfume. Akard had looked in the case at the Rolex watches, but his Timex always told him the correct time.

Conrad Dellifield emerged from the Commander's Club looking as if he had not been traveling all night. His turtleneck sweater had been replaced with a crisp white shirt and a blue and white striped tie. He was clean-shaven and his silver hair was no longer out of place from having slept on it. Conrad Dellifield would be all business from now on. He boarded the plane in the first boarding group. Akard and Zelda-Corrine passed him on the way back to economy class. Dellifield nodded as they went by, much in the same way as he had done on the earlier flight.

The flight from Zurich to Munich was smooth. The Bavarian countryside was visible from the windows of the airplane. Zelda-Corrine had the window seat. Akard needed the aisle seat to spread his long legs. As she looked out the window, Zelda-Corrine remembered all the things she had read about the wonderful architecture of the buildings in the Bavarian Alps. Chief among the buildings was the Schloss Neuschwanstein, a fairy tale castle built by Ludwig II.

She had seen the picture of the castle a hundred or more times on travel posters. The castle was built on an outcrop of rocky land, which is above a gorge in the River Pollat. The travel posters always show the castle against a cloudless blue sky. The castle's towers are framed against a background of fir trees and blue skies. Zelda-Corrine wanted to see the castle for herself so badly that she could taste it.

The plane landed at the Franz-Josef-Straub International Airport. The unlikely three cleared customs and walked through the airport. Akard noticed that there were an abundant number of fast food places and excellent restaurants. He was hungry, but he knew that waiting until he got to town would be well worth the wait. Just walking through the airport was an experience. The passenger lounges, with the polished checker- board floors and the colorful flags hanging from columns, gave a festive look to the buildings. Last-minute shoppers were buying souvenirs to take home, Bavarian delicacies, clothing such as Lederhosen, a Bavarian felt hat with a Gamsbart, or a porcelain doll.

Dellifield hailed a cab and the trio headed for the Maximilianstrasse, the Rodeo Drive of Munich. They were headed for the Kempinski Hotel Vier Jahreszeiten (Four Seasons), one of the grand hotels of Europe. The hotel had housed royalty and heads of state. Certainly, a place that one would expect Dellifield to stay, but Akard was hardly in this league.

The taxi pulled up to the entrance of the Vier Jahreszeiten. The hotel is five stories and the yellowish color that characterizes many of the grand buildings of Munich. Fancy shops line the street beside the hotel. Huge flags hang over the entryway. As Dellifield got out of the car, he turned to Akard and said, "Now, where can you be reached, Akard?"

"What the hell do you mean, where can I be reached? I can be reached right here in this hotel," Akard replied.

"Akard, you certainly cannot expect the Court to allow you to stay in a five-hundred-dollar a night hotel. I am spending my own money to supplement what the court will allow. Remember, I said that you would be paid your usual per diem, but that the rest of the trip would be your responsibility," Dellifield said in a gruff voice.

"We are going to park our asses right here until we get this straightened out," Akard shot back.

"Very well, Akard. You and Miss Paige come with me and I will see if I can find you accommodations nearby," Dellifield said with a sigh.

The doorman, who had been standing watching the scene with some amusement, took the luggage into the hotel. The lobby of the hotel is befitting a place, which, from time to time, houses presidents and kings. Well-dressed people sit in the various alcoves that comprise the lobby. There are businessmen and beautiful women. There are dowagers bedecked in fine jewelry. There are Asians, talking into their cell phones, hurrying through the lobby like water bugs jumping across a pond.

The lobby is dominated by the colored glass dome ceiling. When the sun shines through the glass, a beautiful image is cast upon the lobby. The reception desk is long and made of polished wood. Behind the desk, in the center of the wall, is a large tapestry depicting deer in a forest, with what appear to be mythological creatures.

Dellifield looked like he could fit in with any one of the other guests. Zelda-Corrine was as beautiful as any woman in the room, and a night of travel had done nothing to diminish her good looks. Many of the men in the lobby turned to look as she went past. Zelda-Corrine, sensing that she was being observed, walked particularly erect with her chest sticking out for all to see. Akard, on the other hand, with a day's growth of beard and his wrinkled corduroy coat, would have to pass for an American movie star or be judged someone who was totally out of place.

Dellifield approached an immaculate young man who was stationed behind the registration desk.

"Sprechen Sie Englisch?" he asked.

"Of course, how may I help you, sir?" the young man asked.

"My name is Conrad Dellifield. I am from Dallas, Texas. I have reservations for six nights."

"Yes sir, I have you registered and your room is ready."

"There is another situation. My traveling companions, beside me here, were under the impression that I had made reservations for them as well. Perhaps, you could accommodate them for one night, until they can make arrangements elsewhere?"

"I am terribly sorry, Mr. Dellifield. There is a major trade fair in Munich at the present time and we are totally booked."

"That's terrible," Zelda-Corrine said.

As she spoke, the young man behind the desk got his first really good look at Zelda-Corrine. He was immediately struck by her good looks and the shape of her body. He was imbued with a new sense of urgency.

"Mr. Dellifield, you have a small suite. You have your bedroom and a front room with a door that can be closed to the bedroom. The front room can serve as an office. There is a desk and telephone. The room has an Internet connection. I was thinking that for one night I could have the porter move a roll away bed into the front room. That may be a temporary solution to your problem." The young man smiled at Zelda-Corrine. Zelda-Corrine smiled back and winked.

"I guess that I can live with that, but just for one night," Dellifield groused. This is Miss Paige, whom you seemed to have already noticed. The gentleman is Mr. McCoy. He is here with Miss Paige. Please give them a key to the room," Dellifield added.

"Conrad you are wonderful," Zelda-Corrine said as she pecked Dellifield on the cheek.

Dellifield melted.

"Wonderful," Akard said under his breath. He would prefer that Zelda-Corrine save her charms for him. "Be sure we get a key," he said

A bellman took the luggage to the third floor. Dellifield carefully removed his clothes from his bag. They were wrinkle free. He unpacked his papers and laptop computer and placed them neatly on the desk in the outer room. He took his electric current converter and plugged it into the wall. He then plugged a multiple socketed surge protector into the converter. Lastly he plugged the charger to his cell phone and the adapter/charger to his computer into the surge protector.

Dellifield then took command, as would be expected.

"If we are to live together for tonight as room companions, we must have rules. We only have one bathroom. Even at my age, I would like to see Miss Paige in the altogether, but Mrs. Dellifield would not be happy about that. When Mrs. Dellifield isn't happy, no one is happy. Therefore, please knock before entering the bathroom, except in the middle of the night when I am asleep. Nevertheless, please be clothed when going past me, even if I seem to be asleep.

"I plan to have dinner in my room tonight. I will be preparing for my meetings tomorrow. The remainder of the afternoon I will use to schedule tomorrow's activities. I do not think I will require the presence of either of you until the day after tomorrow. At that time, I want both of you to accompany me to the bank. I need you there as witnesses to what I find. I also want to give the impression that I have a staff traveling with me. Miss Paige, you will be introduced as my executive assistant. Akard, you will appear as my chief of security. In that regard, Miss Paige, please bring a folder with something to take notes. Both of you will dress suitably for the occasion.

"I suggest that you spend part of the afternoon looking for another place to stay. In the long run, it is probably a good idea for us to be in different hotels. Should there be trouble our forces will be separated. If one force comes under fire, the other group will serve as reinforcements. I hope that nothing will happen that will require a rescue operation.

"I trust that you will use the free time of this afternoon and tomorrow to do something fun. Mrs. Dellifield and I try our best to have fun when we travel. She is in much better shape that I am, and I have a hard time keeping up. This is especially true when she is shopping.

"Finally, I know that you think that I am a stuffed shirt. I probably am. I am not, however, a moralist. The idea of the two of you sharing one bed and not being married is of no moment to me. Mrs. Dellifield does not share my views. Accordingly, she would be somewhat shocked to find out that I sanctioned the two of you sleeping together in my suite. Therefore, I strongly suggest that none of us tell her. Are there any questions?"

"None from me," Akard replied.

"Just one," Zelda-Corrine said. "May I hug you?"

"I think that will be alright," the counselor replied.

With that, Zelda-Corrine hugged the lawyer, pressing her breasts against his chest.

Conrad Dellifield IV felt a touch of springtime in his body. He faced reddened. He cleared his throat. "That will be all," he said. He turned away and walked into the other room.

"Save some of that for me," Akard whispered.

"That is the thing that dreams are made of," she whispered back.

"Conrad, we are going to get some lunch and find a place to stay. We will be back sometime tonight. Don't stay up," Akard directed toward the adjoining room.

By this time Dellifield had regained his composure. "Try to stay out of trouble," the response came from the other room.

After the rollaway bed had arrived, Akard and Zelda-Corrine took enough from their luggage to carry them through the night. It was a little brisk outside so they took their coats. Each had a small folding umbrella as well. Akard took out a travel guide and oriented himself to the sights they wanted to see. One thing they both wanted to see was the Neus Rathaus (New Town Hall). The clock in the tower is what every tourist wants to see. It is the fourth largest chiming clock in Europe. A concert is played daily on its bells. Colored figures dance to the music of the chimes. There are two scenes. One is a knightly tournament. The other is called "the Dance of the Coopers" which commemorates the passing of the plague in the epidemic of 1515-17.

Before they went out on the street, they stopped at the registration desk to see if the young man could help them with a place to stay. Zelda-Corrine approached him with a smile that would melt an iceberg.

"Have you been sweet enough to find us a place to stay?" she asked the young man. She had unbuttoned the top button on her blouse and leaned over to give him a good look. The young man about peed in his pants, but he kept his composure.

"I have been able to find you a room at The Hotel Splendid. It is within easy walking distance. It is close to a U-ban station or you can always find a taxi. It is small. It has a small elevator. I am told it is quite romantic. I have marked its location on this map for you."

"Thank you so much. You are such a dear," Zelda-Corrine said as she accepted the map from the young man.

"You are such a dear," Akard muttered under his breath.

The clock tower chimes performed at five o'clock. They had missed the eleven o'clock am performance for this day. Perhaps, they could catch the event in the afternoon. The most pressing need was to get something to eat. There was a nice restaurant within a few blocks of the hotel. Akard had read that it was better to eat where the local people ate. The food would not be as pricy and the meals served with less ceremony. At this point, he did not know where such a place might be and hunger overcame reason.

The restaurant looked expensive and it was. Like most European eateries, it had a fixed priced lunch special. Lunch was still being served. The menu was printed in both German and English. This was a good sign. The fixed price meal started with Krautsalat, a light salad with raw cabbage and a vinegar sauce dressing. The second course was Schweinebraten, a pork chop with potato dumplings on the side. The third course Dumpfnudel, steamed dumplings of leavened dough served with vanilla sauce and fruit. Akard ordered the special without hesitation. Zelda-Corrine opted for a salad and a vegetarian, meat free meal. Both ordered a glass of beer. Zelda-Corrine skipped the dessert.

While Akard and Zelda-Corrine were dining in style Dellifield was eating a sandwich that he had ordered brought to his room. He called the office of Hans Grueber. Grueber had arranged for him to meet Helga's cousins, who were her only heirs, the next morning. After the meeting, Grueber would take Dellifield to lunch. After lunch Grueber had arranged a short hearing before the Probate Judge at the Munich courthouse.

Dellifield knew little about the Brandenberg heirs. He knew they were in their late sixties. Grueber had told him they came from very poor circumstances. How they would communicate was a mystery to him. How he would communicate with the judge was also a mystery to him. One thing Dellifield hated above all others was to be unprepared. He had read and reread all the documents he had brought with him. He knew their contents like the back of his hand. What he did not know was what to expect in court. The judge might ask him a question or two. He could answer the questions. It would be of little use if he were to be asked in German. The same issue applied to the meeting with the heirs. He could answer their questions if framed in English. "To hell with it, Grueber will have to earn his money and get me through it." Dellifield said to himself.

Akard and Zelda-Corrine finished their lunch. The Town Hall chimes, or "Glockenspiel," would give the full dance routine at 5.00 p.m. If they hurried, they could go by the Hotel Splendid, check out the room and still make it to the Town hall in time for the show. The Kempinski was located at Maximilianstrasse 17 while the Splendid was located about two blocks off the same street about six blocks away from the Kempinski, a short hike that was easily done.

The day was cool, not cold. A coat felt good. It also felt good to walk off the lunch they had just eaten. German food is heavy, even the vegetables. After a brisk walk, the two arrived at the Hotel Splendid. The lobby of the hotel, unlike the Kempinski, was tiny. There was a small reception desk. An attractive young woman was at the reception desk.

"My name is Akard McCoy. The man at the desk of the Vier Jahreszeiten said he called and asked about the availability of a room," Akard said.

"Certainly," the young woman said in perfect English. The young woman behind the desk was tall and slender. She had blonde hair which was pulled back on the sides and gathered in back. "Akard is a name I have never heard before," she said.

"It's a street," Akard said.

"A street? You could easily pass for German with your short blond hair and blue eyes, even if you are named after a street" the young woman said.

"I would be happy to be a German if all the women looked like you," Akard said.

"Just tell us if we have a room," Zelda-Corrine interjected.

"Yes, yes, of course. There is a room. Would you like to see it?" the young woman asked.

The young woman took them to a room. The room was filled with antique furniture. The bed was a four-poster with a canopy that could be pulled down on all sides.

"This is lovely. We will take it," Zelda-Corrine said.

"The room will be ready for you tomorrow at 2 pm," the young woman said. "There is a tram stop very close to the hotel. It will take you to the old town center. If you hurry, you can make it to the show at the Glockenspiel."

"Thank you for your help. We will see you tomorrow," Zelda-Corrine said.

"I hope so. I would like to see both of you again," the young woman replied.

When they got to the street, Zelda-Corrine was fuming.

"You certainly went out of you way to be chummy with the help in there."

"Wait a minute. You showed your tits to the guy at the Kempinski. All I did was tat for tit, so to speak," Akard answered.

"There is a distinction," Zelda-Corrine said.

"I can't wait to hear this," Akard replied.

"I let the guy see the top of my tits to get us a room. We already had the room when we got here. You didn't need to invite her to bed," Zelda-Corrine said.

"Look, I did not invite her to bed. This is an argument that even Smoothmouth could not win for me. Let's stop it now and think of all the things we can do in that canopy bed," Akard pleaded.

"Well, alright, I forgive you," Zelda-Corrine said, tossing her hair back. "Let's go see the Glockenspiel."

They caught the tram at the station in front of the hotel, just as instructed. The tram arrived at Marienplatz with plenty of time to reach the Town Hall. There was a crowd gathered beneath the clock tower to see the show. At 5 pm, the 43 bells began chiming. The first figures appeared with the knights circling around the opening in the clock tower. Next, the dancers appeared celebrating the end of the plague. It was quite a show to see. By this time, Zelda-Corrine had gotten over her contrived mad and she and Akard were holding hands.

"Why don't we take in the Hoffbrauhaus this evening?" Akard asked.

"Are you going to get smashed your first night here?"

"No, but a cold beer sounds mighty appealing."

"It sounds good to me, too. Let's look around a while. The shops are still open. I checked this out. Shops can legally stay open from 6 am to 8 pm Monday through Friday, and from 8:30 am to 4 pm on Saturdays. Most of the small shops close for lunch and stay open to 6 pm. So, let's go."

"I might have known you would have the shopping hours down pat. You have a black belt in Karate and also a black belt in shopping."

"Don't be jealous. You have neither."

Akard accompanied Zelda-Corrine from shop to shop. Like most men, he was bored out of his mind. Like most men, he thought of the exercise as getting strokes much like in a golf handicap. Zelda-Corrine looked, felt, picked up and contemplated. At each store she said, as she left, "I'll have to think about it."

As soon as Akard determined he had accumulated enough strokes, he casually mentioned, "Let's go to the Hofbrauhaus."

"Alright," Zelda-Corrine said.

The Hofbrauhaus may be the world's most famous beer joint. It is situated on a narrow street, not too far from the Kempinski. The downstairs beer garden contains a large room with long tables. The ceiling is painted with various scenes. A repeated scene is the enterprise's logo, an HR with a crown above it.

A guest is often seated with a group of people who speak the same language. A guest may also be seated with local citizens. This evening Akard and Zelda-Corrine were seated with what appeared to be some young German professionals. All members of the group spoke English. All of the men noticed Zelda-Corrine.

The discussion eventually got around to the question of where Akard and Zelda-Corrine came from. When the Germans were told that Akard and Zelda-Corrine were from Dallas, Texas, the merriment began in earnest.

"You are J.R," one of the Germans yelled at Akard.

"No, He is my uncle," Akard replied.

It was obvious that German television was still showing reruns of *Dallas*.

"Buy us all a drink, J.R.," the Germans yelled. "You are a rich Texas oil man."

"One round," Akard yelled back.

The beer on tap is served in liter mugs. The bar maids, with arms like lumberjacks, can carry as many as three mugs in each hand. Akard bought a round and the Germans turned their attention to Zelda-Corrine. Most of the young German women are beautiful. A number, however, resemble an overweight Maria from *The Sound of Music*. Apparently the young German men were used to seeing the latter.

"What a beautiful woman. May I kiss her, J.R.?" one of the young Germans asked.

"Ask her," Akard said.

"I don't think so," Zelda-Corrine said.

Undeterred, the young man leaned over to kiss Zelda-Corrine. She grabbed his wrist and gave it a sharp twist. The young man put his head on the table in pain.

"You have to learn that a Southern Belle doesn't bestow favors on strangers," she said.

The young German nodded his assent.

"I'm hungry," Akard said.

"Then you should eat, J.R. We will leave you alone. Texas women are too mean for us," one of the group said. With that, the group finished their beers. Several patted Akard on the shoulder as they left. "Goodbye, J.R. Goodbye Miss Ellie," one said while leaving.

"I did not mean to spoil the party," Zelda-Corrine said.

"The boys were probably just here for a beer after work. I guess they are now used to being whomped on by a girl," Akard replied.

The both ordered a meal consisting of several different types of sausages, potato salad and bread. It does not take many liters of beer before their effect can be felt on the human head and bladder. Akard was feeling the effect on both before he had finished his meal. After relieving one source of pressure, both Akard and Zelda-Corrine were ready to call it a day.

As they were leaving the Hofbrauhaus, they noticed that two of the young Germans had stayed behind. They were well lubricated.

"I still want my kiss," one of the young Germans said as he wobbled toward Zelda-Corrine.

"I don't think you got the message in there," Zelda-Corrine answered, pointing to the building they had just left.

Undaunted, the young man staggered toward her and tried to grab her. She quickly stepped aside, grabbed his arm and flipped him on his back.

She looked over at the other young man. "You want a kiss, too?" she asked.

"No, Miss Ellie. Good evening." With that the young man picked his friend up from the street and they wobbled away into the night.

Akard and Zelda-Corrine walked back to the hotel. The night was crisp. Akard was somewhat uneven in his gait due to his consumption of beer. Zelda-Corrine steadied him as they walked. The more he breathed the cold air, the more sure-footed he became. The hour was late and very few people were in the hotel lobby.

After a bit of fumbling, Akard came up with the key to the room. Upon entering the room, the pair discovered that the door was shut to the bedroom. Apparently, Dellifield had retired earlier and closed the door to the anteroom.

"I think the bathroom is somewhere behind that door," Zelda-Corrine said.

"I need to unload some of the beer," Akard answered.

"I think we are either going to have to take the chance of waking Mr. Dellifield or we find restrooms in the lobby. I need to take off my make up, brush my teeth and get ready for bed," Zelda-Corrine said.

"To the lobby then, I don't want to see him get angry this time of night," Akard said.

The two of them got their toilet articles and headed down to the lobby. The restrooms are located next to the Lobby Bar. The men's room, next to the bar, was more elegant than any place Akard had lived, even in college. Akard washed his upper body in the wash basin and splashed on some after shave. Zelda-Corrine did the best she could under the circumstances. She was hopeful that she and Akard would not be needed in the morning and that she would have the luxury of a warm bath when Dellifield left. The rest of the trip, they would have their own room and no inconvenience.

When they got to the room, Zelda-Corrine put on a cotton gown. Akard stripped down to his usual sleeping attire of boxer shorts and a T-shirt.

When they got in bed, Akard pressed his body next to Zelda-Corrine's.

"Not tonight. You can wait until tomorrow when we have our own room," she said.

"Please?"

"No."

"Pretty please?"

"No."

"Why not?"

"Because I am not in the mood when Mr. Dellifield is in the next room."

"He can't hear anything."

"I do not like to be restricted in my sounds of pleasure when we are making love."

"If he hears, he can't say anything. I have attorney client privilege."

"Akard, I know sometimes you can be a little dense, but if you want a great romp in that canopy bed tomorrow, you will shut up and go to sleep."

"Yes, Ma'am."

Thus ended the debate. Both went to sleep.

# Chapter Twenty

The next morning, Conrad Dellifield arose early. He took a brief shower and then groomed. He then dressed carefully. He was fully mindful of the fact that neither he nor Dr. Hans Grueber had ever met. His suit was a blue, pin striped Corneliani heavy wool suit. The suit had been expertly tailored to fit at the Neiman-Marcus store in downtown Dallas. His shirt was blue striped with white collar and white French cuffs. The shirt was made in England. Fourteen karat gold cuff links in a basket weave pattern held the cuffs together. His tie was a muted gold and powder blue patterned tie of Italian silk. His shoes, made in Italy, were polished to a high sheen.

Dellifield looked at himself in the mirror and exclaimed, "That will do nicely." He gathered his papers and put them in his brief case. When he opened the door Akard and Zelda-Corrine were still asleep. He tried to quietly leave, but Zelda-Corrine awoke and pulled the covers on the roll away bed up around her chin. Akard was still dead to the world.

"I will not be back for sometime. Feel free to use the suite as you wish. Leave word at the desk or on the hotel voice mail where you can be reached," Dellifield said.

"Thank you, Mr. Dellifield. We will let you know," Zelda-Corrine answered.

Dellifield left and went to have the breakfast that was furnished with the room.

As soon as he left, Zelda-Corrine headed for the bathroom. She filled the tub with hot water and looked around the wash basin to see what the hotel furnished. There was a small bottle of scented body wash. She slipped into the bathtub and rubbed the body wash over her body. The shampoo and conditioner in the room were also pleasantly scented. She washed her hair and then rubbed conditioner on it. She then slipped down into the warm water until the water reached her chin.

While she was enjoying the comforts of her bath, Akard emerged looking like something the cat had dragged in during the night. He had not shaven in two days. He was somewhat bleary eyed from over-indulging in the fruit of the hops. Zelda-Corrine was thankful that the toilet was separated from the bathtub by a door. She pulled the shower curtain closed in hopes that he would clean up before she saw him again.

After a few minutes, Akard emerged and started brushing his teeth.

"Next," Akard said.

"Next for what?" Zelda-Corrine replied from behind her fortress in the bathtub.

"Next person in line to take a shower."

"You can be next in a minute." Zelda-Corrine came from behind the shower curtain. She had a large hotel towel wrapped around her torso. Her hair was dripping water and she removed the towel from her body and dried her hair. Akard could barely control himself, but he was determined to be a gentleman and respect her wishes, at least until they got their own room.

Akard jumped into the tub and turned the shower on cold. He hated cold showers. He was afraid that if he did not get in a cold shower immediately, his manhood would show what effect seeing Zelda-Corrine was having on him.

Akard stepped from his shower and shaved. Zelda-Corrine was using the blow dryer on her hair. She had slipped on a robe that was furnished by the hotel. Akard dressed for sight-seeing. He wore corduroy pants, and a turtleneck sweater. Zelda-Corrine emerged wearing dark gray wool pants and a black, ribbed turtleneck sweater. The sweater concealed nothing about the shape that was underneath it.

Conrad Dellifield finished his breakfast. The hotel had an incredible buffet with every dish a person could imagine for breakfast. Around the room were businessmen talking in various languages. Next to his table sat an older woman wearing expensive jewelry. She never looked his way as she was engaged in drinking champagne and working a crossword puzzle.

While he ate, he checked his email messages on his cell phone. There was nothing that could not be taken care by his paralegal or a young partner. He looked over his papers a final time and headed for the offices of Hans Grueber.

Dr. Grueber was a member of an eight member firm whose office was in a four- story building not far from the hotel. It was a pleasantly cool morning, so Dellifield decided to walk to Grueber's office. He arrived at 9:00 am, the precise time that he was scheduled to meet with Grueber and the Brandenberg heirs.

The law office was brightly lit and had a lot of light colored wood on the walls. There was an attractive young woman who greeted him as he entered. She was dressed in a tailored suit in much the same style of clothes as her American counterpart would wear.

"Guten tag," the young woman said.

"Good Morning. My name is Conrad Dellifield. I am here to see Dr. Grueber," Dellifield answered.

The young woman replied in perfect English, "You must be Dr. Dellifield. Dr. Grueber is expecting you. May I offer you anything to drink?"

"No, thank you. I have just had my breakfast," Dellifield replied.

"Then follow me, please. I will show you to Dr. Grueber's office."

Dellifield followed the young woman to the office of Hans Grueber. The office was large. Hans Grueber came from behind a massive desk to greet Dellifield.

"Guten Tag, Dr. Dellifield," Hans Grueber said.

Dellifield paused a moment to look Hans Grueber over. He was a tall and slender man. His three button tailored suit made him look even slimmer. He had pale blue eyes. His face was narrow. He wore rimless glasses. His sandy hair was close cut. His English was flawless.

"Guten Tag, Dr. Grueber. I am not used to being called Dr. Dellifield. In America, we do not use those terms."

"But you are not in America. You are in Germany. While you are here, you will be referred to as Dr. Dellifield. I know about American ways because I received an L.L.M. in international law in America."

Dellifield paused for a moment. It was obvious that the man standing before him was very capable.

"I am impressed with your achievements," Dellifield said.

"Thank you. Please have a seat and we will discuss what needs to be done here in Germany."

"Thank you. I have brought with me the Apostille. I have a basic inventory of the property situated in the United States. I will have to have an inventory of the property in Germany for U.S. estate tax purposes."

Dellifield handed Grueber the Apostille. The German lawyer adjusted his rimless glasses and examined the documents. After he had spent sufficient time to review the documents furnished by Dellifield, he paused as if he was reflecting on what he had just read.

"The documents are in fine order. We can present these to the court after lunch. The court here will honor them and authorize you to act here. We will have a simple hearing in the Court. It will all be conducted in German, of course. I will do all the speaking. If the judge looks your way and addresses you, simply smile."

"I smile quite well. When will I meet the beneficiaries?"

"The beneficiaries are here in another office. I will have them brought in. There is little point in discussing legal matters with them. Unlike their cousin Helga, life has been extremely difficult for them. Both have had health problems which prevented them from working. They are quite poor. I do not want to encourage their hopes of inheritance until we have had an opportunity to view the contents of the lock box."

"I can quite understand your reasoning. I would do the same thing myself, if faced with a similar situation."

"Neither has married. Her name is Anna Zweig. His name is Stephan Zweig. They do not speak English, I will tell them who you are and why you are here. I will explain to them that no one can tell them what their inheritance will be until the assets are located and all taxes are paid."

"Fair enough, you are a brother attorney and I will trust you to do the proper thing."

Hans Grueber picked up his telephone and said some words in German. Shortly thereafter, another woman employee entered with two older people. The years had not been kind to Anna Zweig or to Stephan Zwieg.

Anna Zweig was somewhere in her sixties or maybe older. She was younger than her cousin Helga Brandenberg, but she had not had any comforts that surrounded Helga. Her hair was a mousey brown streaked with gray and had no style. It was more like the coat of an animal, with no sheen. She wore no makeup. The lenses of her glasses looked like the bottom of a soda bottle and were scratched. Her eyes were magnified by the thickness of the lenses, and they gave her a bug-eyed facial expression.

She was still wearing her coat. It was worn almost threadbare. In places the material shone with wear. Beneath the coat was a rumpled dress. She did not wear stockings. Instead she had some long black socks that stopped below her knees. When she sat down you could see the skin between the top of her socks and the hem of her dress.

Her brother was dressed no better. He was a dumpy little man. A well worn all-weather coat was under his arm. You could see the family resemblance. The only difference was that he was not wearing glasses. His hair may have been dyed. If it was a natural color, it was one that Dellifield had not seen before.

He was wearing a black suit that had not been in style in years. He had on a white dress shirt with no tie. The ends of the shirt collar were frayed. His shoes were turned up on the ends from age. On one shoe the sole was beginning to separate from the upper part of the shoe.

These were not the class of people that Dellifield was used to seeing in a law office. Certainly not the type of people he would see in his office. He did feel a sense of satisfaction knowing that the inheritance would dramatically change the lives of the siblings he saw before him.

Grueber spoke to the brother and sister in German. They smiled and each extended a hand to Dellifield. He shook their hands and smiled back. Grueber continued to address the pair in German. From time to time the siblings would look in the direction of Dellifield and smile. Dellifield would nod and smile back.

After a twenty-minute discussion between Grueber and the Zweigs, they all arose from their chairs. Dellifield got up as well. The brother and sister shook hands with Dellifield again. Grueber paged his secretary. The secretary entered the room and led the Zweigs away.

"They are the only heirs of Helga Brandenberg," Grueber said.

"You are sure of that?" Dellifield replied.

"I will present affidavits to the Court this afternoon stating that to be the facts," Grueber said.

"Why so few heirs?" Dellifield asked.

"Most of the siblings of Helga's parents were killed in World War II. Some of their children were also killed. I have only been able to locate two cousins who are from the maternal side of Helga's family," Grueber replied.

"They appear to be impoverished," Dellifield said.

"Anna and Stephan had little education. They were a source of embarrassment to Helga and her mother. This is what I have been told anyway. They have no idea the amount of property they may receive. Anything they get will excite them a great deal," Grueber explained.

"They will do quite well from the property located in the United States. I have no idea of what is located here. That is where you come in," Dellifield said.

Grueber then spent time going over papers and scheduling a meeting for the next day at the bank.

Akard and Zelda-Corrine had spent the morning sight seeing. They first had breakfast at the hotel. They wanted to have one breakfast at the grand hotel. Dellifield had already left when they emerged from the room.

After breakfast they walked around until the Residenz opened. The Residenz was the home of the Wittlesbach dynasty until 1918. The buildings are traced back to 1385. It would take several days to thoroughly explore this complex. The buildings house the Residenz museums. The buildings have three facades and many court yards.

The Ancestral Gallery contains 121 portraits of the Wittlesbachs. The Schatzhammer contains the famous jewel-encrusted statute of St. George mounted on his horse with his sword drawn.

"I love this place," Zelda-Corrine said.

"It is a far cry from my digs in Deep Ellum," Akard replied.

"Does this make you think about how you live? People actually lived here, this was their home."

"Yeah, it makes me think that my entire net worth would probably not buy one of the paintings in here."

"Maybe some day we could win the lotto."

"Some day I might be the King of England."

"I know I sound silly, Akard, but it is fun to dream."

"No prince ever had a better princess than I do."

"You are sweet, Akard. Let's keep sight-seeing while we have the chance. You keep dreaming and later I will make your dreams come true."

Conrad Dellifield and Hans Grueber had lunch at a trendy place, not far from Grueber's office.

"May I try my German?" Dellifield asked.

"It is not necessary, the waiter will speak English," Grueber replied.

When the waiter approached, Dellifield spoke in fractured German.

"Guten Nachmittag," Dellifield said.

"Good afternoon," the waiter replied.

Dellifield said, "Duffen wir um Ihre Speisekarte und Weinkarte bitten."

"You may have a menu and wine list, sir. It would be easier for both of us to speak English," the waiter said.

Grueber looked down at the table with a sly grin on his face. Dellifield, never a loss for words, acquiesced. "An admirable suggestion, I will let you choose my lunch. Just accompany the meal with a glass of your fine white wine."

"This is Bavaria, Sir. Let me suggest that the food you order is more suited to beer than to wine," the waiter nodded.

"Then beer it will be," Dellifield said.

Grueber nodded to the waiter and said, "The same."

It was a good decision. The waiter brought out an excellent meal. The first course was a light cabbage salad with a vinegar sauce dressing. The main course was Weiswurst, a white sausage with sweet mustard. This is a renowned Bavarian dish. The dessert was a hot plum strudel. Dellifield enjoyed every bite. When the two lawyers had finished lunch, they went to the building housing the probate court. Since they had extra time, Grueber showed Dellifield the more impressive court buildings.

The New Justice Building houses the appellate courts. It is located near the train station next to the Palace of Justice. Although it is a newer building, it follows the architecture of many of the older buildings. It has a pitched roof with some Gothic features. It has a clock tower. The appellate courts begin on the second floor.

Next to this building is the Palace of Justice. It houses the civil courts. It is a magnificent building with an exterior that resembles a palace. It has a greenish metal roof. There are statues along the roof line. Inside, the courtrooms are small. At the front of the courtroom are three chairs. The center chair seats the chief judge. There are no juries. On either side are two other chairs that seat the other two judges who may or may not be legally trained.

In front of the judges are two tables. One is marked "Klagler" for the attorneys for the plaintiff. The other is marked "Beklagter" for the attorneys for the defendant. The witness sits in a chair between the two tables. There is little or no cross-examination of a witness allowed. On the wall behind the judges is a crucifix required by Bavarian law to be in the courtroom.

After the tour, Dr. Grueber took Dellifield to a non-descript building about two blocks away. This building housed the probate court. The courtroom was small.

Dr. Grueber announced that he was ready to proceed in the case of the matter of Helga Brandenberg, Deceased. The judge appeared and the attorneys rose to their feet. The judge motioned them to sit.

Dr. Grueber addressed the court and handed the judge the Apostille, which Dellifield had given to Grueber. The judge reviewed the document along with other documents, which Grueber had prepared. The judge would question Grueber, and Grueber would respond. Occasionally, the judge would glance at Dellifield and seem to address him.

After about fifteen minutes, Grueber handed the judge a paper, which the judge signed. The judge then looked directly at Dellifield and addressed him in German. Dellifield could only comprehend a few words, but the judge was smiling. Dellifield took this as a good sign. The judge rose and left the bench. The attorneys rose as the judge left the courtroom.

"What did the judge say to me?" Dellifield asked.

"He said that you had done a good job," Grueber responded.

"What do we do next?"

"I will get certified copies of the Judge's order to present to the bankers in the morning. This will be your authority to act. This will allow you to take custody of the property and to distribute the assets to the beneficiaries at the proper time."

"Very good, I hope to determine what belongs to the estate and work with you on paying any appropriate taxes and costs, including your fee."

The two lawyers got the necessary papers to carry out the needed tasks. They shook hands and left for different destinations.

After the two o'clock hour had passed, Akard and Zelda-Corrine started thinking about moving to their new hotel. It was mid-afternoon when they went back to the old hotel. At the Kempinski they discovered that Dellifield had not returned.

When they reached the room, they found that their belongings had been carefully packed. On the top of Akard's suitcase was a note from Dellifield. The note said. "The Kempinski car will take you to your hotel. Call the bellman when you are ready to leave Meet me back here this evening at eight o'clock. I will take the two of you to dinner. We will discuss the game plan for tomorrow morning at the bank. Dellifield."

"The man does have style," Zelda-Corrine said.

"Don't get use to thinking that way. He will find a way to change your mind," Akard replied.

"Don't be such a cynic. I am ready to settle in at our new place."

Akard called the bell desk. A smartly dressed employee took their luggage downstairs and loaded it into the hotel's black Mercedes. The driver took them to the Hotel Splendid and took their luggage into the lobby. Akard tipped him an amount larger than his customary gratuity.

They were greeted by the same young woman who had been at the desk the day of their arrival in Munich.

"Welcome back. Your room is ready. Do you need help with you luggage?" she said.

"No thanks, we can manage," Zelda-Corrine answered.

"The elevator is small," Akard said.

"Don't be a wimp. Use the stairs."

"I am just trying to avoid a hernia. I need to save my strength for what lies ahead when we get to the room."

"Wishful thinking."

"You carry your bag and I will carry mine."

"Cool."

Getting the luggage to the room was not as difficult as Akard had imagined. He was a strong man. Zelda-Corrine was a strong woman. Akard believed that she was just showing off for the girl downstairs. Whatever the intent, they were in their room with the luggage.

Zelda-Corrine removed her belongings and neatly placed them in drawers or hung them in the closet. Akard unpacked, but not as methodically or neatly.

Zelda-Corrine removed her clothes down to her panties and bra.

"You know it will be late when we get back tonight. We have an appointment in the morning. The thought occurred to me that the canopy bed could be used for something besides sleeping," She said.

Akard set a new speed record for removing his clothes. They ended up in a pile on the floor.

"Did you have something in mind or do you just enjoy standing in the middle of hotel rooms naked?" Zelda-Corrine asked.

Akard did not reply. Instead he pushed her down on the bed and kissed her passionately.

"I guess you do have something in mind," Zelda-Corrine said.

Akard gently removed her under garments and kissed her on her neck. She pulled his face to hers and kissed him for a long time. The next hour was spent with the canopy drawn around the bed. Only the two of them knew what was going on. The sounds that came from behind the drawn canopy indicated that it was pleasurable.

There was a period of time when there were no sounds. This was an indication of exhaustion or just the quiet time reserved for savoring what had gone before. Only the two of them knew for sure what was going on when they were sequestered from the world and all its cares. That is the best way for a man and a woman to enjoy their love making, something that is personal and something that belongs only to them.

Akard and Zelda-Corrine finally emerged from the canopy bed and faced the prospect of having dinner with Dellifield. Knowing that Dellifield would be dressed to the nines, each of them dressed nicely as well. In European countries, if a person is not known to the locals, then that person is judged by the clothes that he or she is wearing. The way that you are dressed affects the service that you receive.

Akard wore his blue blazer with gray slacks. Zelda-Corrine had on a royal blue two piece wool dress. Akard looked at himself in the mirror and looked over at Zelda-Corrine.

"Not bad for two hicks from Dallas," he said

"We are not hicks. Hell, we have Neiman-Marcus," she replied.

"It is show time. Let's go," Akard said.

It was cool and Zelda-Corrine was not wearing walking shoes so they took a cab to Dellifield's hotel. When they arrived at the hotel, Dellifield was waiting in the lobby. He was dressed in a dark blue suit with white shirt and striped tie.

"Thank you for coming," Dellifield said in a courtly manner.

"Thank you for having our luggage packed and a car to take us to our hotel. That was sweet," Zelda-Corrine said as she pecked Dellifield on the cheek.

"Gag," Akard said under his breath.

"Did you say something Akard?" Dellifield asked.

"I'm sorry, I said thanks," Akard replied.

"You are welcome. I suggest we have dinner here at the hotel and discuss our plans for tomorrow." With that Dellifield motioned them toward the hotel's formal restaurant.

After some pleasant dinner conversation about the sights of Munich, Dellifield got down to business.

"I met with the heirs today. They can certainly use any thing they get from this estate. The property in the United States will be substantial. I have no idea what we will find at the bank in the morning. I will do most of the talking. Akard, I want you to carefully observe everyone in the room. I want your take on the body language of each of the participants in the conference. If you notice anything that causes you alarm, make a note of it.

"Miss Paige. Please take notes. I am sure that a person your age and training will not know shorthand. That is not important. Write down key phrases that will be of help to us after the meeting.

"It is most important to remember that Europeans are very formal. One does not address a stranger by his Christian name, unless invited to do so. I will refer to the lawyer, Grueber, as Dr. Grueber. He will be there to be sure that we do not take away any of the assets that he feels belong to his clients. I will make sure that he does not take anything before all taxes and debts are paid.

"The bankers may have their own counsel at the meeting. They will make sure that everything is in compliance with what their lawyer says. There may be six or seven people in the room. Akard watch them all, except our little group, of course."

"Tell me again who Akard and I are supposed to be," Zelda-Corrine said.

"Akard works for me as a security consultant. This may be a hard concept for them to grasp. I want to put them on notice that this estate will be handled properly. If, and I say *if*, Akard's suspicions are correct that something sinister surrounds the death of Helga Brandenberg, the word will get around to leave us alone. You are to be my legal assistant. Just dress in a suit, if you brought one, and leave the rest to me," Dellifield said.

"I am a born actress. I have to be to put up with Akard," Zelda-Corrine said.

"I am sure you are, my dear. I suggest we all get a good night's sleep and be fresh for the venture tomorrow." With that admonishment, Dellifield motioned for the check. The trio exchanged pleasantries and parted for the night.

When Akard and Zelda-Corrine got back to their room, Akard had a question.

"You are a natural born actress, huh? Were you acting in bed this afternoon?"

"That is a woman's secret."

"Humbug."

# Chapter Twenty-One

*The Deutsche-Bayern bank is a short distance from the Kempinski.* Akard and Zelda-Corrine had a continental breakfast at their hotel and then met Dellifield at his hotel. The three of them walked to the bank. The bank occupies several floors of a modern building. Grueber was waiting for them in the lobby. He told the group that they would be meeting in a conference room on the third floor. There would be three people representing the bank.

Gerhart Scheer would be the senior bank officer at the meeting. A junior officer present would be Helmut Hentsch. Hentsch had been the bank's representative assigned to Helga Brandenberg's account. The third member of the group was the bank's lawyer, Erich Moltke.

After this explanation, the four of them went to the third floor of the bank. Grueber approached the receptionist and had a brief conversation with her in German. The receptionist rose from her desk and Grueber motioned to the group to follow him. Grueber and the Americans were shown into a large conference room. The room had a large dark wooden desk in the center. Positioned on one side of the table, standing, were the bank's representatives.

Gerhart Scheer took the lead and introduced his colleagues to the American group. The introductions were in English. While he was speaking, Akard was studying the group. Scheer was a slight man. He was completely bald on the top of his head. The hair he had left was closely cut. He was wearing a gray three- button suit with a navy, gold and green striped tie.

Erich Moltke could have passed for an American lawyer. He was tall and thin. He was wearing a black pin striped suit accented by a solid gray tie. He looked all business.

The third member of the German group, Helmut Hentsch, was a young man. He was wearing a solid black suit with a solid black tie. He was of average height, but very well built. His blond hair was extremely short. It seemed odd to Akard that he seemed to be studying the American group with the same intensity that Akard was studying the German group.

Grueber, in turn, introduced the Americans. He introduced Dellifield as the lawyer from Dallas, Texas, who was handling the Estate of Helga Brandenberg. Dellifield was wearing a tailored navy blue suit with a patterned Hermes tie.

Grueber introduced Akard as a security specialist came along to be sure that all assets were accounted for. Akard was wearing his discount store gray suit with a subdued tie. Akard noticed that Hentsch gave him a piercing look when Grueber explained Akard's position.

Last, but not least, Grueber introduced Zelda-Corrine as Dellifield's legal assistant. She was wearing a well-fitted Navy blue St. John's suit. (The only one she owned). She was wearing a white blouse under the jacket. The material of the St. John's outfit did nothing to hide the nature of the figure beneath the clothing. This was a fact that had not gone unnoticed by the Germans.

After the introductions the parties seated themselves at the conference table. Grueber presented the Apostille and the certified copies of the orders from the Munich probate court. Erich Moltke read them carefully. Everyone sat silently while he examined the papers. When Moltke had finished, he spoke to Scheer in German. When the conversation ended, Scheer addressed the group.

"We find everything to be in order. We are prepared to treat this matter as if it were taking place in Texas. Herr Hentsch will accompany you to the lock box area in the basement of the bank. You may take as long as you wish to inventory the contents, if any, of the box. If you have any questions, Herr Hentsch will be glad to be of assistance."

With that pronouncement, the group exchanged pleasantries and disbanded. Dellifield, Grueber, Akard and Zelda-Corrine followed Hentsch to the basement of the bank. The lock box area was large and guarded. Hentsch gave the proper instructions and the group was admitted to the secure area. No one had a key so a locksmith was on hand to open the box. The old mechanism was removed and a new locking devise was installed.

When the door to the box was opened it revealed a pull out drawer about the size of a filing cabinet drawer. Hentsch grabbed the handle to the drawer. Before he opened the drawer he stated, "And now you will see what you have come all the way to Munich to see, an empty box." With that announcement Hentsch pulled out the box and opened the top.

"Mein Gott!" Hentsch exclaimed.

He took the box into a small room with a table and four chairs surrounding the table. It was clear that the weight of the box caused even a strong young man like Hentsch to strain under its weight. He placed the box on the table and opened the lid. The eyes of five people were fixed on the contents of the box.

Grueber began to systematically remove the contents. Dellifield asked Zelda-Corrine to make a list of each item as it was removed. At the top of the box were bearer bonds. Most of them were old and payable in Deutsche Marks. The bonds ranged in face value from 10,000 DM to 50,000 DM. The total was over 3,000,000 DM.

The next layer in the box was banded bundles of Deutsche Marks. The bundled cash came to a total 1,775,000 DM. The final layer consisted of shiny golden one-ounce coins. It took a while to count the coins. The final count was 400 coins. At $600 per ounce that came to $240,000. Helga had not been in the box to convert the Deutsche Marks to Euros. The bank could do the conversion.

Zelda-Corrine had her hands full keeping up with the tally. Once the initial list had been made of the bonds and their face amount, the serial number of each bond was listed. The cash was not listed by serial number.

Akard noticed that Hentsch was making his own list. This seemed odd to Akard. He could photocopy the list that Zelda-Corrine was making. Once the box had been inventoried, Grueber and Dellifield agreed that the contents would be left in the box at the bank until time for distribution to the heirs.

A new lock had been installed on the face of the lock box by the time the inventory was completed. The locksmith had left two keys to the box. Hentsch was about to hand the two keys to Dellifield when Akard interceded.

"I will take one of those," Akard said.

Dellifield looked annoyed but said nothing.

Hentsch looked at Dellifield for guidance.

"It is proper for my security man to keep a key, but only I can get into the box," Dellifield said.

"Can you tell me what Helga Brandenberg's will said?"

"She had no will," Dellifield said.

"Of course, she had a will. She and I discussed her will on many occasions. You are mistaken," Hentsch said, in an angry tone of voice.

"I am sorry to disabuse you of that thought, but she had no will," Dellifield said firmly.

Hentsch gathered his composure. "May I ask who gets this property?"

"You may ask, but that will be a matter of court record in due course. Until that time, the names of the heirs are confidential," Grueber interjected.

"Very well, may I ask how she died?" Hentsch said.

"She took her own life," Dellifield responded.

"No, she would not have done that. I knew the woman. She had much to live for," Hentsch said.

"The medical examiner ruled her death a suicide. If you have information which would indicate otherwise, please let us know," Akard said.

"I have no information about her death," Hentsch replied.

"Thank you for your help in this matter," Dellifield said, extending his hand to Hentsch.

Hentsch extended his hand, but not eagerly. "May I have the bank car take you to your hotel?"

Before Dellifield could answer, Akard spoke, "We are all at the Vier Jahreszeiten. We will walk. Thank you anyway."

Dellifield looked puzzled but did not contradict what Akard had said.

Hentsch accompanied the group to the lobby floor. There he said his good-byes and returned to the elevator. It was now one o'clock in the afternoon. Dellifield invited Grueber to have lunch. Grueber replied that he had much work to do at his office. Dellifield asked a clerk in the lobby to make a copy of the list that Zelda-Corrine had made of the lock box contents. The clerk obliged and Dellifield gave Grueber a copy.

The two lawyers agreed that nothing would be done with the contents of the lock box until the United States estate taxes had been paid. The two of them would meet again the next morning to see if there were any other assets in Germany, which would be a part of the Brandenberg estate. The lawyers shook hands as they left the bank.

Dellifield then addressed Akard, "What was going on in the bank? Why do you need a key? We are not all staying at the same hotel."

"Trust me on this, Conrad. Something is strange about Hentsch. The more we keep him in the dark, the better off we will be."

"He did seem to know a lot about Helga Brandenberg. I was surprised that a young banker would have that much information about someone that he would seldom see in person," Dellifield answered.

The three of them walked back toward the hotel. They had walked a short distance when they had to stop for a red light. When the light turned green, Akard still had his eyes fixed on the building across the street.

"Akard, come on, we will miss the light," Zelda-Corrine said.

"Come back a minute. I see something I think I recognize," Akard said.

Zelda-Corrine and Dellifield retreated back to the street corner where Akard was standing with his eyes still fixed on the building across the street.

"Akard, what are you looking at?" Zelda-Corrine asked.

"Look at the building across the street," Akard said.

"Alright, I see a building. There are a lot of buildings in Munich. What is so special about that particular building?" Zelda-Corrine said.

"Remember when Nell said what she had found in Helga's apartment. There were multiple copies of the front page of a Munich newspaper. There was a picture of a tank in front of a shell-pocked building. I could not figure out why Helga would have kept pictures of a newspaper sixty years old. The building in the picture is the building across the street," Akard answered.

"Are you sure that is the building? You said it has been sixty years," Dellifield said.

"Look at the stone work above the windows. You can see where something has been used to fill in holes. There are different colored bricks in a number of places. This is a three story building. The one in the picture is three stories. This is the same building. I am sure of that," Akard said.

"Then let's go investigate," Dellifield said.

The three of them crossed the street and looked for the entrance to the building. It appeared to be an apartment building. They found the entrance to the building. The entry door led into a narrow hallway. There were old mailboxes on the wall in the hallway. Above the mailboxes was a faded metal sign. The letters were barely legible. The sign said "Brandenberg."

"Akard, I do not give you enough credit," Dellifield said.

"I am pretty smart for an acknowledged dumb ass," Akard said.

"My hero, the dumb ass," Zelda-Corrine chirped.

"Perhaps we can find a manager and determine who owns this building." Dellifield said.

It did not take too much detective work to find a manager. A man came out of a door down the hall and approached the group. The man was middle-aged. He was wearing a brown sweater and brown wrinkled slacks. His shoes may have been shined in this century, although judging by their appearance, it was doubtful. His face was almost without color. His reddish-brown hair stood straight up as if he had just removed his finger from a light socket.

The man said something in German that no one seemed to grasp.

"I think he said 'May I help you?'" Dellifield said.

"I speak some English. I am the manager. What do you want?"

"I am the court-appointed representative of the Estate of Helga Brandenberg. She died in the United States. We think she may have some ownership of this building," Dellifield said.

"Do you have papers?" the man asked.

"I have the papers from the German probate court which allows me to act on behalf of the Brandenberg estate in Germany," Dellifield said.

"Come to my office and I will look at your papers," the man said.

Dellifield, Akard and Zelda-Corrine followed the man to his office. The office was cluttered with papers. The desk, or that part of it that was visible beneath the papers, was marked with cigarette burns. There was a telephone on the desk. There was no sign of a computer. A manual typewriter was on a small stand behind the desk. It made one wonder how anyone could do business in this manner, in this day and time.

There was a radiator by the window. That would supply the heat. On top of an ancient filing cabinet was an electric fan. Its blades were covered with a dusty grease-like substance. That explained the air conditioning. The people in this building were not living high on the hog, although the rooms might be nice. One should not jump to conclusions.

The manager picked up a battered pair of reading glasses from the cluttered surface of the desk.

"The papers, please," he said.

Dellifield opened his brief case and pulled out a certified copy of the order which allowed him to gather the assets in Germany. The manager studied the order carefully. He made notes on a pad of paper that was on his desk.

"What do want to know?" the man said in a stern voice.

"I want to know if Helga Brandenberg owned any interest in this building?"

"She is, or was, the owner. This was the family apartment house. Her grandparents were the first owners. Her parents lived here. Helga lived here until she went to America. I have been here a long time. My family also lived here. When Helga went to America, she asked my father to manage the apartments. When he got old, I took over the management," the manager said.

"I found no record of this building in her files. Her bank accounts did not show any deposit of rentals," Dellifield said.

"I did not send rentals to America," the manager said.

"Did anyone pay any taxes on this money?" Dellifield asked.

"I would not know the answer to that question," the manager said.

"Where were the rentals deposited?" Dellifield asked.

"Each month after I pay the bills, I deposit an amount in a bank in Zurich. I maintain a small reserve account at a local bank in Munich. Every three months I go to Zurich and secure a certified check made payable to Helga Brandenberg. The account in Zurich is very low after I withdraw the funds. I just withdrew funds last month," the manager replied.

"Where do you send the funds?" Dellifield asked.

"I do not send the funds. Her agent picks up the check and I do not know where the funds go from that point," the manager answered.

"Who is the agent?" Dellifield asked.

"He is a young banker named Hentsch," the manager replied.

"Bingo," Akard said.

"I do not understand," the manager said.

"No one does. May I see one of the returned checks?" Dellifield asked.

"There is no returned check. I get a copy of the certified check at the time it is issued. No copy is returned to me," the manager said.

"Thank you. You have been most helpful," Dellifield said.

The trio departed for a late lunch. Over a light German lunch, they discussed the events of the morning.

"I told you there was something fishy about that Hentsch fellow," Akard said.

"Do not jump to conclusions, Akard. Everything may be quite legitimate," Dellifield replied.

"Did you know about the apartment house? No. Did anyone at the bank say anything about the money from the apartment rentals? No. Did we find any evidence of a bank account in the United States where the money from the bank account in Zurich was deposited? No. We know that someone named 'Herman' made monthly deposits for Helga. Is Hentsch the same person as Herman? Was Hentsch disturbed that Helga left no will? Yes. Was Hentsch disturbed that Helga's death was the result of her taking her own life? Yes. Don't let them bullshit you, Conrad," Akard said.

"You may be right. Go to Grueber's office. I want him to follow up on the bank account in Zurich. He may want to talk with the apartment manager at greater length. It is obvious that there is more here than I can accomplish on this trip. The most I can devote is a few more days. I promised my wife that I would be back in Dallas for the Garden Club dinner dance," Dellifield said.

"I think it is sweet that you are going to do that for your wife," Zelda-Corrine said.

"It is a matter of self preservation," Dellifield answered.

"I think you are just a softie at heart," Zelda-Corrine responded.

"Could we stop this line of talk? I am about to get sick," Akard said.

"I do not know why I associate myself with such a person of low class. However, in as much as you are here, Akard, make yourself useful. I want you to go over to Grueber's office and fill him in on what we found out about the apartment. See if he can get a line on the bank account in Zurich," Dellifield said.

After lunch, Akard and Zelda-Corrine parted from Dellifield. Dellifield was going back to his hotel room to check messages and make any necessary telephone calls on his overseas cell phone. Before they parted, Dellifield gave the pair directions on how to get to Grueber's office.

Zelda-Corrine suggested that they walk to Grueber's office, to exercise away some of the calories that came from eating German food. This was in spite of the fact that she was wearing high heels. As they walked along the street, Zelda-Corrine would stop to look in store windows. She liked to look in the windows of the upscale clothing stores and the jewelry displays. Akard would periodically let forth a sigh, but he did not verbally object.

Akard began to notice that whenever the two of them would stop to look in a window a young man, who seemed to be following them, would also stop.

"The next dress shop we come to, we are going in," Akard said.

"I can't believe that you said that. With all the sighing you have been doing, that would have been the last thing that I world expect from you," Zelda-Corrine said.

"I am pretty sure that we are being followed. Turn you head slightly to the right. Point toward the window, but look and see if you can spot a twenty-something man in a black leather jacket."

"You mean the man who is looking in the window about thirty yards away?"

"The one and only."

"I knew it would take something drastic to get you to go into a dress shop."

"Just do it."

"Yes, sir."

The next shop that they came to, Zelda-Corrine pointed out a dress in the window. The two of them entered the shop and Zelda-Corrine began to feel fabrics. A shapely saleswoman approached and said something in German.

"I am sorry, we do not speak German," Zelda-Corrine said.

"It is not necessary. Everyone in this shop speaks English. May I show you something in particular?" the woman replied.

"I would like to try this one on, please," Zelda-Corrine said.

"Certainly," the saleswoman said.

"Oh brother," Akard said.

"Just trying to help you out," Zelda-Corrine said, as she headed for the dressing room.

Zelda-Corrine went to the fitting room and Akard thought he would sneak a peek at the ladies underwear. A common male trait exercised when men are killing time while women shop. He also positioned himself to see out the window without being seen himself. The man in the black leather jacket was not in front of the store.

He was, however, across the street keeping an eye on the store while talking on a cell phone. Akard could hazard a guess that the man was reporting the situation to someone higher up. This man was too easily spotted to be a pro.

"Thank you for your help. I may come back and get this." Akard heard Zelda-Corrine say.

"Have you been having fun looking at underwear?" Zelda-Corrine asked Akard.

"I have been keeping an eye on the guy across the street."

"Yeah, sure, one eye on him and the other on the undies."

"We're out of here."

As they walked along the street, Akard and Zelda-Corrine would stop and look in a window. The man, who was still across the street, would stop when they would stop. He would pretend to be looking in a window himself, but he was constantly looking in the direction of Akard and Zelda-Corrine.

Akard decided to test the old Western adage of "never corner a man meaner than you are." Akard could see that he was larger than the man in the leather jacket. He felt comfortable that he would prevail in any encounter. If he could not, he would let Zelda-Corrine whip his ass.

"We are going to pay our friend a visit," Akard said to Zelda-Corrine.

"Are you sure that is a good idea?" Zelda-Corrine answered.

"This guy has been looking in the window of a stationery store for ten minutes. He does not look like a man of letters to me. I have no idea if he has been following us or not. I figure if we go stand next to him, he is going to leave or wait until we move on and follow us again."

"Reluctantly, I do your wishes."

Akard and Zelda-Corrine crossed the street at the first convenient place. As they approached the stationery shop where the man was standing, they got a closer look at him. He was about five feet ten inches tall. He was wearing a black T-shirt barely showing under his zipped up black leather jacket. His black hair was closely cut. His face was hardened beyond his years. He wore heavy black boots. Barely seen above the collar of his jacket was some sort of black tattoo.

Akard walked up and stood next to the man. The man never looked at Akard, but instead, studied Akard's reflection in the window. Both men stood staring into a stationery store. Neither spoke. Suddenly the man turned and slipped his hand inside of Akard's coat. His movement was so swift and unexpected it caught Akard off guard.

Akard tried to grab the man's hand as he withdrew it from the inside of Akard's coat. The man pulled free and broke into a run. Akard started to follow, but he knew the man had too much of a head start. The man sprinted only a short distance before he was picked up by a passing automobile.

"He was a pickpocket," Zelda-Corrine said.

"Not just any pickpocket. He only went for the pocket that I had placed the key to the lock box in." Akard answered.

"Did he get the key?"

"No. When I left the bank I put the key in my wallet. I moved my wallet from my back pocket and placed it in the front pocket of my pants."

"Do you think he has been following us just to try and get that key? That seems too far fetched."

"It could be that he is just a pickpocket. I hear that cities in Europe are full of them. You don't hear about it being that much of a problem in Germany. It is obvious that someone was helping him. Think for a minute of who knew where I put the key to the lock box."

"There were you, me, Conrad, Grueber and Hentsch."

"Exactly, but why would he want to try and get the key. The only person who can get in the box is Conrad. The three of us, plus Grueber and Hentsch, all know the contents of the box."

"I can't answer your question, Akard. Perhaps we should just go over to Dr. Grueber's office like we were asked to do and quit worrying about the pickpocket. He did not get anything and neither one of us is hurt in any way."

"You are right, as usual. The nature of my business is that I expect the worse in every situation. It has kept me alive for thirty-two years."

Grueber's office was off the Thierschstrasse, not to far from the Hotel Splendid, where the two of them were staying. In the lobby of the building there were several brass nameplates bearing the name Rechtsanwalt, the German word for lawyer. One nameplate had several names including the name of Dr. Grueber.

The two of them went to the floor that housed Grueber's office and entered. A young woman greeted them and Akard explained that they did not speak German but that they were there to see Dr. Grueber.

"I am sorry. Dr. Grueber has not returned from a meeting that he had this morning with an American lawyer. I have been expecting him. He had an appointment with a client that he missed. I have tried to reach him on his mobile telephone, but he has not answered," the young woman said.

"That seems odd. We left him some time ago after a meeting at the bank. He said he was coming back to his office," Zelda-Corrine said.

"I cannot explain where he is. I hope nothing has happened to him. I am sure he got distracted. Perhaps an emergency arose and a client called him on his mobile telephone," the young woman responded.

At that moment, another woman entered the room and motioned the receptionist to come over to her. The two women engaged in an animated conversation in German. The second woman seemed highly agitated. The young woman looked over at Akard and Zelda-Corrine and then continued her conversation with the other woman. The younger woman seemed unsure about telling Akard and Zelda-Corrine about the conversation that was taking place. Finally, she approached the two of them.

"There has been an accident. Dr. Grueber may have been struck by an automobile. He has been taken to a hospital," she said.

Akard thought a moment and exchanged glances with Zelda-Corrine. He was concerned, but he did not want to show the already rattled young woman how concerned he was.

"Can you tell us the name of the hospital where Dr. Grueber has been taken? We are very concerned for him," Akard said.

"Dr. Grueber's wife is a doctor. She will see that he is well cared for," the young woman replied.

Akard paused and thought again. He was having concerns that Dr. Grueber being struck by an automobile was not an accident.

"We came all the way to Munich to meet with Dr. Grueber. I am the security man for Dr. Dellifield. I would feel much better about our visit here if I could check on Dr. Grueber personally."

"Very well, he has been taken to the Park Hospital near Cosima Park. It is off of the Vollmannstrasse. You will need to take a taxi."

Akard pondered whether he should even take the time to visit a man he barely knew. He had a gut feeling that the attempt to pick his pocket and this accident were somehow related. He decided to call Dellifield and get his reaction. Before he left the law office, he placed a call to Dellifield at the Kempinski. After three rings, Dellifield answered the telephone. Akard filled him in about the attempt to pick his pocket on the way over to Grueber's office. He told him about the accident involving Grueber. He expressed his fears that the attempt to pick his pocket and the accident were related.

"I hardly know the man, Conrad. His wife is a doctor. Should I go check on him at the hospital?" Akard asked.

"The man is invaluable to our case. I want him to know that we care about his condition. By all means, go to the hospital. Convey our concerns to his wife," Dellifield replied.

"Look, Conrad, if they, whoever they are, are out to get us, they will come after you. Don't take any chances. We will be by the hotel after we check on Grueber."

"I am probably on the safest street in Munich. I will be careful."

Akard and Zelda-Corrine left the office of the law firm and caught a cab to the hospital. Traffic was beginning to pick up because it was nearing the rush hour. Public transportation is very good in Munich and the main streets are wide, yet the automobile traffic is still heavy. The taxi driver spoke enough English to take them to their destination. The Taxi driver pulled the cab up to an entrance marked "Notaufnahme."

Germany has one of the best health services in the world. Ambulances arrive promptly when called. If a person can arrive at a hospital by himself, he goes to the entrance marked "Notaufnahme." This means Accident and Emergency. Less serious cases can be handled by one of the many private clinics.

Akard paid the taxi driver and he and Zelda-Corrine entered the hospital. At first they had some difficulty finding a person who spoke enough English to make themselves understood. Akard made a mental note that perhaps it was unreasonable to expect someone to speak

English in Germany, especially when a German would not be shown the same courtesy in the United States.

After some delay, a person who spoke English fluently was located. The person who spoke English was an athletic-looking woman. She had short blond hair and was almost six feet tall. She was thin and appeared to be around forty years old. Akard explained to her that he was here to inquire about the condition of a lawyer named Dr. Hans Grueber. The woman was wearing a dark suit with a gray turtleneck sweater. Akard guessed that she was an administrator of some kind.

"I am sorry but I cannot release information about a patient to someone other than his family," the woman said.

"I understand. Please listen, just for a moment. I came here with a lawyer from the United States. We met with Dr. Grueber this morning. His input is essential to our trip. I have been told that his wife is a doctor. Could you check and see if she could possibly spare us a moment?" Akard replied.

"I will see. Please, do not expect her to come see you. What is your name?"

"McCoy, Akard McCoy."

The woman gave him a skeptical look, turned on her heels and left.

Akard and Zelda-Corrine took a seat on the chairs in the waiting room. They discussed how long they should wait, what Akard might say that would mean anything to Grueber's wife, and how to express sympathy for someone they hardly knew and have it mean anything. After about thirty minutes elapsed, a woman wearing a white coat approached. She appeared to be in her late thirties or early forties. She was about five feet eight inches in height. Her hair was reddish-brown, cut short. She was very pretty in spite of her sad look. She had obviously been crying.

She approached Akard and Zelda-Corrine. Her English was good although punctuated with a German accent.

"Are you Mr. McCoy? I am Hans Grueber's wife."

Akard replied that he was McCoy. He introduced Zelda-Corrine. He explained the meeting earlier in the day with her husband. He told her that they had come by to check on his condition and to convey the concerns of Conrad Dellifield. He asked about her husband's condition.

"He is still unconscious. He has some brain swelling. The next few hours will tell us if an operation is necessary. Thank you for coming here. But now, I need to get back to my husband's side."

Akard mulled over whether he should ask one question. He knew that it would sound insensitive on his part. He finally decided to ask anyway.

"When your husband was brought to the hospital, did they also bring his briefcase?"

"I am sorry but I cannot answer that question. I don't know why you would ask. I have not seen it. I must get back."

Grueber's wife left without speaking further. Zelda-Corrine gave Akard one of those looks that said, "Why am I with this clod?"

"Whatever possessed you to ask a question like that? The woman's husband may have to have serious surgery. She was obviously distraught."

"I thought about it before I asked the question. Someone tried to get the key to the lock box. Someone struck Grueber with a car. I did not ask if the person who hit him stopped. I should have. It could be that someone tried to kill him and took his brief case because it had the inventory of the lock box inside. Hell, I just don't know. I may be tilting at windmills. At any rate, we need to check on Conrad."

"We can check on Conrad, but first, I am going back to our hotel and get out of these damned high heeled shoes."

# Chapter Twenty-Two

$\mathbf{D}$*arkness had fallen by the time Akard and Zelda-Corrine had* changed clothes at their hotel. Zelda-Corrine told Akard that she was tired of being dressed up and changed into something more casual. She put on slacks, a sweater, comfortable walking shoes and a leather jacket. Akard put on comparable clothes but his did not cling to his body the same way that Zelda-Corrine's clothes fit her form. After some discussion they decided that they would walk down to the Kempinski and fill Dellifield in on what they had learned at the hospital. They had also decided that if the people at the Kempinski did not like the way they were dressed, tough.

The walk from the Hotel Splendid to the Kempinski takes about ten minutes. Massive buildings line both sides of the street of the Maximilianstrasse. At one time they were government buildings. Now they house museums. When Akard and Zelda-Corrine arrived at the hotel, they proceeded to Dellifield's room. A knock at the door produced no response. Akard waited about thirty seconds and knocked harder. Still, there was no response.

"He may be down in the restaurant," Zelda-Corrine said.

"We'll check," Akard answered.

The two of them hurried to the hotel restaurant, which is on the left side of the lobby when coming into the building. Dellifield was an easy man to describe. By this time, Akard was sure that the hotel staff knew his name. A check in the restaurant yielded no clue as to the whereabouts of Dellifield. The next trip was to the desk of the Concierge. Akard and Zelda-Corrine waited in line until the man at the concierge desk had given directions in German to a well-dressed, middle-aged couple. When he had finished giving directions, the hotel employee turned his attention to Akard and Zelda-Corrine.

"May I be of assistance?" the man asked, while keeping his eyes focused on Zelda-Corrine. In as much as he paid so much attention to her, Zelda-Corrine assumed that he must be addressing her.

"We are trying to locate a friend of ours who is a guest of the hotel. His name is Conrad Dellifield," she said.

"Mr. Dellifield was here about thirty minutes ago. He said something about needing to take a walk. He hoped to take a walk and then drop by the hotel of some business associates. I assume that you are the persons he was discussing," the man at the desk answered.

"Did he say where he might walk?" Akard asked.

"He asked me how far it was to the Isar River. I told him that it was an easy walk and that on the other side of the river was a green area that was a small park. He asked directions to the Hotel Splendid. I would guess that his plans were to stop at the Hotel Splendid coming back from his walk," the man said.

"Damn it. It is dark outside. I am worried about Dellifield. Let's see if we can find him," Akard said.

He and Zelda-Corrine thanked the man at the desk and headed up the street toward the Isar River. There is a traffic bridge on the Maximilianstrassse that crosses two rivers. It is probably just a small fork in the Isar. The bridge is illuminated by lamp posts, but the river, which is some fifty feet below the bridge, is dark and foreboding at night. A small waterfall is just past where the river passes under the bridge.

Akard and Zelda-Corrine opted to check the hotel after they walked to the river. As they got within about 100 yards of the bridge, they saw the figure of a man approaching the bridge from the other side of the bridge. As the man passed under the first lamp post Akard recognized the figure of Conrad Dellifield.

"Conrad," Akard yelled. At that moment, a dark automobile stopped opposite Dellifield. To men jumped out and started pulling him into the car. In the struggle, Dellifield threw something into the river.

Akard and Zelda-Corrine raced to the scene. The two men over came Dellifield's resistance and pushed him into the car. Akard almost reached the car when it made a U-turn and headed the opposite direction. Akard could see Dellifield still struggling. His hair, which was never out of place, was mussed and his face was beet red. As the car sped away, Akard heard Dellifield yell, "Akard, my medicine."

Akard and Zelda-Corrine ran after the car, trying to get a license number. The car was too fast. After they crossed the bridge and ran a distance, they stopped to catch their breath. They then noticed that the car had reversed direction and was headed their way.

"Run into the green belt. Let's make them come after us," Akard said.

Both Akard and Zelda-Corrine were in excellent physical condition. They felt their chances were better if they could defend themselves in a wooded area. They sprinted toward the park area. The car parked on the street, but it was a distance away from where Akard and Zelda-Corrine were headed.

Two men got out of the car and ran after Akard and Zelda-Corrine. They did not appear to be armed. At least they did not have a gun in their hands. Akard motioned for Zelda-Corrine to get behind a bush while he waited to confront the attackers. It was fairly dark in the area Akard had chosen to make his stand. The two men approached, each now having a knife in his hands. One was the man who had followed him earlier in the day. The other appeared to be darker in complexion.

Neither man said a word. They circled Akard, taking turns lunging at him with their knives. They were getting ready for the kill when Zelda-Corrine emerged from the bushes and kicked one of the men in the kidneys. He doubled over in pain. Akard took the opportunity to plant his size thirteen shoe under the man's chin.

Now the hunter became the hunted. One man, the man darker in complexion, was on the ground semi-conscious. The other man broke and ran toward the car. Akard gave chase, but gunfire came in his direction from the car. The car was too far away for the shots to be accurate, but Akard knew when he was beaten. The second man reached the car and the car sped away.

Akard felt that someone must have heard the shots and the men in the car could not risk being caught. He then realized that he had left Zelda-Corrine alone with the goon who had attacked them. He sprinted back to the woods. The man had gotten up and was making an attempt to get Zelda-Corrine. He was still woozy from the blows he had taken.

The man would stumble and lunge at Zelda-Corrine and she would punish him with a blow to some part of his body. Akard folded his arms and decided to watch the show. After a number of well-delivered karate blows from Zelda-Corrine, the man wobbled toward Akard. The man's face was battered. He reached out to grab Akard and fell to the ground. He fell face forward to the ground. Akard put a knee in his back, removed his belt and pulled the man's arms behind his back. He secured his arms by pulling his belt tight around the man's wrists.

Akard looked at Zelda-Corrine. "Would you mind letting me have your panty hose?" he said.

"Have you lost your mind?" she yelled back.

"Look, I have given my belt to the cause. I need something to tie up his ankles. Please go behind a bush and remove them."

"It is cold out here. Find something else."

"I promise to buy you another pair tomorrow. Please, help me out."

"I have already helped you out, but, alright."

Zelda-Corrine went behind a bush and complied with Akard's request. She threw the panty hose at his feet. "My ass got cold," she said.

Akard bound the man's ankles together with the panty hose and then turned him over. The man was coming around and stared at Akard with hate-filled eyes.

"Why, you're a damned Arab," Akard said to the man.

"I am not an Arab. I am a Turk," the man answered.

"Well, pardon my mistake, Mr. Turk. Why did you take our friend?" Akard asked.

"I have nothing to say," the man answered.

"I was afraid you might say that. I think that a nice dip in a cold river might change your mind," Akard answered.

With than admonition, Akard grabbed the man's feet and started dragging him along the grass toward the river.

Zelda-Corrine started to pick up the man's knife from the ground.

"Leave it there. If the police come here, I want only his fingerprints on the knife." Zelda-Corrine nodded and followed along as Akard dragged the man toward the river. As they approached the river, Akard asked Zelda-Corrine to take the man's feet while he got him by the shoulders.

"Now, Mr. Turk, we are going to throw your ass into the river. I hope you have gills because you are going to need them."

Akard swung the top part of the man's body while Zelda-Corrine swung his legs.

"On the count of three, toss his ass in," Akard said.

"Fine by me," Zelda-Corrine answered."

"One. Two…"

"No," the man yelled.

"Who asked you to take our friend?"

"I do not know."

"Time for me to go back to counting."

"No, please, I have never met the man. He promised to give money to our cause if we helped him. The other men work for him."

"Is this man a German?"

"Yes."

"Is his name Hentsch?"

"No. They call him Herman."

"Where are they taking our friend?"

"I do not know. I was only to help get some American. They would then drop me off. Money would be delivered to our group tomorrow."

"Well, Mr. Turk, I don't think you or your group will ever see any money. They probably planned to kill our friend and you as well, and blame it on you."

"Akard, I think there is a police car up on the street. A light is being shined on the area," Zelda-Corrine said.

"Time to go fill them in, maybe they can find Dellifield before he gets killed."

Akard dragged the man back to where the fight took place and Zelda-Corrine went to get the police.

As Zelda-Corrine walked toward the police car, Akard bent over and got in the face of the man on the ground.

"Did your friend try to pick my pocket this afternoon? Did you run over a German lawyer this afternoon? Tell me, or so help me, I will pitch you in the river."

"You are too late. The police will be here soon, and I will tell them that you attacked me because you are a Muslim-hating American," the man said.

"Look, pal, I don't know you well enough to hate you. I must admit that I have developed a certain dislike for you since you and your buddy tried to kill me. Frankly, between you and me, I would like to beat the compound shit out of you. The difference between you and me is that you hate me without even knowing what kind of guy I am. I am actually a pretty nice fellow when you get to know me. You just hate because that is all you know how to do, you ignorant son of a bitch. But enough chit chat. Tell the police whatever you want to tell them." Akard gave the man a short kick in the ribs. Short enough that he was sure the German police had not seen him do it.

Zelda-Corrine approached the two police officers whom had gotten out of their car and were walking toward her.

"Gutten Abend," one of the officers said.

"Sprechen Sie Englisch?" Zelda-Corrine said.

"Yah, a little," the other officer said. "What has happened here? We had a report of gun fire in this area," he asked.

Zelda-Corrine did her best to explain the situation. She told them about the American lawyer who had been kidnapped on the bridge. She described, in detail, Dellifield's appearance. She told about the reason for the trip to Germany. Lastly she told about the two men who had attacked them.

Zelda-Corrine and the two officers came to the place where Akard was standing guard over the Turk. The Turk began yelling that he had been assaulted and called names by the two Americans. Akard confirmed what Zelda-Corrine had previously told the officers and directed them to the knife that was on the ground. One of the officers went back to the car and got an evidence bag to contain the knife.

Akard looked at the two officers who could pass for twins. Each was of average height and well built. Both had short sandy-colored hair. They wore the uniform of the Polizei. The uniform consisted of khaki pants, tan shirt and Luftwaffe-style hat. Each wore a side arm and had a radio on his belt. In other words, but for the uniforms, they could pass for a compact version of Akard McCoy.

One of the officers shined his flashlight into the Turk's face.

"This man has been injured," he said.

"That's what happens when you pick on someone that's of the opposite sex. She worked him over pretty good. Of course, he was just trying to kill her," Akard explained.

The other officer bent over and noticed that the man ankles were tightly bound with pantyhose.

"What is this?" the officer asked while removing the pantyhose.

"Those belong to me, but feel free to keep them. Sport, here, is buying me a new pair," Zelda-Corrine answered.

"This is all very unusual. We must take you all to the police headquarters," the officer holding the pantyhose declared.

The two officers got on each side of the Turk and escorted him to the police car. Akard and Zelda-Corrine followed suit. The police car was not made to hold five people, especially when three of them had been waging war among themselves. One of the officers called for another car. In a short time, the other police car arrived and two other officers got out. The first two officers took the Turk with them and the other two officers took Akard and Zelda-Corrine with them.

The police station was about ten minutes away from the scene of the fight. Unlike American police stations depicted on television, there were no prostitutes sitting around waiting to be booked. Akard and Zelda-Corrine were ushered into the office of the police commander. He was in a tailored uniform. He was tall and thin. His black hair was flecked with gray. He face was long and narrow. His nose was thin and came to a sharp point.

"Please have a seat and tell me what has happened," the commander said.

Akard and Zelda-Corrine took turns relating the events of the day. They told of the reason for the trip. They talked of the meeting at the bank, the accident involving Dr. Grueber, the kidnapping of Dellifield and their attempt to stop the car. They talked about the two men who had assaulted them in the park.

"You believe that the accident involving the German lawyer and the kidnapping of the American lawyer are related?" the Commander asked.

Akard explained that he was a detective who had been hired to prevent this type of event from happening. He showed the commander his private detective license and his permit to carry a concealed weapon.

"This will not allow you to carry a firearm in Germany," the Commander said.

"He does not intend to carry a fireman," Zelda-Corrine said. "We want you to find our friend before he is harmed. I want to know what a Turk is doing trying to kill us. Aren't we all in N.A.T.O? I want to take a hot bath."

The Commander did not want to argue with an outraged woman. He tried to calm her down. "This man, who you say assaulted you, is wanted by the police. He is a member of a group that wants to over throw the democratic government of Turkey and install a religious state. We will try to find your friend. I must notify the BND," the Commander said.

"The who?" Akard asked.

"The Bundensnachrichtendienst is our equivalent of your C.I.A. They will take part in the investigation if any form of terrorism is involved," the Commander explained.

"Tell them this, then." Akard then went into great detail about his theory as to why Helga Brandenberg was killed in Dallas. He told of finding the apartment house that no one knew about. He explained why he thought Hentsch was involved in the whole scheme. He told about finding the name "Herman" in Helga's diary and that he believed Hentsch was Herman. He stated it was his belief that Hentsch wanted the millions in the lock box for himself or for his cause, whatever it was, and that he had duped the Turk into playing along. He suggested that the police assign a guard to Dr. Grueber at the hospital. Of the five persons who knew the contents of the lock box, one was in the hospital, one was kidnapped, one was a banker and the other two were sitting across from the commander.

"You tell a rather imaginative story, Herr McCoy. One would think that it came from one of your American detective stories. Nevertheless, I will assign a guard to Dr. Grueber if his wife consents. I will see that no one other than Dr. Dellifield can enter the lock box. I cannot go storming into a well-respected bank and accuse the bankers of such conspiratorial actions on their part. There is nothing that can be done tonight." The Commander said that he would be in touch and assured Akard and Zelda-Corrine that everything that could be done to locate Dellifield would be done.

The Commander called for an officer to take Akard and Zelda-Corrine back to their hotel. Zelda-Corrine let it be known that she was starving. Akard was almost afraid to walk the streets at this time of night. A lot of time had passed since they first set out to find Dellifield.

"Take us to the Vier Jahreszeiten, please," Akard told the driver.

"Why are we going there?" Zelda-Corrine asked.

"First of all, we still have a key to Conrad's room. The room is where his medicine is. I hope that his telephone is still there. Sooner or later someone is going to try and contact us. Conrad threw something in the river. My best guess is that he was smart enough to toss the key to the lock box away. That may keep him alive. We have the other key. I don't know how they could use it, but they will think of something. They are either going to try and get the key from us by force or negotiate for it. And lastly we are going to have room service and charge it to Conrad's room."

"Cool," Zelda-Corrine replied.

The policeman let Akard and Zelda-Corrine out in front of the grand hotel. The night crowds along the Maximilianstrasse are much like the people walking in New York City at night. For the most part, the people are extremely well dressed. A steady stream of luxury automobiles passed along the street. People were still drinking at the bars of the fancy restaurants that line the boulevard.

The jewelry stores had removed the fine gemstones, Rolexes and expensive baubles from the windows. The boutiques still displayed the fashions of the day. The art galleries displayed works of art that would hang in only the finest homes. Akard and Zelda-Corrine, for the first time, looked completely out of place. They had changed into their casual clothes. They had been in a fight and looked the part. Zelda-Corrine had not seen herself in a mirror and was afraid to look. Akard's pants were dirty and grass-stained.

Akard and Zelda-Corrine entered the hotel lobby. The lobby was full of well-dressed people, socializing and laughing. Perhaps there was a party at the hotel. Akard and Zelda-Corrine worked their way through the crowd looking down and hoping that no one would notice them. They made their way to the elevators and reached the floor where Dellifield's suite was located. Akard unlocked the door and, at last, the two of them had escaped public humiliation.

The suite was neat, as one would expect. Sitting atop the nightstand next to Dellifield's bed was a plastic box with a day of the week marked on each separate lid. Within each compartment was the dosage of medicine that Dellifield needed to maintain his health. Sitting next to the medicine container was a mobile telephone.

Zelda-Corrine took a long hot bath. Akard ordered a hearty meal from room service. Both pondered the fate of Conrad Dellifield.

# Chapter Twenty-Three

*onrad Dellifield had no hot bath or room service waiting for him.* After the encounter with Akard and Zelda-Corrine, the man with the tattooed neck had joined the other man in the car and they had sped away with their prey. A hood had been placed over Dellifield's head and he had been shoved to the floor of the back seat.

His captors conversed in German and Dellifield could understand a few words that they were saying. His college German had long since fallen out of use. German in good times is a hard language to comprehend. When you have a hood over your head and you are in fear of your life, your comprehension level diminishes accordingly.

What Dellifield was able to pick up was that his captors did not know what to do with him. Apparently they were aware that he had tossed away the key to the lock box. One of the men had seen him do it. They had not counted on Akard and Zelda-Corrine being present at the grab. The man who was not driving was having an excited conversation with someone over a cell phone.

At first, the car seemed to be stopping on occasion. This would indicate that they were in the city. Later, the car was being driven at a high rate of speed. This indicated that they were on a highway outside of the city. The car slowed, apparently to exit. Then, they proceeded at a lesser speed through some winding roads. Wherever he was being taken, Conrad Dellifield knew that he would not be easily found or rescued.

Dellifield also knew that there had been three men in the car when he was grabbed. He saw Akard and Zelda-Corrine and they had seen him. Two men had left the car and only one returned. While the other two men were in the park, the third man had put a gun to Dellifield's head and placed a hood over his head. He had been ordered to crouch on the floor of the back seat.

This was not the way that Conrad Dellifield IV was accustomed to being treated. These men had no manners. He was hungry. The men smelled bad. He sensed that his heart was going out of rhythm. He was more worried about a stroke killing him than he was about his captors killing him. He knew that he would have to rely on all the tricks that he had learned in almost forty years of law practice.

His main hope was that Akard and Zelda-Corrine had survived the attack in the park and had not been injured by the gunfire from the car. He was encouraged by the fact that one of his captors had not returned from the park. Akard was not his cup of tea, but he was resourceful. He was not afraid to kill a person. He had done it before. Yes, Akard would save him. That was the hope that sustained him.

After a period of time driving down winding roads, the car came to a stop. Dellifield was rudely pulled from the car. He was taken up three outdoor steps to a door. One captor knocked on the door and someone came to the door. A brief conversation took place in German. Dellifield could understand enough of the conversation to learn that whoever answered the door was not pleased to see the other two men with a captive in tow.

Dellifield was led to a narrow stairway. He could hear noise and smell the aroma of German sausage cooking. He could smell beer. He stomach reacted with pangs of hunger. *"I must be in a tavern or beer hall,"* he thought. He was pushed up a narrow flight of stairs. His shoulders were constantly hitting the sides of walls. His heart was pounding from the climb. He was gasping for air through the hood over his face.

Dellifield had tried to guess how many floors he had climbed before he was stopped. He could not any longer hear the noise or smell the food. A door was opened and he was shoved inside. One of the men said something in German and nudged him in the ribs with a pistol.

"I do not speak German," Dellifield said. He was not about to let his captors know that he could understand anything they were saying.

"I am leaving you here. Someone will be outside of the room. If you make a sound or try to escape you will be killed. Your body will be ground up and you will be served as part of the sausage downstairs. Do you understand? A man said in a heavy German accent.

"Perfectly, I need food and medicine," Dellifield answered.

"You are a dead man. Do not concern yourself with trivial matters," the man said, as he shut the door.

Dellifield removed the hood from his head. There was no light in the room. He could see only because moonlight was coming in a tiny window. There was a toilet and a wash basin off the room. Dellifield turned on the water in the basin and it ran a rust color. He let it run until it cleared a little. He cupped his hands and lapped up the water. It tasted metallic. He spit the water out of his mouth. He ran some into his hands and splashed the water over his face. He saw that there was a bed in the room. He intended to get in the bed as soon as he looked out the window.

The window was small and dirty. He judged that he was about sixty feet or more above the pavement. Wherever he was, it was old. Below him was a small outdoor beer garden. The weather was still too cold for people to be outside. Dim lights hung above the empty tables. He guessed that he was at the top of a structure that came to a point. The window was in a bay like area and he could see a slanted slate-like roof on either side of the window.

Far below was a cobblestone street. The building in which he was being held appeared to be at the confluence of two narrow streets.

There was an upper and lower street. Across the street was an ancient stone clock tower. The clock said nine-thirty. He tried to guess how far he might be outside of Munich, but he had no clue.

He felt his way back to the small bathroom and relieved himself. He let the water run until it became almost clear. He did not care what it looked like or tasted like. He drank some out of thirst.

Conrad Dellifield fell on to the bed. For the first time in his life, he was going to bed hungry. He said a silent prayer that the next morning he would be alive and still have his wits about him.

# Chapter Twenty-Four

Akard and Zelda-Corrine had gone to sleep in Conrad's room after eating the meal brought by room service. They were awakened by the ringing of the mobile telephone that was on the nightstand opposite the bed.

"That may be the kidnappers," Akard said. He answered the telephone cautiously.

"Hello." Akard said.

"Who is this?" a woman with a Texas accent said.

"Akard, who is this?" he answered.

"This is Mrs. Dellifield. It is after midnight and I have not heard from my husband. Is this the right number? The woman asked.

Akard covered the telephone with his hand. "Oh shit. This is Conrad's wife. What in the hell am I going to tell her?"

"I don't know. Think of something. Don't let her know he has been kidnapped. She will worry herself to death," Zelda-Corrine said.

"I am sorry Mrs. Dellifield. Conrad had a hard day and went to bed early at his hotel. The battery of this telephone is going bad and he asked me to see if I could find a new one while he was in a meeting today. We are in different hotels or I would try to reach him now. You go to bed and I will tell him you called as soon as I see him," Akard said.

"It is just not like him not to call. I hope he is alright. Is he taking his medicine?" Mrs. Dellifield said.

"I am sure he just fell asleep. He is fine," Akard said, hoping he was more convincing than he sounded.

"Well thank you, I guess. I am still worried. I hope he will call. Good bye."

Akard felt terrible about having to lie to Dellifield's wife. Someone had to find Dellifield soon. It would be tragic if he died and his wife did not know about the danger he was in.

"We have to do something," Akard said.

"I agree, but what?" Zelda-Corrine asked.

"I am going to call Carter."

"Mark Carter, the man with the F.B.I.? I didn't think he liked you."

"I don't give a rat's ass whether he likes me or not. I put my life on the line for him in Italy and he owes me."

"Don't be surprised if he hangs up on you."

"He never should have given me the number to reach him at anytime. I am going to call him."

Akard dialed the number that Carter had been given him when Akard was working with the F.B.I. in a previous case. The stakes were probably higher in that case, but Akard would try and make a good argument for calling him in the early morning hours in the U.S.A.

The telephone rang and a gruff voice answered, "Carter."

"Carter, this is Akard McCoy."

"Is this a joke?"

"Carter, I am sorry to call you at this time of night. I am in a situation in Munich. I am way over my head."

"Good night, Akard."

"Please don't hang up. This is serious, and it may involve something of interest to you."

"You have five minutes."

In the next five minutes Akard talked as fast as he could, telling the story of the trip, his suspicions about the neo-Nazis, and the events that had happened since arriving in Munich. He left out no detail. When he had finished, he anxiously waited for a reaction.

"McCoy, you amaze me. You would screw up a wet dream. We cannot get involved in the internal affairs of a German investigation. The police and the BND are first class. I can't help you," Carter said.

"Carter, I just talked with Dellifield's wife. I told her he was OK. I am afraid that Dellifield will be dead before they can get an investigation off the ground. Surely, you know someone who can help."

"Alright, I feel for the guy. There may be someone who can help. Lyman Welsh is in Germany now."

"Lyman Welsh, the alleged wine merchant?"

"The one and only."

"How can I reach him?"

"You cannot. I have your number on my caller I.D. If he is available, he will contact you. I will also call my contacts at the BND and pass on the information you have given me. That is the best I can do. Do not call me again."

"Thanks Mark. Zelda-Corrine sends love and kisses."

"That woman must be mad to hang around you. Good night."

Akard turned to Zelda-Corrine. She had her head propped up on her hand leaning on her elbow. She was naked. Akard knew this was not a time for romance, but, damn, she looked good.

"Carter can't really do much, but Lyman Welsh is in Germany. He may contact us," Akard said.

"That British pompous ass?"

"He is a pompous ass. He is also a professional killer, if the need arises. He knows his way around every corner where intrigue may be."

"Let's hope he calls."

The next morning Zelda-Corrine did not want to get dressed in the same clothes that she had on the night before. The thought of walking through the lobby in the morning with no make up and wearing the same dirty clothes that she had on the night before was too much. She lay down of the bed and pulled the sheet over her head.

"Akard, you are just going to have to go to our hotel and bring me some different clothes. Bring me the pants suit I wore on the flight over here and a white turtle neck sweater. I have my leather jacket here. Bring back my make-up bag. It will not take you too long. I will order a continental breakfast for us. It will be here when you get back," Zelda-Corrine said, from underneath the sheet.

"Women!" Akard said under his breath. He put on his dirty clothes and headed for the Hotel Splendid. On the way, he tried to sort out what he could do to help find Dellifield. One thing, for sure, he was going to do was to go to the bank and see if Hentsch was at work.

The Maximilainstrasse was beginning to have crowds of workers and people stopping off for coffee before work. The air was colder than it had been before, but it felt good on Akard's face. It helped clear his mind. At the street you turn off of the Maximilianstrasse to go to the Hotel Splendid there is a traffic circle around a large statute. The electric trolley makes a turn there.

Akard stopped for the light and was standing in a crowd waiting for the trolley to pass. Just as the trolley made its turn, someone shoved Akard from behind. He was staring at the headlight of the trolley when someone grabbed his arm and pulled him to safety. A large man in a black coat held him steady. People in the crowd had gasped and shouted. The would-be assailant had run into the U-Ban station and quickly blended in with the crowd.

Akard was shaken. He could be dead or on his way to a hospital to join Dr. Grueber. He regained his composure and shook the large man's hand.

"Danke," Akard said.

"Bitte," the man answered and then he walked away.

When Akard pulled his hand back, there was a card in it.

The card had no name, address or telephone number. It had three handwritten letters on the card. "BND."

"Son of a bitch," Akard said to himself. "Someone is doing something."

"*This does not make any sense. Why try and knock me off before they get the key? I guess whoever it was thought he could pretend to be helping me while I was dying and go through my pockets. He could probably hang around to assist when help came. Yeah, he could hang around to be sure I was dead. Well boys, you are messing with the wrong guy,*" Akard thought to himself.

Nothing was hurt about Akard except his pride. A few people who were standing at the corner checked to see if he was hurt. When the light changed, the crowd moved on. The large man in the black coat had blended with the morning mass of humanity. Akard thought, at first, that he would check the underground station of the U-Ban, but he realized that he had no idea what the person or persons who shoved him in the path of the trolley looked like. Instead, he decided to continue the short distance to the Hotel Splendid, get his shower and change his clothes. Nevertheless, he gave an occasional glace over his shoulder to see if someone was following him. One thing for sure, the lock box key would no longer be on his person. He would leave it locked up at the desk of the Hotel Splendid.

Akard went to his room and showered. He felt much better. He put on some casual clothes and picked up his all weather jacket. He picked out the outfit Zelda-Corrine had asked him to bring back and put it in the plastic sack that had held the scarf she had bought in Zurich. He went by the desk and the beautiful blonde was at the reception desk. He gave her the lock box key and told her under no circumstances was she to give the key to anyone but him.

"Where is your wife this morning?" the blonde asked.

It sounded strange to Akard to hear someone refer to Zelda-Corrine as his wife. It was a logical assumption. Akard had not listed Zelda-Corrine separately when they registered. Zelda-Corrine did not wear a wedding ring or an engagement ring. Perhaps, that was something he needed to address.

"She left earlier this morning. I am going to meet her for breakfast."

"Did she leave without her clothes?" the girl behind the desk asked.

Without answering, Akard headed back to the Kempinski.

While Akard and Zelda-Corrine had been enjoying the comforts of the Kempinski, Conrad Dellifield IV was not having nearly as rosy a time. It had gotten much colder during the night. There was no heat in the room he was in. His heart was beating irregularly. Even though the room was cold, he had been sweating. His shirt was wet from the perspiration. His hunger from the night before was only magnified by the hours that had passed. For the first time, he was concerned that he might really die. His thoughts were interrupted by the turning of a key in the lock on the door. The man with the tattoo came in. He had his pistol in hand.

"You have made things very complicated, Herr Dellifield. If you had not thrown away the key, you might be a free man by now," the man said to Dellifield.

"Don't bullshit me about setting me free. I'm a lawyer. We specialize in bullshit. You need me to trade for the key that my security man has. If you had been successful in getting the key from him, I would be dead by now," Dellifield said.

"It will be necessary for you to contact him and arrange for the delivery of the key," the man said.

"I will not do anything on an empty stomach. You bring me some food and we will discuss the situation," Dellifield said.

With that, the man cuffed Dellifield across the mouth. The warm taste of blood ran between his teeth.

"You do not dictate terms. I tell you what to do and you do it," the man said with much anger in his voice.

Dellifield thought carefully before he said anything else. This was not like being in court. In court, there was a third party deciding the outcome of a trial. Either the judge or the jury would determine who won. Here, the clear advantage was with the younger and stronger man holding the gun.

"You make a good point. However, you should know that I have a heart condition. You have taken me away from my medicine. My heart is out of rhythm now. You can feel my pulse if you do not believe me. If I die or have a stroke, I am of no use to you. You can save me a great deal of suffering by just shooting me now," Dellifield said, waiting for a response from his jailer.

The man put the pistol to Dellifield's head and felt his carotid artery. He could feel the strong, but irregular, beat of Dellifield's heart.

"I have no medicine. If you die, you die."

Dellifield pulled the dirty sheet over his head.

"Then get it over with. Shoot me and then you can explain to your boss that you could not get me to co-operate. You try to get the other key from McCoy. I suspect that someone has already informed you that is a more difficult task that kidnapping me."

Dellifield waited for the report from the gunfire and was ready to meet his maker. Instead of hearing gunfire, the man yanked back the sheet and grabbed Dellifield by the throat. There was fire in his eyes when he spoke.

"I will get you some food but you must do exactly as I say."

"Fair enough." Dellifield would say anything to stay alive a little longer and to get some food.

The man shoved Dellifield hard onto the bed and left. The sound of a key was heard turning in the lock after the man left the room.

In the meantime, Akard had walked back to the Kempinski. He was walking across the lobby when he heard the crisp, stilted voice of an Englishman.

"McCoy, old boy, how are you?" the voice said.

Akard turned around. Sitting in a chair with his six-foot-five frame fully relaxed, was Lyman Welsh. He was dressed in the clothes that Akard had seen him wear before. He had on a double-breasted blue blazer with dark gray slacks. His blue-striped shirt with white collar was opened at the neck. A red and blue paisley ascot was around his neck. His curly, sandy hair was combed back.

Akard thought that Lyman Welsh was a fop whose condescending manner toward Akard was almost intolerable. As intolerable as Lyman Welsh could be, Akard was extremely happy to see him. Akard eagerly went over to where Welsh was now standing and shook his hand vigorously.

"Lyman, I am really glad to see you," Akard said.

"I am sure you are, dear boy. Mr. Carter was quite agitated when he called me this morning. He said I might find you here. I am told that you find yourself in a messy situation. It is one that should be left to the local police," Welsh said.

"Then why are you here?" Akard asked.

"Dear boy, things have been a bit dull for me lately. The wine business has been somewhat slow," Welsh answered.

"You mean you are between assignments with MI-6."

"Never say such a thing in public. Someone might think I am a spy."

Akard lowered his voice to a whisper. "That is because you are one."

"I am a wine merchant, just as I was when we met in Italy, but enough of this. Tell me about the mess you find yourself engaged in at the present time."

"Zelda-Corrine is waiting for me upstairs. She has ordered a continental breakfast. Please join us."

"I have already had mine. I would enjoy getting out of the lobby to discuss matters. I would also enjoy seeing your lovely friend again. I must admit some surprise in the fact that she is still associating with you."

The two men went up the elevator to Dellifield's room. Akard knocked at the door before entering.

"Who is it?" Zelda-Corrine said, from the other side of the door.

"It's Akard. Are you decent?"

"No, you have my clothes. Why?"

"I have someone with me. "

"Hand me my clothes and wait a minute." She opened the door slightly and took the plastic bag containing her clothes.

The two men waited outside the room while Zelda-Corrine got dressed.

When she had dressed and put on her makeup Zelda-Corrine opened the door, hoping to see that Dellifield had returned. Instead, she saw the imposing figure of Lyman Welsh. She was saddened by the fact that Dellifield was not at the door. She, like Akard, was happy to see Lyman Welsh. She gave him a hug.

"I have breakfast inside. Will you join us?" Zelda-Corrine asked of Welsh.

"I have already eaten, thank you, but I would have a cup of coffee."

"Please take mine. It is too strong for me anyway," Zelda-Corrine said.

Lyman Welsh accepted the offer of the coffee and doctored the drink with cream and sugar. "Please have your breakfast, and tell me about the problems you are having," he said.

Akard and Zelda-Corrine took turns telling Welsh everything they could think of concerning the events that had happened since they had arrived in Munich. When Akard got to the part about being pushed in front of the trolley earlier in the morning, Zelda-Corrine dropped her fork.

"My God! What would I have done if you had been killed? Akard, we need to get out of this now. Let the police take care of things from now on," Zelda-Corrine said tearfully.

"I am afraid it will not be that easy," Lyman Welsh said. You see, by now the police will have made it quite clear to the bank that no one can enter the lock box other than Mr. Dellifield. If, as you believe, Hentsch is behind the kidnapping, then he will have to figure out a way to get the key. He will try to find some way to get in the box without Dellifield. It will not be a simple thing for him to do. Dellifield is probably smart enough to realize that he can trade his safety for the key but he is deluding himself. I am sure that these people, whoever they are, intend to kill all three of you. I am encouraged that the BND may be at work. They are good, very good. Is there anything that you have failed to tell me?"

Akard and Zelda-Corrine both thought hard. Finally something occurred to Akard that he had not mentioned.

"Two things I forgot. Early in the case, when we were back in Dallas, I found a small piece of paper concealed in a flashlight in Helga Brandenburg's apartment. There were two words written in German. In English it translated to 'intersection 12.' I assumed it was a location of a map. The other is that Dellifield has a heart condition. His medicine is on the night stand in the bedroom," Akard said.

"My best guess is that it is an exit from one major road onto another road. Do you have a map?" Welsh asked.

"I have one," Zelda-Corrine said. She went to her purse.

She brought back a map of Munich and the surrounding areas. Welsh studied the map carefully. There were numbers shown around the map at various places indicating exits off of major highways that ringed the city. There was a number twelve on the map. It indicated a road that led to the Airport.

"This is just one map. Another map might show different exit numbers, but for now, this is the best we have. The heart condition that your friend has is very troubling. I think we are going to have to wait until someone contacts you. The man's heart condition is probably bothering them as well. Perhaps, they will call your hotel," Welsh said.

"I think he will give them his cell phone number. Dellifield is smart. He knows that there is a caller I.D. that will retain the number of the caller. Once we have that, the police or the BND may be able to trace the telephone to the caller," Akard said.

"Good point, Akard. We can only hope his captors really are that stupid. In the meantime, I think you need to pay a visit to your banker friend. Shake him up a bit. If he leaves the bank, I will follow him. We will keep in touch by mobile telephone. Here is my number I have written down. Give me the number of Dellifield's telephone," Welsh said.

"I don't know it," Akard replied.

"Give me the telephone," Zelda-Corrine said. "You push this little button here and the number is displayed. Akard is not a technical wizard. Zelda-Corrine wrote the telephone number on a small piece of hotel note pad and handed the number to Lyman Welsh.

Welsh folded the paper and placed it in his shirt pocket.

"Akard, I want you to go to the bank and shake up Hentsch. Do not tell him about me or the BND. I am sure that you will handle the situation very well. I want him to run. Then I will follow him and see where he leads me. If you get a call, let me know the caller's telephone number immediately," Welsh said.

"Will do, but Lyman, you are about as inconspicuous as an elephant in a punch bowl," Akard said.

"Dear boy, you continue to underestimate me. On a coat rack in the lobby hangs a well used, black trench coat. In one of the coat pockets is a gray crushable hat. I can walk stooped over and no one will notice me. I'm off. Keep me posted. I will be lurking somewhere around the bank. If you should see me, which I doubt, please show no sign of recognition. Lyman Welsh left Akard and Zelda-Corrine wondering if Lyman Welsh was real or just imagined.

# Chapter Twenty-Five

Conrad Dellifield could smell the food before it reached the room. It had a foul, greasy odor. He still had the taste of blood in his mouth. He had looked around in the dim light of the room for some type of weapon, but he had found none. He had tried to bring his heart beat back to normal by total relaxation of his body and deep breathing. To some extent he had slowed the rate of the beat of his heart, but it would not return to normal sinus rhythm.

The man with the tattoo came into the room carrying a dirty plate containing two burned, greasy sausages. There was a stale piece of bread and a glass of cloudy water. The man placed the plate on the bed and put his pistol to Dellifield's head.

"You will answer each question I ask. At anytime I think you are lying, the meal will be covered with your brains. Do you understand?" the man said.

"Ask your questions," Dellifield said, as he grabbed a sausage and ate it like a hungry dog. He almost choked on the foul taste of the sausage. Grease shot forth into his throat and he gagged. He thought he would throw up, but he chewed more slowly and was able to overcome the taste.

"Where are your friend and the woman?"

"They are at the Kempinski."

"Where does he keep the key to the lock box?"

"The last time I knew, before you kidnapped me, he had it on his person."

"Is he armed?"

"He has no weapon other than his fists."

"Does the woman carry a weapon?"

"She has no weapon."

"She fights like a man."

"I would not know. She does secretarial work for me on a contract basis."

"Where is Helga Brandenberg's will?"

"We were unable to find one or any reference to one. There is a presumption in law that when a will was last in the possession of the testator, and if it cannot be found, it is presumed to be revoked."

"You destroyed it."

"I did not. Why should I? I never met the woman. I was appointed by the Court because she had no will."

"How did you find out about the lock box in Munich?"

"I had her diary translated and it contained a reference to the bank and the lock box. The judge of the court in Dallas knows about the box. The woman who translated the diary knows about the box." Dellifield then told his first lie. "I have informed my office and the Court of the inventory of the lock box. You cannot kill everyone who knows about the cash and bonds. You are wasting your time."

The man grabbed Dellifield by the hair. "You are not in control here. I am. I will be the judge of the outcome of the contents of the lock box. If you want any more food you will answer my questions without comment. Who killed Helga Brandenberg?"

"It was ruled a suicide. The police have no interest in the case. She took an overdose of drugs."

"You do not think it was a suicide."

Dellifield considered what he would say next. The longer he talked the more he got to eat. Even if he gave the information he had about the death of Helga Brandenberg, he felt there would be nothing this man could do to use the information. He decided to tell him what he knew, but first he grabbed the piece of stale bread. The bread had a sour taste. He took a small bite and chewed it slowly. He then answered the question.

"I suspect that someone found out that she was financing some neo-Nazi activity here in Munich. That 'someone' caused her death."

"Who knows of your suspicion?"

"It will take me a while, but let's see, the judge in Dallas, everyone in my office who has worked on the case, the lawyer here in Munich. The two people here with me in Munich. I am sure by now that the police in Munich know since they, no doubt, have your colleague in custody at this very hour. That's the short list. I probably forgot a few."

"I want to know who killed her."

"That, no one knows."

"If you want to live another minute, you will tell who you think killed her."

"Since you put it that way. I suspect, only suspect, that an elderly man who lived down the hall from her was responsible. His name is Jacob Franks. I have reason to believe that he was a survivor of one of Hitler's death camps, and he found out what she was doing and eliminated her."

"There were no death camps. That is just Zionist propaganda. My grandfather was an officer in the German army. He told me on many occasions that the Americans, the English and the Russians made films to depict death camps to justify their aggression against the Fatherland."

"I guess the memorial outside of town called Dachau is a figment of the imagination of these aggressors?"

"Talk no more of this. You are a prisoner of the Fourth Reich."

"Then, as a prisoner, I demand to be treated under the rules of the Geneva Convention as it relates to prisoners of war."

"You are a spy. You have no rights."

The tattooed man then left the room. He apparently was outside of the room making a telephone call. To Dellifield, it seemed clear that the tattooed man had no idea what to do with him except to abuse him until further orders. He was puzzled about the whereabouts of the third man. Three men had grabbed him off the street. One man did not return to the car. Two men brought him to the present location. The only contact he had was with the tattooed man.

Dellifield also wondered where he was. Since the early morning hours, he had heard the roar of jet engines. He was close to the airport, but he had no idea which direction he was from the airport. What he hoped was that he would be asked to contact Akard and that a plane would take off during the conversation. A lot of things had to fall in place for him to be rescued. He let his mind wander back to Dallas. His wife must be wondering what had happened. He had always faithfully called her whenever he was away on business. He had to be back in Dallas for the Garden Club Ball in three nights. If he got away and missed the Ball, he might as well die in Germany, because if he missed the Ball his wife would kill him anyway.

His reflections were short-lived because the tattooed man reentered the room.

"If you want to live any longer, it will be necessary for you to contact your security man. If you try to give any indication of where you are, I will shoot you immediately. What is his hotel room number?"

"He will not be there. He will be looking for me. The police probably have the hotel telephone line bugged waiting for someone to call. You do what you want. I am in room 334 of the Kempinski. I do not know the number of the hotel."

"You must have a mobile telephone. What is the number?"

*"Surely the man is not this dumb. He would not have been left in charge of me if he were that dumb,"* Dellifield thought. He gave him the number without hesitation.

The man dialed the number. After three rings, Akard answered. He heard the voice of a man speaking with a heavy accent.

"We want the key to the lock box," the voice said.

"Go to hell," Akard answered.

The tattooed man slapped Dellifield across the face. The sound of contact from the blow was heard by Akard, as well as Dellifield's groan. By this time, Akard had made a note of the caller's telephone number.

"I will kill your friend if you fail to listen."

"You kill him and the lock box key goes to the BND."

"You will make no contact with the authorities. If we see a policeman anywhere near this place, your friend will die."

"You made it impossible to control that when you left the Turk with us. We were not going to baby-sit him. You fired the gunshots. That brought the police. The Turk has probably already sold you out to save his own skin."

"You treat the situation as a game. We can kill you and the woman anytime we choose. I have lost patience with you."

The man hung up on Akard. Akard called Lyman Welsh and gave him the telephone number of the caller. He told Welsh about the threat to kill Dellifield if the police became involved.

"I am ready to kill those bastards," Akard told Welsh.

"In your country, there are two massive stone lions guarding the Beaux-Arts building of the New York Public Library. They have been named Patience and Fortitude. No one doubts your fortitude. You are lacking in patience. The kidnappers have made a huge mistake. I now have their cell phone number. I will give the number to the people who can trace its location. We have to accept the fact that your friend may be killed. We can lessen the chance of his losing his life if we find him. Go lean on Hentsch."

Akard turned to Zelda-Corrine and said, "Put Conrad's medicine in your purse. We are going to pay a call on Hentsch. It is time for him to know what we think and to see how he reacts."

"Are you going to tell him we have the kidnapper's telephone number?"

"No, we are going to tell him about how we think the kidnapping, the assault on Grueber, and the attempt on my life are all tied together."

Zelda-Corrine took Dellifield's medicine from the top of the bedroom table and placed the containers in her purse. Akard told her that he was tired of being unarmed. About two doors down from the Hofbrauhaus is a small shop, which sells a wide variety of knives. Akard and Zelda-Corrine had passed the shop on several occasions. In the window were knives of every shape and form. Some looked particularly vicious. The shop was only a little out of the way in route to the bank.

At the shop, Akard asked to see a number of different knives. He opted to get one in a scabbard that would hang on his belt. He would have to keep his coat buttoned at all times. He could not go in a building that had metal detectors. He got a smaller, yet equally effective, knife for Zelda-Corrine to slip in her purse. After securing the weapons, the two of them headed for the bank.

When they reached the bank, Akard asked if Hentsch was available. After a short wait, Hentsch came to the front and greeted them warmly. *"This guy is a cool customer,"* Akard thought to himself.

Hentsch ushered the two of them into his office. After several minutes of pleasant conversation and inquiries about how Akard and Zelda-Corrine were enjoying Munich, Hentsch got down to business.

"What brings you here today? I expected to see Dr. Dellifield. It is a pleasure to see you here even if I do not know the nature of your business." Hentsch said.

"There is a problem. A lot has happened since we left your office yesterday. First, we found out about an apartment house that you failed to mention as well as the fact that you collect the rent. Then, someone tried to pick my pocket and get my duplicate of the lock box key. Next, Dr. Grueber was hit by a car and is in the hospital, and someone kidnapped Mr. Dellifield. The kidnappers tried to kill Miss Paige and me. We caught one of the attackers and he is in police custody. Stop me at anytime if you already know all of this. If this is Munich hospitality, we will stay in Dallas from now on," Akard said with all the dramatic license he could muster. Akard ignored the admonition of Lyman Welsh not to mention the BND.

"You are joking, of course," Hentsch said.

"Some joke. The police and the BND didn't think it was a joke." Akard could see the uneasiness showing in Hentsch's face.

"You know of the BND? I am surprised that the BND would be involved in a matter of this sort. The events you mentioned are surely not all related," Hentsch noted.

"We only know that a man from Turkey tried to kill us. The police told us that would be of interest to the BND," Zelda-Corrine interjected.

"I received an order from my superiors this morning that no one, other than Dr. Dellifield, could enter the lock box. I just assumed that was a request from Dr. Dellifield. How can I be of assistance?" Hentsch asked.

"We thought that you might know something about this, since only five people were in the safety deposit box area when the inventory was taken. Only those five people knew who had keys. One of those persons is unconscious in the hospital. One is missing. The other three are here in this room," Akard said glaring at Hentsch.

"Surely, you do not think that I had anything whatsoever to do with the events you described?" Hentsch gave his most innocent look.

"I do not make those decisions. That is for the police. I am sure they will ask you the same questions," Akard said pointedly.

The telephone rang on Hentsch's desk. He asked that he be excused. Akard and Zelda-Corrine stepped into the hallway outside of Hentsch's office. He shut the door. Akard and Zelda-Corrine could hear Hentsch almost shouting into the telephone. He heard one word of the conversation, which must have the same meaning in German as it does in English. That word was "Idiot."

Hentsch came out of his office. His face was red with anger, yet he was totally composed.

"I am sorry to have to leave. My mother is ill. If I could take you to one of the other Bank officers, perhaps, he might think of something that would help you and the police find your friend."

Hentsch said something to the receptionist in the lobby of the office suite and left. Just before he disappeared from sight, he took out his mobile telephone and started dialing a number.

Akard took out Dellifield's telephone and called Lyman Welsh.

"He's running. I told him about the BND," Akard said when Lyman Welsh answered his telephone.

"I have him on my radar screen. I will let you know where he leads me. Perhaps you were right to tell him about the BND. It had the proper effect," Lyman Welsh answered.

Lyman Welsh was in the bank lobby when Hentsch got off the elevator. He hurried out the front door and Welsh fell in behind him. It had started to rain. It was a hard rain. Welsh was glad to have his hat and all weather coat. Hentsch opened a large black umbrella. There were numerous black umbrellas opened with people crowded together on the street. This would make it very difficult for Welsh to distinguish the figure of Hentsch from all the other people with opened black umbrellas on the street. Lyman Welsh was a pro, and a lot of people carry umbrellas in his native London.

Hentsch entered an underground parking lot. He appeared to have been talking on the telephone the whole time since he had left the bank building. Fortunately, Lyman Welsh had parked in the same underground parking lot. It was more than luck. He had inquired where bank customers usually parked their cars when visiting the bank. He had studied each floor of the three-level parking garage and found a place that was marked reserved for bank employees. He had even been able to find a vacant parking spot on the same floor.

Hentsch got into a black Mercedes. Welsh got into his gray BMW. Welsh waited in his car for Hentsch to leave. Hentsch was still talking on his telephone. Welsh wondered if the telephone reception was very good in the underground lot. Finally, Hentsch left the parking lot and Welsh followed.

The rain was still coming down in buckets. There were a lot of black Mercedes on the streets. The rain had made traffic pile up. Welsh was having a difficult time keeping from losing Hentsch's car in the traffic. Welsh had to keep a sufficient distance behind Hentsch so as not to be noticed, yet remain close enough not to lose his quarry.

Hentsch left the main thoroughfares and headed down a narrow street. He parked his car in an alley and went inside a nondescript building. Welsh pulled over to park and hoped that he would not be asked to move his car. After a short wait, Hentsch emerged from the building with two other people. Each of the other people had an umbrella, and it was difficult for Welsh to determine much about them. What he could determine was that one was an older man and the other was a young woman.

When the trio drove away, Welsh continued his tailing of Hentsch's car. Hentsch got back on a main road and exited off a major artery. The exit was marked 12. The road that Hentsch now took led to the airport. Welsh thought back to what Akard has said about the slip of paper that he had found in the flashlight in Helga Brandenberg's apartment. Wherever Hentsch was headed, it was obvious to Welsh that it was a safe house for whatever nefarious activity that Hentsch was involved in. Probably Helga Brandenberg had been a visitor to this very place. It was now up to Welsh to find the place. When he found the safe house, he was sure he would also find Conrad Dellifield.

Hentsch had spent a lot of time on the telephone. Welsh had taken the opportunity to use his phone while waiting for Hentsch to pick up his passengers. He had called his contacts with the Munich police department and the BND. He asked them to find out Hentsch's telephone number and then find out with whom Hentsch had been talking.

Even though it was cold and rainy, Hentsch was sweating profusely. Nothing had gone as he had planned. Now he had one last chance to pull his plan out of the fire.

It had all started six years before. He had just joined the bank. He was assigned the account of Helga Brandenberg. She visited the bank about once a year. The first year she came, he had used all his charm to endear himself to her. He would call her at her apartment from his office and talk with her before she went to bed. She was a lonely woman, and she enjoyed his calls.

Gradually, she became more and more dependent upon him. On her third visit to see him in Germany he had taken her to dinner. She drank too much wine and told him about how her parents had been treated after the War. Hentsch had been very attentive. He belonged to what could be classified as a young neo-Nazi group. An idea began to formulate in his mind. He would help her get even with the regime that had mistreated her parents. In his view, Germans were never destined to be governed as a democracy. They would follow a strong leader. They had conquered Europe once before and they could do it again.

That night, he went back to her hotel with her and made love to her. She was over seventy, but he closed his eyes and made her groan. Helga was in love, in love with a dream. She was a young woman again and she had a young lover. Hentsch then began to use his power over Helga. He took over the management of her apartment house. He put some of the profit in her account and kept the rest. He got funds from her regularly under the pretense of financing Nazi web sites in the United States. He did, in fact, do that through a number of subterfuges, which would prevent from being traced back to him. He kept far more money than he spent on Helga's causes.

Hentsch would let Helga compose the messages on the Web sites. She could spew as much venom over the Internet as she wanted. She could log on to a web site and look at her compositions. She sent more money to Hentsch. All communications by email were sent to the code name "Herman." This was the name that she called him by, even in intimate telephone conversations. He had used her funds to become a leader in radical groups. No one knew him by a name other than Herman. By day he was an up and coming banker. At night and on weekends he was a terrorist.

Hentsch became friends with a like-thinking man who owned a tavern and rooming house in a small village not far from the airport. By word of mouth, various radical groups would learn of the tavern and rooming house and it became the locus for their meetings. That was where he had met the Turk and the man with the tattoo. The Turk belonged to a fanatical group that wanted to overthrow the democratic government in Turkey and establish a religious State. The tattooed man, whose name was Fritz, had been raised by his grandfather, who had been a member of the Nazi SS.

Hentsch had given both these men money and they became his henchmen. There was a third man in the group. He was a former convict who hated any form of establishment. This man was a friend of Fritz. His name was Adolph. Hentsch did not know if that was the man's real name or if he had dubbed himself that after Hitler.

The more deeply Helga fell in love with Hentsch, the easier it became for him to influence her. He convinced her that if she left her fortune to him, he would use it to shape Germany into the country that she had known as a girl.

Now everything had turned to shit. Some one must have destroyed her will. He had plans for that money. Those plans did not include building a new Germany. He could care less. He had used his extreme views to build a following. He knew it would be just a matter of time before his alter ego was discovered. He had made plans to go to America and live with Helga until she died, if it became clear that someone was getting to close to the truth.

His hope was that Helga would die and he would get the money. As soon as he got it, he would leave for a warmer climate, just as the

Nazis of old had done after the War. He would go to a South American country that had no extradition treaty with Germany. It would have worked, but for the fact that a Jew had killed her and probably tore up her will. The tattooed man had told him the name of Jacob Franks and where he lived. He now had only a short time to get the money from the lock box and leave the country. He would eliminate the only people who knew about the contents of the box. In addition, he would have the Jew who had messed up his plans killed.

Hentsch had made contacts with radical groups in the United States. He had help with his Web sites from American radicals who were anti-government and full of racial hatred. One of his telephone calls had been to a Klansman in Texas. They discussed killing the Jew. The Klansman said that he knew just the people to do the job. They were out on bail for parole violation. They needed money to pay their lawyers. They lived within forty-five minutes of Dallas. They were brothers. Their names were Monroe and "Goose". They would do the job for $5,000.00. Hentsch had his secretary wire the funds to a bank in East Texas, giving her the order while he was driving.

His plan had to work. He believed he was smarter than the Americans. He had figured out a way to get the key from McCoy and how to get the money and bonds from the lock box. His passengers held the solution.

While Hentsch had been ruminating about his past and his future, he passed the airport exit. The rain was pounding down. Lyman Welsh was relying on the tail lights of the Mercedes in order to keep up. The driver of a car on his left apparently realized that he had missed the airport exit and cut in front of Welsh to make the turn. Welsh did what he could do to avoid a collision. When his car swerved on the rain soaked highway to miss the other car, he ended up in a ditch. The tails lights of the Mercedes disappeared in the rain. Welsh had lost Hentsch.

# Chapter Twenty-Six

Akard and Zelda-Corrine ate lunch at a small café just off of the Marienplatz. The rain was still coming down when they had finished eating. Akard told Zelda-Corrine that he would step a few doors down to a small shop and buy an umbrella. Zelda-Corrine told him that she would stand under the overhang of the shop next to the café and look in the window. Akard hurriedly went to get an umbrella.

Zelda-Corrine was looking at the display in the window when she became aware of a man standing next to her. Before she could get a good look, she felt a sharp pain in her arm and a burning sensation. The man's face began to blur. She thought she had caught a glimpse of the man before. He was one of the men in the car that was used in the kidnapping of Dellifield.

Zelda-Corrine felt her legs giving way. The man put his arm around her back and placed his hand under her armpit. The scene around her began to get foggy. It seemed as if the people around her were walking in slow motion. The rain was running off of her leather jacket in sheets. She walked or was half-dragged to a car. Her hands were taped behind her with duct tape. She was rudely shoved into the back seat of the car. She lost consciousness.

Akard came back with the umbrella only to discover that Zelda-Corrine was not where he left her. *"She has got to be shopping,"* Akard thought to himself. He walked all around the area but could not find Zelda-Corrine anywhere. Finally, he went into the shop where Zelda-Corrine had been looking in the window.

Akard asked the woman in the shop if she spoke English. The woman answered that she did.

"I am looking for a woman who was standing in front of your store. She was admiring the goods in the window. I thought she might have come in here," Akard said.

"Was she a very pretty woman?" Akard was asked.

"Yes, she is a very pretty woman," Akard answered.

"I noticed her looking in the window. I was hoping she would come in and buy something. She went off with a man. She seemed to be unstable on her feet. It was like she had too much to drink," the woman said.

"Jesus! They have her, too," Akard exclaimed.

"I am sorry. I do not understand," the woman said.

"Thank you. You have been very helpful," Akard said.

Akard was a man alone with his thoughts. The pounding rain pouring off his umbrella only added to his dismal thoughts. He would be lost without Zelda-Corrine. He raged inside. He wanted to hit somebody or something. He then remembered what Welsh had said about patience and fortitude. His courage was not needed now. If Zelda-Corrine was to be saved, he needed to rely on his Texas know how. Akard dialed the number of Lyman Welsh's mobile telephone. Lyman Welsh answered on the second ring.

"They have Zelda-Corrine."

"What?"

I said, "They have Zelda-Corrine."

"When did it happen?"

"A few minutes ago. I went to get an umbrella. When I got back she was gone. A sales clerk in the store where she was looking in the window said that she walked off with a man. Zelda-Corrine looked as if she had too much to drink. He probably drugged her someway."

"Akard, I lost Hentsch. He picked up an older man and a woman and then headed toward the airport. I have called my connections and they are tracing the location of the cellular telephone that was used to call you. In the meantime, I want you to go to the police and tell them what has happened. We are going to need all the help we can get. Hentsch knows that we are aware of his involvement. He is running out of time. Call me if you learn anything that will help."

"We have to find her, Lyman. We have to find her."

"We will, old boy. We will. I promise you that we will."

Akard went to the police station he had visited the previous day and gave a complete account of what had happened. The police were courteous, but did not give any indication that the events Akard described were of immediate concern. He could almost understand their reluctance. How were they to know if Zelda-Corrine had been kidnapped or if she had just too much to drink and left with an attractive man? They told him to notify them immediately if anyone called. In the meantime, they would open a file.

Akard walked out into the rain. He could not hold back tears. They were tears stemming from the thought of losing Zelda-Corrine. They were tears of anger and frustration. He lowered his umbrella and let the rain wash the salty tears from his face. He would be patient, but when he got down to the nutcutting he would take no prisoners.

The drug used on Zelda-Corrine was beginning to wear off. She was still groggy. Her hands were taped behind her and her mouth was taped closed. She was uncomfortable, slouched down on the back seat of a small foreign car of some type. She could hear the rain bouncing off the roof of the car. Sheets of rain rolled past the windows of the car. Outside, the sky was black as night. It reminded of her of some of the frog-strangling rains that would come in the middle of the day in Texas. Sometimes, they would be accompanied by a tornado.

She could not think clearly. The man who was driving said nothing. As her head cleared, she tried to get a glimpse of his face in the rear view mirror. At one point, headlights from the car behind them illuminated the inside of the car in which she was riding long enough for her to see her captor's face. He appeared to be about forty. He might have been younger. His face was hardened by years of prison life. What hair he had was closely cropped. It was beginning to gray around the temples. His meanness was evident in his face.

Zelda-Corrine felt a tinge of fear. She had a black belt in karate. She might be able to hold her own against the man driving, if she were given a level playing field. She did not have that luxury at this point. Twisting her hands only made the tape get tighter. She decided to try to relax and wait for an opportunity to escape.

# Chapter Twenty-Seven

The telephone call from Hentsch had awakened the Klansman in the middle of the night. He, in turn, had roused the Johnson brothers from a drunken sleep. The thought of getting $2,500 for killing a Jew appealed to them. They did not realize that the caller was taking half the fee as middleman. None of them realized that the F.B.I. had a telephone wiretap on the Klansman's telephone.

The agent listening in on the telephone intercepted the call from Germany. He, in turn, alerted his superior about the call from Germany. The German caller had given the name and the address of the man that he wanted killed. The agent's superior had alerted the Dallas police about the call. The Dallas police planned to send two detectives to the high rise to wait for the would-be assassins.

Another F.B.I. man called the BND headquarters and gave them the telephone number of the German caller. It would just be a matter of time until Hentsch was located. He just needed to continue to make more telephone calls.

The Klansman was so sure that the money would be wired to his account that he told Monroe and Goose to take care of the old man as soon as possible. The Johnson brothers had once had jobs as plumber's helpers. They had quit because work disagreed with them. It was far easier to be petty criminals. They would steal a car or truck and sell it to a chop shop. Occasionally, they did some muscle work to collect for a loan shark. They had killed before. They just had not gotten caught.

Monroe got out their old gray uniforms that had "Ace Plumbing" on the back. The thousand beers consumed since they last wore the uniforms made them fit snugly. Nevertheless, they were able to get into the uniforms as long as they did not button the bottom buttons on the shirt. They discussed how they would kill the old man and decided they did not need to take guns. Besides, they were about to have their paroles revoked because of being caught with a gun. They decided that they would just hold him down and place a pillow over his face. They high-fived and left for Dallas.

It was the five thirty in the morning when the two Dallas police detectives arrived at the high-rise apartment house on Turtle Creek. They went up to the twentieth floor and knocked on the door. After some minutes, a weary Jacob Franks opened the door. The two detectives were shocked by what they saw. It was an emaciated old man gasping for air. He had oxygen running through a tube connected to his nose.

"Yes, gentleman, to what do I owe the pleasure of your company so early in the morning?" Franks asked.

The detectives explained why they were there. They told him that they had reason to believe a person or persons were being sent to Dallas to kill him. That someone from Germany had ordered that he be killed. They would be happy to stay with him until he got dressed and then they would take him to a safe place.

"I am an old man. I survived the Nazi camps. I have no fear of death. In fact, I would welcome death at any time. No, gentlemen, thank you for your concern, but I will stay here."

"Suit yourself. We will be around. If you see anything that alarms you, call downstairs. We will be in the lobby," one of the detectives said.

Jacob knew that his killing of Helga Brandenberg would soon be discovered. Why else would the call for his death have come from

Germany? Dying would be welcomed. He slowly walked to his bedroom closet. With great difficulty he lifted a box off of the shelf in the closet. He took the box down and removed its contents from an oily rag. In his hands, he was holding a model '98 Luger. He had removed the pistol from the body of a dead German guard when the death camp had been liberated. He had concealed it and took it with him when he left Germany. For years, he kept it only as a reminder of what he had been through.

Jacob was not even sure it would fire. Years before he had fired it on a pistol range. He cleaned the gun every year or so. He had bought bullets for it within the last ten years. He removed the clip from the box and inserted it into the handle of the pistol. With great effort, he pulled back the receiver. There was now a bullet in the chamber of the pistol.

The two detectives had taken up positions in the building. One was in the lobby. The other was in a stairwell two doors down from Jacob's apartment. At six o'clock, Monroe and Goose pulled up to the rear service entrance of the apartment house. They had gone unnoticed by the detective in the lobby. No one was attending the service entrance as they pried the door open with tools they had brought with them.

They entered the building and found the stairwell.

"Shit, we ain't gonna walk up twenty floors," Monroe said.

"We are if we are gonna get paid," Goose answered.

The two killers began their difficult climb up the twenty floors. Each one of the thousands of beers they had consumed during the years seemed to be loading them down. They were breathing heavily. Neither said a word. Goose was in better shape so he was about one floor ahead of Monroe. When Goose got to the nineteenth floor, the detective heard his heavy breathing.

"OK, come up here with your hands up," the detective said.

Monroe froze in his tracks. The detective walked down a few steps and motioned Goose to come up toward him. Monroe hid where he could not be seen. Goose walked up the stairs with his hands over his head. The detective stepped toward him and was about to put handcuffs on him when Monroe hit him on the head with a wrench. Monroe picked up the detective's gun and put it in the waist of his pants.

"Let's get this over with," Goose said.

It was six-twenty in the morning when Monroe knocked on the door of Jacob Frank's apartment.

"Who is there?" A voice from inside the apartment said.

"We are here to check your plumbing," Goose said.

"Come in. The door is unlocked."

There were no lights on in the apartment. It was dark inside. Jacob Franks was in his recliner. His hands were resting on a tray. Over his hands was a pillow. Under the pillow, he was holding the Luger with both hands.

"Where are you, old man?" Goose asked.

"I am here." Jacob said softly.

"We're here to kill, you old man," Monroe said.

The would-be killers were trying to get their eyes adjusted to the darkness of the room. Jacob Franks had learned to see in the dark in the years he spent in the death camp. He saw them much more clearly than they saw him. The two moved toward him.

"I see you now, old man," Monroe said. That was the last words he would ever utter. The first shot caught him square in the chest. The recoil from the pistol had almost thrown it from Franks' fragile hands. He steadied his grip and fired at Goose. The shot hit him in the abdomen. He bent over and clutched his middle.

Monroe was dead on the floor. Goose staggered toward Franks. The second shot aimed in his direction caught Goose in the neck. He fell over backwards and joined his brother on the floor in death.

A fourth shot was fired. This time it entered the brain of Jacob Franks. The bullet had ended his suffering. It also insured that no one could question him about the death of Helga Brandenberg.

The detective in the stairwell came to and went to the apartment. People in bathrobes were standing in the hall looking at the bloody scene in Franks' apartment. The detective's partner joined him and called for medical attention for his injured associate. In due course, the bodies would be taken away. In due course, when the Klansman arrived at the bank to get his funds, two men in suits with guns would be waiting for him.

# Chapter Twenty-Eight

The car transporting a drugged Zelda-Corrine arrived at the safe house in the late afternoon. The rain had made it difficult for the driver to leave Munich proper. Traffic had been slow near the airport because traffic had slowed to observe silver BMW that was being pulled out of the muddy median by a wrecker.

The third man gained entry to the safe house when the landlord let him and his prisoner in the back door. The landlord was showing signs of disgust. A silver haired man had been brought in the night before. Earlier, Hentsch had arrived with two strangers. Now Adolph was ushering in a woman with rain soaked hair who was unsteady on her feet. The landlord was not a happy camper. His involvement with radical causes had been mainly for the money. It was true that he did not like the German tax system, but his allegiance to radical causes stopped short of kidnapping and possible murder. This time Herman had gone too far. This could mean prison, but the landlord was more frightened of Herman and his comrades than he was of prison. He let Adolph and the woman inside.

Zelda-Corrine was shoved and pulled up the same flight of stairs that Conrad Dellifield had traversed the night before. When the pair reached the top of the stairway, Zelda-Corrine was pushed into a small room across the hall from the room in which Dellifield was being held. Standing in the room were a young woman and the tattooed man. Adolph removed the tape from Zelda-Corrine's wrists and steadied her by holding her arm. The woman came over and removed the leather jacket from Zelda-Corrine. Next, the woman removed the top of the pants suit Zelda-Corrine was wearing followed by the sweater, and finally, the slacks.

Zelda-Corrine stood shivering in the cold room wearing nothing but her bikini panties and bra. The woman said something in German and Adolph left the room. He returned shortly with a baggy flannel shirt. The woman draped the shirt over Zelda-Corrine and buttoned it up. Zelda-Corrine was still drugged enough that she was seeing faces and hearing voices, but she felt as though she were outside her body viewing the scene as a spectator. She would have loved to show her martial arts prowess to the assembled group, but her body would just not co-operate.

Zelda-Corrine was rudely shoved down on the bed. Her hands and feet were bound to the posts at each end of the bed. She was helpless to do anything except watch and hope her head would soon clear. The young German woman plugged in a hair dryer and methodically dried the wet parts of Zelda-Corrine's clothing. When she finished, she removed her own clothing and replaced her clothes with those of Zelda-Corrine. She did stop at one point and stuffed a substantial amount of tissue into her bra. When she had finished, she produced a make-up kit and mirror.

The German woman spent quite some time with her make up. She would look at Zelda-Corrine and then look at her self in the mirror and apply a touch of make up. Sometimes, she became dissatisfied with her work and started over. Finally, she was happy with her work. When the woman had applied the last dab of lipstick, she tied her short black hair in back. She then reached into the bag and pulled out an auburn colored wig. Placing the wig over her head, she adjusted it to fit. When she had finished, she spread out her arms and accepted the applause from Adolph and the tattooed man. The German woman now possessing enhanced breasts and a wig could pass for Zelda-Corrine. On a dark and rainy night, she would fool anyone, including Akard McCoy.

The trio consisting of the German woman, the tattooed man and Adolph turned off the light and left the room. Zelda-Corrine was helpless. The flannel shirt covered her body to just above her knees. She was cold. The coldness was making her head clear. Maybe that was not a good thing because now she was beginning to appreciate how desperate her situation was. The trio had overlooked one part of her wardrobe. Adolph had picked up her purse from the car. Somehow, it had been kicked under the bed. So no one had looked to see what was inside the purse.

The three conspirators added a fourth to their gang before they entered the room where Dellifield was held. The fourth member was the older man. The four of them gathered in the small room. When Dellifield first saw the German woman, he thought she was Zelda-Corrine. The light was dim, but as he saw the woman came closer, he knew her features were too harsh to be those of Zelda-Corrine. Dellifield's chest tightened. He was already weary from the irregular beat of his heart. He was now faced with the prospect that someone was taking the place of Zelda-Corrine. He had heard the voices coming from the room next door. He had not heard Zelda-Corrine's Texas accent because her mouth was still taped shut. He feared she was dead.

Dellifield looked at the older man in the room. He had silver hair. The man's face was sullen. His eyebrows were much bushier than those of Dellifield, and he was slightly shorter. Dellifield fell back on the bed and shut his eyes. It was obvious. If the woman was to be Zelda-Corrine, the man was to be a duplicate of him. The woman said something in German and the tattooed man pulled Dellifield upright on the bed.

The German woman then began the task of making her confederate resemble the American lawyer. She clipped and trimmed his eyebrows. She went over and combed Dellifield's disheveled hair. Next, she ordered Adolph to produce shaving cream and a razor. She shaved Dellifield. This was the one part of his captivity he did not mind. In fact, the hot lather seemed to perk him up.

The woman then studied the clean-shaven Dellifield for some time. She cut and combed the other man's hair. She removed the circles under his eyes with artfully applied make up. The one thing she could not do was change the color of his eyes. Dellifield had steel blue eyes. The German man had brown eyes. It mattered little. On a dark and rainy night, no one would get close enough to see the man's eyes. When she had finished, the man put on a white shirt and tie and a double-breasted blue suit. This struck Dellifield as very odd. The woman was wearing Zelda-Corrine's clothes. Dellifield was still wearing the casual clothes he was wearing the night before. His question was answered when the man picked up Dellifield's jacket. It covered the suit coat, and when zipped up to the top, concealed the shirt and tie.

When the makeover was completed, Dellifield was left alone. He silently got up from the bed and placed his ear against the door. He heard a conversation, and recognized a different voice. It was Hentsch. He talked to the group in German. Dellifield could make out a few phrases. One thing he determined was that Hentsch was leaving to catch a plane to Zurich. It would be the last flight from Munich to Zurich for the evening.

He then heard a one sided conversation in English.

"Mr. McCoy, listen very carefully," said Hentsch

"Keep your remarks to yourself."

"I assure you that both of your friends are alive and well."

"No, that is not acceptable. You will do as I say."

"If you continue to threaten me, I assure you, your friends will be killed."

"Be at the Englischer Gardens on the path way to the Japanese Tea room at nine tonight. You must be alone. There will be no police. You will give the key to the man who is escorting Miss Paige and Herr Dellifield. The man will be armed. If you do not do as you are told, all three of you will be shot."

"No more from you. Nine o'clock."

Although Dellifield had heard only one side of the conversation, he could only imagine what Akard had said.

Hentsch was departing. Adolph was to take the two actors with him to the Englischer Garden. He would get the key and give it to the actor. The actor would empty the lock box in the morning and bring the contents to Zurich. Then, Hentsch would meet him at the baggage claim and receive the carry-on bag with the money and bonds inside. Everyone would be well paid for his or her part in the drama once lock box contents were delivered to Hentsch.

Dellifield could only understand parts of the conversation. He understood Englischer Garden and Zurich. He knew that "Gepackanspruch" meant baggage claim. He had seen the signs in the airport.

Then Dellifield heard something in German he understood only too clearly.

Those words translated into English, were shocking. They meant, "Kill the lawyer. Kill the woman."

# Chapter Twenty-Nine

*It had taken a while for Lyman Welsh to extract his car from the* muddy ditch he had landed in while pursuing the black Mercedes. During the time that it took to be pulled from the ditch, he had talked constantly with operatives of the BND. They had traced the telephones to a tavern and boarding house in a small village, not to far from the airport. It had been several hours since he had lost contact with the Mercedes. The rain had not lessened in intensity. If anything, it had gotten heavier.

Welsh made his way to the village. Police were headed in the same direction, but he had a head start on the police. He hoped he would recognize the address he had been given. When he came to the village, he saw that it consisted of a number of old buildings. Akard had told him that he heard an airplane in the background when he received the call from Dellifield's captor. One of the tallest structures in the village was a yellow building with large cross-timbers beginning at the third floor of the stucco exterior. The building narrowed at the top almost to a point. Beneath each window was a window box. The window boxes contained flowers, but it was difficult to tell what type of flower because of the heavy rain.

In front of the building was a small beer garden. There was no one outside. The dim lights above the beer garden flickered in the heavy rain. The windows above the main floor intrigued Welsh. The building did not appear to be a private dwelling. This had probably been a public house serving spirits for centuries. The noise from the tavern would probably drown out any calls for help from an upper floor, if a hostage were able to sound an alarm of any kind. There was an address below the tavern sign that matched the address from which the telephone calls had been made.

Welsh weighed his options. Should he go into the tavern by himself or should he wait for the police to arrive? He decided to go in alone. If Dellifield and Miss Paige were being held there, time was running short. He parked his car on a side street below the building and walked up a steep cobblestone street to the entrance to the beer hall. Opposite the building was a clock tower. The clock said 8:30. He removed the Glock from his coat pocket and slid a round into the chamber.

The rain was running off the brim of Welsh's hat when he reached the door of the tavern. He walked inside and surveyed the crowd. The crowd was thin, probably because of the heavy rain. Three skinheads dressed in black leather jackets occupied a round table in a dark corner. Two darker-skinned men with black beards sat close to the bar. Other than the five customers and the bartender, Welsh could see no one else in the tavern. He had more bullets in his automatic pistol than there were patrons in the bar. Welsh felt good about the odds.

Welsh walked to the bar and, in German, ordered a beer. The bartender looked Welsh over with a great deal of suspicion. He was unaccustomed to having strangers in his bar. The man standing across the bar from him did not look like a German. He looked like an Englishman. The customer had a pale complexion and sandy colored eyebrows. His enormous left hand bore a ring with a blue dragon over a white setting. The bartender could not see the customer's right hand because it was concealed in his rain-soaked coat pocket.

The bartender handed Welsh a glass of draft beer. Welsh took his right hand out of his coat pocket and removed his wallet. He placed three Euros on the top of the bar. Welsh had drawn the attention of the other patrons in the bar. Five sets of eyes looked him over. Welsh walked to a small table located where he could closely watch the other customers. Welsh set his beer on the table and walked to the corridor leading to the restrooms. He noted that past the men's restroom was a back door. Several feet from the back door was a stairway. Welsh went into the men's room and after a short wait, flushed the toilet. As he was leaving, one of the skinheads entered. The skinhead looked Welsh directly in the eye, but said nothing.

Welsh returned to his table and sat down. He was wary that someone might have slipped something into his drink while he was gone. There was a plant in a large container next to his table. When the other customers were not looking, he would pour some of the beer into the container housing the plant. He moved his chair so that he could look at the back door. No one was going to come or go through that door without being noticed by Welsh.

Four floors above the tavern, another drama was playing out. The tattooed man was about to carry out his instructions. The man entered Dellifield's room. Dellifield braced for the worst and closed his eyes. Dellifield was breathing in gasps. His heart was beating faster in irregular beats. The tattooed man bent over and felt the pulse in Dellifield's neck. "*Why waste a bullet on a dying man?*" the assailant thought. His main concern was on raping Zelda-Corrine before he killed her. The old man could wait. In his haste and lust for Zelda-Corrine, the tattooed man forgot to lock the door to Dellifield's room.

Dellifield had been spared for the moment. He now forced himself to concentrate on finding a weapon. He had searched the room thoroughly and had found nothing. He fell back on his bed. The ancient springs let out a groan. The thought struck Dellifield that this bed was much like the one he had slept on when he was a boy. He eased himself out of bed. With great effort, he lifted the ancient mattress and springs. He was looking at dusty wood. The dusty wood was a series of bed slats. Slowly and silently he removed one of the slats and blew the dust off one end. He eased the door open a crack.

Next door, the tattooed man was looking at something Dellifield could not see. The tattooed man was looking at Zelda-Corrine clad only in her underwear and the flannel shirt. The man looked at Zelda-

Corrine who was bound and gagged and helpless to fend him off. The man's face had a ghost like grin. His malevolent eyes were fixed on her crotch. As he removed his shirt, Zelda-Corrine could see the full repulsive tattoo that began on the back of his neck. It was a cobra. The tail began at his neck and it coiled over his shoulder and had its puffed out face in the center of his shaved chest. The cobra's fangs had drops of venom trickling down the man's abdomen.

The man addressed Zelda-Corrine in English. "At least you will die a happy woman. You will die knowing that you have made love with a real man."

Zelda-Corrine struggled with her bindings, but struggle just made the bindings dig into her skin. The man removed his pants and bent over Zelda-Corrine. He set his pistol on the nightstand next to the bed. He took the index finger of each hand and started to pull down her bikini panties. The tattooed man was too engrossed in his lust to notice that Dellifield had taken a position behind him. (Conrad Dellifield had taken up golf when he was a teenager. Every Saturday morning that he was in town and time permitted, he joined his regular golf foursome at the Royal Oaks Country Club.)

Dellifield's swing speed had slowed with the years, but on a good day he could carry the creek on the ninth hole, hitting from the blue tees. Dellifield grasped the bed slat as if it were a driver. The tattooed man had almost pulled Zelda-Corrine's panties to her pubic hair when Dellifield struck his first blow.

Whap! He had carried the creek on number nine. Dellifield had slowed his back swing, just as Randy Smith, the pro at Royal Oaks had taught him. The blow caught the tattooed man at the base of his skull just above his neck. The man turned to see what had hit him. Whap! It was a seven iron to the green. The follow through caught the tattooed man under his chin and his head recoiled from the blow. In his mind, Dellifield made his putt for a birdie and was ready to tee off on number ten. The tattooed man lowered his head. Whap! It was a perfect drive down the middle. The blow removed the man's left eye. Blood streamed down the man's chest. The cobra was even more gruesome with blood covering its hooded face. The man was staggering toward Dellifield. Dellifield imagined himself 190 yards from the green on number ten. His five wood caught the man square in the throat and the man collapsed on the floor, gasping. The man was choking on his own blood.

Dellifield was fighting for breath as he removed the gag from Zelda-Corrine's mouth. Zelda-Corrine was crying hysterically.

"My purse is under the bed. There is a knife in there. Your medicine is in there, too. Hurry," she said.

Dellifield got the purse and opened it. He removed the knife and cut the bindings that had tied Zelda-Corrine to the bed. She got up and rubbed her wrists. Dellifield removed the tablets of Norpace and Coumadin. He swallowed three hundred milligrams of Norpace and seven and one-half milligrams of Coumadin without water. He was catching his breath when the tattooed man, with blood streaming from his eye and mouth, raised his moribund body from the floor and lunged at him. Zelda-Corrine screamed. She picked up the pistol from the nightstand and fired a shot into the chest of the tattooed man. The bullet entered at the bloody cobra's head. The tattooed man took a half a step forward and died, as his hands slid down the chest of Conrad Dellifield.

"Make love to that," Zelda-Corrine yelled.

The gunshot and Zelda-Corrine's scream were heard in the tavern below. The bartender grabbed a shotgun and headed up the stairs, with Lyman Welsh in pursuit. The bartender had made it up one flight of stairs before Welsh overtook him. With one hand, Welsh grabbed the shotgun. With the other, he threw the bartender down the stairs. The bartender lay in a crumpled heap at the foot of the stairs. Welsh could not tell if he was alive.

A skinhead, with pistol in hand, was coming up the stairs. The skinhead stopped cold in his tracks when he realized that Lyman Welsh was pointing a shotgun at his head. Welsh said something in German and the skinhead dropped his gun. That action saved the skinhead's life. What the future held for the man was in doubt, because a policeman was taking hold of his arm. Welsh said something in German to the policeman who seemed satisfied with what he had heard. Welsh then bounded up the stairs to check out the gun shot and the woman's scream.

When Welch reached the room where Dellifield and Zelda-Corrine were, he saw a grotesque sight. Zelda-Corrine was standing beside the body of a man lying face down in a pool of blood. She held a gun in her hand. There were bindings still tied to her wrists and ankles. She was barely clad beneath a baggy flannel shirt. Welsh put down his shotgun. He untied the bindings. He took off his all weather coat and wrapped it around Zelda-Corrine's shoulders.

Conrad Dellifield was sitting on a bed. He was breathing in quick gasps. Beside him on the bed was a bloody board. The walls of the room were splattered with blood.

"Well, I guess something rather spectacular took place here. I think we need to get you to a hospital, old boy," Welsh said addressing Dellifield.

"I will be alright. I just need to rest and let the medicine do the work. What time is it?" Dellifield asked.

"It is ten minutes before nine. Why ask the time now?" Welsh asked.

"Akard is walking into a trap. Hentsch is behind all of this. He plans for a confederate to get the key to the lock box from Akard. Hentsch has left for Zurich. The confederate has a man and a woman with him who is made up to look like Miss Paige and me. Akard thinks he is making a trade, our lives for the key. In reality, they plan to kill him. When they get the key, the actor playing my part will remove the contents from the lock box in the morning. He will deliver the contents to Hentsch in Zurich. We must reach Akard," Dellifield said.

"No problem. I'll give the lad a jingle on your telephone. I will also notify the police. Akard will be delivered safely into our midst," Welsh said.

# Chapter Thirty

*Akard had gone to his hotel and picked up the key to the lock box. He* then took a cab to Englischer Garden. The Garden had gotten its name because it was laid out in the manner of English landscaped grounds. It is one of Europe's largest city parks. It was the vision of an American officer, Benjamin Thompson, who was retained by the Bavarian Elector Karl Theodor. Thompson became Bavaria's Minister of War. He ordered the swamp lands around the Isar River drained for military use. Later, it became a municipal park.

Akard directed the cab driver to let him out on the Lerchenfeldstrasse. The rain had let up some, but he still required the use of an umbrella. As he walked past the Rumford Memorial, the cellular telephone started vibrating. He took shelter next to the Memorial and removed the phone from his coat pocket.

"Hello. This is Akard."

"Mr. McCoy, this is Nettie Dellifield. I am most distressed that my husband has not called me. Please get him for me, right now," the voice on the other end said.

"To be honest, Mrs. Dellifield, he is not with me right now. I expect to see him shortly. I will tell him to call you immediately when I see him."

"Tell him I am very anxious to talk to him."

"I assure you that I will, just as soon as I see him."

Lyman Welsh had gotten a busy signal when he tried to call Akard.

Akard slipped the telephone into his pocket. When he stepped from behind the monument, he saw three people approaching him. On the path about one hundred yards away, were two men and a woman. The woman was holding an umbrella, as were the other two. As they got closer, he saw that one man had gray hair. The woman had auburn hair. They were seventy-five yards away. There was one thing that Akard was sure of; these two people were posing as Zelda-Corrine and Dellifield. He had been watching how Zelda-Corrine swayed her hips when she walked for over two years, and Dellifield almost strutted. This was a trap. He knew that the third person would be armed. He had a knife on his belt, but his Beretta was back in Dallas. He ducked behind the monument.

"You are not fooling me, assholes! You had better give up. The place is crawling with police." Akard had no idea how close to being right he was. The police were in the garden but they had not reached the scene, yet.

The two imposters separated themselves from Adolph. He pulled out his pistol and ordered them to his side. Akard removed the knife from the scabbard. He took a two Euro coin from his pocket.

"If you want the key you are going to have to go after it."

Akard stepped from behind the monument and threw the coin as far as he could into the grass. Adolph fired a shot at Akard and it barely missed his head. Akard pressed himself against the monument. Adolph ran toward where the coin had landed. The two imposters took off running. Adolph was smart enough to realize that he could look for the key later. He knew where to find the imposters. The foremost thought in his mind was to kill Akard. He started walking toward the monument, firing as he walked.

Bullets ricocheted around Akard. He tried his best to conceal himself from Adolph. Just as Adolph was closing in on Akard's hiding place, a giant bolt of lightening illuminated the sky, followed by an ear-shattering clap of thunder. This startled Adolph for only a moment, and that was all Akard needed. He threw his knife at Adolph, catching him in the right shoulder. Adolph's right arm was immobilized. He was in the process of switching the gun to his left hand when Akard hurled himself at Adolph's body. Adolph managed to fire another shot, but the bullet went harmlessly into the ground. Adolph pulled the trigger one more time, only to hear the click of an empty chamber.

Akard and Adolph were sprawled out on the ground. Adolph was trying to remove the knife from his shoulder. Akard was momentarily shaken. His chin had hit Adolph's knee when he tackled him. Adolph freed himself from Akard's grasp and stumbled away. The police had heard the shots and were running toward the two men. Adolph saw the police and picked up his pace. Akard shook off the cobwebs and headed after Adolph.

Adolph was headed toward the Eisbach. The Eisbach is a waterway that runs through the Garden. The swift running water is always chilly. Nevertheless, local citizens practice surfing there. Adolph was getting weak from loss of blood. It would be madness to try to cross the Eisbach. That was particularly true when the steep banks would be slippery from the heavy rains. Adolph stumbled inexorably toward the dark, swift flowing waters. As he reached the edge of the water, he yelled, "Heil Hitler" Adolph plunged to sure death into the churning waters. It was April 30th, the anniversary of Adolph Hitler's death when he purportedly shot himself in the right temple on April 30, 1945.

Akard was joined at the scene by German police officers. He and the officers watched the rain swollen Eisbach take Adolph beneath the black surface. The policeman who seemed to be in charge asked Akard if he was alright. Akard affirmed that he was. The policeman also told him that they had two German citizens in custody, each had denied any wrong doing, but that it would all be straightened out at police headquarters. The time was nine eighteen.

Akard reached for the cellular to call Lyman Welsh to determine if Zelda-Corrine and Dellifield had been rescued. When he pulled the telephone from his pocket, he found that it was in pieces. The telephone was victim of the hard fall Akard took while tackling Adolph. He would have to wait to find out the fate of Zelda-Corrine and Dellifield. Mrs. Dellifield's call would go unanswered.

The police ushered Akard and the two imposters into cars and drove them to the police headquarters. Captain Horst Raeder was on duty.

"Mr. McCoy, please tell me what was going on in the park tonight. I understand there was shooting and one man is missing," the Captain said.

"You should know most of the story. Your men were sent to the scene. You have a woman in custody who is wearing my fiancee's clothes. I want to know if my fiancée has been harmed," Akard said.

"Mr. Dellifield and Miss Paige are fine. They are being brought here as we speak. Please, tell me why you were in the park."

"I was telephoned and told that if I wanted to see Zelda-Corrine and Dellifield alive again, I would meet a man in the Englischer Garden. I was to exchange their safety for the key to the lock box at the bank. The kidnappers ran in two ringers. I saw that the imposters were not who they were supposed to be and that is when the shooting started. Some man I never met is in the Eisbach. I doubt if he is still alive. That is about it."

"I have men looking for a body in the Eisbach. It will most likely be morning before we find anything."

"What about Hentsch? I know damn well he is behind all of this. Have you caught him?"

"We have information that Herr Hentsch has gone to Zurich. Our investigation is incomplete. We will know more when your two friends arrive."

"What about those two dummies that were posing as Zelda-Corrine and Dellifield?"

"Once again, we do not have enough information to charge them with a crime at this point."

"That bitch in there is wearing my girl's clothes. If you want me to, I can tell you the name of the labels inside the clothes. I want you to make her take them off and give them back. I bought that leather jacket myself. It came from Neiman-Marcus. Check it out."

"We will take every thing you say into account when we complete our investigation."

The conversation was interrupted by the arrival of more police.

Three people were with the police, Zelda-Corrine, Conrad Dellifield and Lyman Welsh. Dellifield was eating something. It looked like a sausage sticking out of a folded over piece of bread. Zelda-Corrine was wearing Lyman Welsh's coat. The hem of the coat was just above her ankles. The sleeves of the coat hung over her hands.

When Zelda-Corrine saw Akard she ran over and threw herself into his arms. She started sobbing.

"It was awful. They had me tied to a bed. The man with the tattoo was going to rape me. Conrad beat him almost to death with a board. Then I shot him. He is dead. I shot him. There was blood everywhere. Thank God you are alive. We tried to warn you. I want to go home," she cried.

"I am so sorry all this happened. Thank God you are OK. We will go home soon," Akard said.

"We have to get Conrad to a hospital. He saved my life. He got some medicine in him, but he has had a hard time," Zelda-Corrine said.

"Nonsense! I will be fine. All I have done since I was kidnapped is lie on a bed and get selective beatings. If I can get some rest tonight, I will be fine. I must be back in Dallas tomorrow evening. I will sleep on the plane. I have to stop in Zurich to change planes. That is where I plan to get even with Herr Hentsch. That imposter son-of-a bitch was going to meet him at the baggage claim when the noon flight arrives. I can do that and catch the 1:30 flight to Dallas and make my deadline. I want to see the bastard's face when I give him a bag full of newspapers," Dellifield said.

Akard had never heard Dellifield curse before. There was also fire in Dellifield's eyes. Maybe that was the fire that had made the man a successful trial lawyer when he was a young man.

"I need to call my wife. Where is my telephone?" Dellifield asked.

"I am afraid it was a victim of the fight I had in the park. Just before the fight started, your wife called asking for you. I told her you would be calling when you got an opportunity to do so," Akard said.

Dellifield was about to ask the Captain if he could use a telephone when the Captain ushered Lyman Welsh into his office and closed the door. Captain Raeder asked Welsh to tell him everything he knew about the kidnapping, the bloody scene at the tavern, and the turmoil in the Englischer Garden. Welsh told him everything that he knew to the best of his ability. The Captain explained to Welsh how the BND had intercepted telephone calls and traced the telephone to the tavern in the small village. Explaining to Welsh how the BND operated was like Welsh telling the Captain about MI-6. Both men were familiar with the intelligence agencies of each other's country.

While they were talking, the tattooed man's cellular telephone rang. Welsh had removed the telephone from the tavern. Welsh handed the telephone to Captain Raeder who carried on a conversation in German, trying to disguise his voice as much as possible. When the conversation was over, he turned to Welsh.

"That was Mr. Hentsch. He wanted to know if the three Americans were dead. I told him that they were. He outlined the plan for the imposter to go to the bank and remove the contents from the lock box. He is to trade the cash for a cashier's check Hentsch has arranged with the bank for a cashier's check to be cut in the morning. He knows the amount of the check from the inventory. The check is payable to the Estate of Helga Brandenberg. Hentsch has forged court papers which show him to be the representative of the estate. He will open an estate account at a bank in Zurich and draw on the funds at a later date.

"The imposter will then catch a flight to Zurich and deliver the contents of the box to Hentsch. He will carry as many of the bonds as he can on his person. The rest of the bonds are to be packed in a carry-on bag and brief case. Magazines and newspapers are to be mixed with the bonds. He knows the amount from the inventory. He promised that his associates would receive a sizable bonus for jobs well done. Hentsch is feeling pretty smug. He should not brag in such detail," the Captain said.

"Herr Dellifield has had a rough go of it. He will have to go to the bank and then meet Hentsch in Zurich. I hope he is up to the task. Will he need to return to Germany?" Welsh asked.

"I am sure that there will be an inquiry. The two imposters will have to answer for their part in the crimes. Herr Dellifield will need to return to Germany soon to finish his work on the estate. I have checked with the hospital and Dr. Grueber is responding to treatment. He will have recovery time, but his wife is a capable doctor. In time, he will resume his practice," the Captain responded.

"What will you need from Mr. McCoy and Miss Paige?" Welsh asked.

The Captain responded, "I will need their statements. They will likewise have to return to Germany, if they want to see the imposters prosecuted. There may be others involved in this matter. The tavern owner will have to answer for his actions. He may be the key to finding terrorists organizations in the city and elsewhere. For now, I think Herr Dellifield should get some rest. He has a busy day ahead of him."

Lyman Welsh went out of the Captain's office and tried to explain the situation to the group. Dellifield was coming around. His heart was still out of sync, but it was beating much more slowly.

"Mr. Welsh, I thank you for all your help. I am sorry we had to meet under such circumstances. I would be much obliged if you had a telephone I could use. I need to call my wife," Dellifield said.

"Certainly, this telephone is somewhat tricky to use. Let me dial the number for you," Welsh said. Welsh dialed the number given to him by Dellifield. A woman answered and Welsh handed the telephone to Dellifield. Only one side of the conversation was heard.

"Hi, sweetheart, it's me."

"Yes, I know you have been worried about me. I am fine."

"I will tell you all about it when I get home."

"I will be there without fail. I may be too late to go to the party from home with you. I will meet you there before you are introduced."

"Yes. I love you too. Goodbye."

Dellifield was now ready to go to his hotel, take a shower and go to bed. Welsh told him exactly what the plan was for the next morning and his meeting with Hentsch in Zurich.

"One more thing, you will have to wear the imposter's suit. Hentsch will expect to see you in the clothes he furnished," Welsh said.

"My God, man! You must be kidding! The man has been in the rain. He may have urinated in his pants or worse when he was captured. That is too much to ask," Dellifield said.

"I will take you to the hotel. I will get the clothes and have the hotel clean them overnight. This is important. We do not want Hentsch to run. You are going to be the imposter of the imposter. He needs to be caught red-handed. He will be arrested," Welsh said.

"Very well, but you are asking a lot," Dellifield said.

"I want my jacket back from that bitch. She can have the rest of the clothes. I want to leave now. I am tired of being half naked," Zelda-Corrine said.

"I will take you and Akard to your hotel, after we drop off Mr. Dellifield. I will get your jacket and the suit and tie the imposter was wearing," Welsh said.

Welsh had driven his rent car from the tavern. He got their various belongings, took Dellifield to his hotel and arranged for the suit to be cleaned. He then took Akard and Zelda-Corrine to their hotel.

Dellifield took a shower and went to bed. He slept soundly. Akard and Zelda-Corrine went to their hotel. Lyman Welsh said that he would pick up his coat in the morning.

Akard and Zelda-Corrine went into their room. Each breathed a sigh of relief.

"Akard, I want a hot bath. Then I want a back rub. I want you to hold me close, but I cannot make love tonight. I have been through too much, and I am going to sleep late. We said our good-byes to Conrad. His job is not finished, but ours is for the time being. I have also thought about going home. I came here to see Neuschwanstein and, by God I have earned the right to see it," Zelda-Corrine said.

"I am your fairy godfather and I will grant your wishes. I will change the plane reservations in the morning. We can shop for a new outfit tomorrow. The next few days are for a good time. By the way, I love you more than I can ever say. When they took you, I died inside," Akard said.

"I know. I felt the same way when we could not reach you in the Englischer Garden. I could not help crying when I saw you. One other thing, from now on you are going to show Mr. Dellifield proper respect. He saved my life. He could have lost his helping me. I am ready to get rid of this damned shirt and take a bath."

"Yes, ma'am."

In Zurich, Hentsch was finishing off a glass of port and smoking a

Havana cigar. In about twelve hours he would be rich. He would send a token amount to his confederates and keep the rest. He would get the money made payable to the estate and open an account in Zurich. The bonds would be cashed and the proceeds wired to an affiliate bank in South America. Hentsch was a banker. He knew just what to do.

It had been a good run, not as good as he had expected. He had counted on getting Helga's entire estate. She had given him a lot of money and some of it he had used to spew hate venom. He had used her money to acquire a following of true believers who would follow the man named "Herman" with blind obedience. He had made contacts with hate groups in the United States and had sent them money when it suited his purposes. It also gave him credibility with Helga. It was a shame to leave a new Mercedes at the Airport in Munich, but he owed about what it was worth. His bank had financed the purchase.

He looked at his plane tickets and smiled. He finished his drink, put out his cigar and then turned his attention to the hooker who was sitting on the side of his bed.

# Chapter Thirty-One

*T*he next morning found Zelda-Corrine sleeping in Akard's arms. They had fallen asleep completely exhausted, both physically and mentally. It would be ten o'clock before they awakened. On the other hand, Conrad Dellifield was up and packed by seven thirty. He was standing in his underwear when Lyman Welsh knocked at his door. Dellifield opened the door. Standing there was Welsh, with a suit and tie freshly cleaned and pressed. Welsh was pushing a cart that had a hearty breakfast on it.

Dellifield ate the breakfast like a freed prisoner-of-war. Normally, Dellifield displayed impeccable manners. This morning, however, he wolfed the food down and slurped the coffee. While he ate, Welsh went over the game plan. Dellifield would go to the bank as soon as it opened. He would take a carry-on bag and a briefcase with him. He would pretend to fill them with the contents of the box, but would leave the assets in the box until his return trip to Munich. The suitcase and the briefcase were to be filled with cut up newspapers. Dellifield would go directly from the bank to the airport. His own luggage would already be checked. On arrival in Zurich, he will meet Hentsch at the baggage claim and give him the bag and briefcase. Hentsch would then be arrested.

"Herr Hentsch has rather messed his knickers," Lyman Welsh said. "His confederates sang like canaries during the night. The two actors gave all the details of their complicity in the crimes. The man from Turkey blamed everything on Hentsch when he discovered that he was being used and that Hentsch had planned all along to take the money for himself. The tavern owner wanted no part of attempted murder and kidnapping. He blamed Hentsch for everything. The tavern owner will not get off that easily, though."

"Hentsch reminds me of Uriah Heep out of Dickens. I am going to enjoy seeing his face in Zurich. Give me that damned suit. I guarantee I am changing clothes in Zurich," Dellifield said.

Dellifield changed into the ill-fitting double-breasted suit. He wore a plain white shirt and the tie that the imposter had been wearing. Dellifield checked out of his hotel and Welsh drove him to the bank. Welsh furnished him with the rolling bag and briefcase that Hentsch had given to the actor. The police had recovered them and given them to Welsh. Dellifield went into the bank and presented his key. He was shown into the safety deposit box area. The attendant used her key and Dellifield's key to open the box.

Dellifield took the box into a small room and closed the door. He took the amount of time he felt necessary to empty the box and then replaced the box. He went through the charade in case Hentsch called anyone at the bank to check on the imposter's actions. He called the attendant and the box was locked again. Dellifield then left the lock box area with the bag and carrying the briefcase. He went to a teller and told her he would no longer need the cashier's check. If Hentsch called about the check, the teller was instructed to tell him the check had been issued.

Welsh picked Dellifield up at the bank and drove him to the airport. In route Dellifield, carefully filled the bag and the briefcase with the cut-up paper that Welsh had furnished for that purpose. On the way he and Welsh discussed Dellifield's ordeal.

"You know, old boy, you do not look too much worse for wear. I can see some slight bruising on your face. Perhaps it will go away before your gala tonight. It should be dark enough that you won't attract too much attention. In addition, no one will be paying any attention to you anyway," Welsh said.

"I guess it is fine now to make light of the situation. The facts are that a young woman was almost raped and murdered. I beat a man almost to death. The terrible thing was that I almost enjoyed it. I was paying back every bully I had known in my life. Then Miss Paige shot the man. I doubt that it was necessary. I think the beating I gave him would have killed him anyway. I am sure that I will have dreams about it as long as I live," Dellifield said.

"In my line of work, killing becomes routine. I suppose that I can justify what I do. I rarely try anymore. Someday, I will have to give this life up for something more sedate. I do not look forward to that day. Try to forget what happened. There are times when situations demand that ordinary men become extraordinary. Anyone faced with the same circumstances would have acted in the same manner," Welsh opined.

"Perhaps, you are right. I became a lawyer because I believe in the rule of law. Without law we have no civilization. The people who kidnapped me hate the law. They only respect violence for the sake of violence. The rage I showed toward the dead man took me away from the civilized person I have always believed myself to be. I hope to return to my old self as soon as possible," Dellifield said.

"You will. Your respect for the law is too ingrained for you to lose it over this one incident," Welsh said.

"I pray that you are right," Dellifield answered.

Welsh reached terminal two at the Munich airport. He summoned a porter to help Dellifield with his luggage. Dellifield had his two carry-on bags. Welsh had persuaded him that he would have to wear the imposter's clothes all the way back to Dallas. It would not do for Hentsch to see Dellifield with clothes draped over his arm.

"Safe trip old boy. Put on a jolly good show, as we British say," Welsh said.

"Goodbye, Lyman. Thank you for the encouragement. I can take it from here."

Dellifield cleared security and boarded the plane for Zurich. Even though it was only a thirty-five minute flight, he took his seat in the First Class section. He had some orange juice and relished the knowledge that his heart was back in sync.

Hentsch rolled over and saw that the hooker was still in his bed. He checked his wallet and determined that nothing was missing. The woman was good looking, in a cheap sort of way. She was very talented in the way she satisfied his desires. Hentsch though this was only a portent of things to come. He would be in South America. He had heard the women there were hot. He would have the money to have any woman he wanted. The thought of the South American women aroused him again. The woman in his bed took care of his needs.

This was going to be a great day for Hentsch. His physical needs had been more than adequately cared for. He tipped the hooker in an appreciative manner. She left the room and Hentsch had breakfast brought to his room. After eating, he checked his passport and airline tickets. He was scheduled to leave Zurich the next day. He had banking matters to take care of today. He might even have the same hooker come back for one more night. He was young. He could stand up to the task. He dressed and hired a taxi to take him to the airport.

Conrad Dellifield's plane landed about the same time Hentsch reached the airport. Dellifield was seated in the small first class section of the Swiss Air plane. He was one of the first passengers off the plane. He headed toward the baggage claim area. Hentsch was in route to the same place. Dellifield saw Hentsch before Hentsch saw him. He walked toward the baggage carousel. Hentsch finally saw Dellifield and walked his way. Dellifield faced the carousel with his back toward the direction from which Hentsch was approaching.

Hentsch stood beside Dellifield and said, "Haben Sie das Geld?"

"Nicht heute Arschloch. That means not today asshole," Dellifield answered.

"Dellifield!" Hentsch said.

Dellifield turned around and said, "Surprise! Herr Hentsch, you are in one shit load of trouble, to coin a Texas phrase. These bags are full of newspaper. Those two men in the blue jumpsuits, boots and sub-machine guns are about to arrest your young ass. The sad thing is, you are probably a pretty good banker. You just used your talents the wrong way."

"What happened to my men?" Hentsch asked.

"Well, son, I am sorry to tell you that two of them are dead. The rest of your pals are being held by the police," Dellifield answered.

"Damn you, Dellifield. Damn your friends that you brought with you," Hentsch said.

"That is not a very neighborly thing to say. If you ever get out of prison, you will have to learn some manners if you want to visit us in Dallas. I think these two gentlemen here want to take you away. Nice visiting with you." The two policemen took Hentsch away. He never said goodbye to Dellifield. Before the police left, Dellifield gave them the two bags filled with newspaper. Somewhere along the line, they might be needed as evidence.

Dellifield made his way to the shopping area of the airport. He never intended to wear the imposter' suit to Dallas. He bought a pair a casual slacks and silk jacket. He went up to the Commander's Club and took off the suit and tie. He changed into his new clothes. He folded the old suit and put it in the shopping bag that had held his new clothes. He would mail the suit and tie back to the police in Munich to be used as evidence. He put the plastic bottle containing a day's dose of medicine in his pant's pocket. He stayed in the Commander's Club until time to board the plane to Dallas. Before he left the club, he called his wife and assured her he would be home in time for the dinner and dance.

# Chapter Thirty-Two

*Zelda-Corrine rolled over on top of Akard, who was still sleeping.* She gently blew on his face until he awakened.

"Akard, do you ever get over killing someone?" she asked.

"That is one hell of a question to wake up to."

"I'm sorry, but things are just now sinking in. I killed a man."

"No, you did not. Dellifield had already killed him. You just put him out of his misery."

"You know, I guess neither Conrad nor I will ever know who really killed that man."

"That's good. Both of you can feel guilty from now on."

"It is not a matter of guilt. He deserved to die. That is, if anyone deserves to die."

"You need to get your mind off of things. We will go shopping."

"Yea! I can do that. Before we do that, I need something more."

"Let me guess."

There was nothing to guess about. Zelda-Corrine reached down and guided Akard inside of her. Their lovemaking was not rushed. It was not athletic. It was sweet and meaningful. When they had finished making love, they showered, dressed and went to breakfast. They left Lyman Welsh's coat at the front desk with instructions to thank him for the use of the coat. After breakfast, as promised, they went shopping. Clothes were very expensive. Zelda-Corrine bypassed the small shops and went to a large department store. The rain had stopped and she wanted something bright and spring like. After all, it was May Day.

The terrible rain of the day before had given way to bright sunshine. Akard and Zelda-Corrine went over to the Englischer Garden. The dastardly scene of the night before was no longer present. The two of them walked hand in hand along the pathway until they got near the Rumford Memorial. Police had the area roped off and were looking the area over carefully.

"To the rear, March," Akard told Zelda-Corrine as he turned her around. "I have no desire to revisit the scene from last night. I will have a chance to relive it enough, if we have to return for trials."

"Akard, I want to go to the hospital and check on Dr. Grueber," Zelda-Corrine said.

"Why?"

"Because, he was the first victim of this violence. You, me and Conrad are all physically fine. Time will tell how we fare mentally. I just want to see how he is doing."

Akard felt she was right and the two of them took a taxi to the hospital. They checked at the desk and found out that Grueber was still in intensive care. They asked if his wife was available. In a short time, Grueber's wife, the other Dr. Grueber, came out to meet them.

"We wanted to see how your husband was doing," Zelda-Corrine said.

"The swelling in his brain is much better. I will probably have him moved to his own room tomorrow. I have every hope that he will fully recover. The police came here last night and visited with me briefly. I understand that the men who did this to my husband are now dead," the doctor said.

"That is true," Akard said.

"They also told me that the two of you had narrow escapes yourself. I am glad that you are unharmed. I must get back to my husband," the doctor said.

"Tell him to get well. Dr. Dellifield will need his help to finish the work here," Akard said.

"I shall. Goodbye," the doctor said.

"I feel much better now," Zelda-Corrine said. "Now I am ready to have fun. I want to book a tour to Neushwanstein in the morning. Tonight, I want to drink beer and listen to an oom-pa-pa band."

"That you shall, my dear," Akard said. And that they did.

That evening Akard and Zelda-Corrine partied. The plane carrying Dellifield back to Dallas was delayed because of storms in the Dallas area. Hattie Dellifield resolved herself to the fact that she was going to spend her special night alone. She needed to be at the hotel by 6:00 for the reception and the dinner started at 7:30.

Dellifield looked at his watch constantly. He very seldom was asked by his wife to do something special for her. This night was to be one of the highlights of her life. She had worked countless hours to help beautify Dallas. This night was to be her reward.

"You seem to be obsessed with the time," the flight attendant in the first class section said.

"I am. It is terribly important that I be at a dinner tonight at 7:30," Dellifield answered.

"The Captain just let us know that the weather has cleared in Dallas and that we should land at 6:45."

"I need a telephone, badly," Dellifield said

"You cannot use a cell phone, but you can use the one in the back of the seat in front of you. Just use your credit card," the flight attendant said.

Dellifield called his long-suffering secretary, Gwendolyn. He asked her to go by his house. She had worked for him for twenty years. Her work was her life. Usually she was home alone on Saturday night. He gave her the code to get in the gate that granted access to the driveway to his house. He told her where his tuxedo was in the closet. He asked for a shirt that had a front that required no studs. He told her which drawers held his cuff links, tie and cummerbund, and black socks. He asked her to bring his black patent formal shoes, and to arrange to meet him at the baggage claim. It was the second time in one day that he had met someone in that area, he mused to himself.

She agreed to arrange for a limo to pick him up at the airport. He would give her the baggage claim checks and she would bring the luggage back to his house. Dellifield would give her a night at the Mansion for her and a friend for her trouble.

"I could not help but overhear your conversation," the flight attendant said. "You have a bruise on the side of your face. You should not be seen in public like that."

"What can I do?" Dellifield asked

"Step inside the galley area. I can put some of my makeup over the bruise and it will not show," she said.

Dellifield was humiliated, but he agreed. The flight attendant skillfully applied the makeup to Dellifield's face. When she was finished, the bruise no longer was visible. He thanked her and went back to his seat trying to hide his face as much as possible.

The plane landed and Gwendolyn met Dellifield as planned. She gave him his attire. A limo was waiting. Dellifield thanked Gwendolyn profusely and told her she would be rewarded.

"It's just part of my job," Gwendolyn said, trying not to show her affection for Dellifield.

Dellifield dressed in the limo. He reached the hotel at 7:28. He ran to the grand ballroom. The head table was being introduced. One by one, the officers were introduced. Dellifield was at a dead run when he saw that all officers but his wife had made their way to the head table. Nettie Dellifield now had the spotlight on her. She was wearing a beautiful green dress. Her diamond earrings were sparkling in the spotlight. She seemed to have tears in her eyes.

"And now, ladies and gentlemen, let's give a big Dallas welcome for Mrs. Conrad Dellifield IV, the President of this organization. She is escorted by her husband, Conrad Dellifield IV," a voice rang out over the ballroom.

Nettie Dellifield lifted her chin and prepared herself for the humiliation of walking in alone. She was not alone, however, because as she took that first step into the limelight, Conrad Dellifield had locked her arm around his. They walked into the room receiving a standing ovation from the crowd. There were no longer tears in Nettie's eyes. She was beaming and waving to the crowd with her free arm. At her side was Conrad Dellifield IV. He had not a hair out of place. He was in his element.

"You look beautiful, my dear," he said.

"I could just kill you," she said.

"Someone has already tried that."

"What?"

"I will tell you later. Tonight is your night and I love you."

"I love you, too, Connie."

Dellifield kissed his wife on the cheek. The crowd applauded louder.

Before the evening was over in Dallas it was the next morning in Munich. Akard and Zelda-Corrine had booked a tour to Nueschwanstein Castle. Before they left the hotel, they picked up an envelope that had been left for them by Lyman Welsh. Inside the envelope was a letter that explained that Akard and Zelda-Corrine would probably be called back to Munich for trials. That was particularly true in the case of Hentsch. Welsh said in the letter that he would not be available to testify because, as far as Germany was concerned, he did not exist.

Nueschwanstein Castle was the brainchild of Ludwig II of Bavaria. He dragged Bavaria into financial ruin by building one country house after the other. This castle was his dream of an old German castle. His subjects believed he was insane. He drowned in the Stamberger See under mysterious circumstances at age 42.

The heavy rains and now the brilliant sunshine had caused the snow in the fields to melt. Wild flowers were beginning to bloom. It was the type of day that Zelda-Corrine had dreamt about. During the bus ride to the castle she had locked her arms around Akard's left arm. She sat by the window of the bus and enjoyed each magnificent view. The snow-capped mountains glittered in the sunlight. She pushed out of her mind the thoughts that had haunted her about the kidnapping and the tattooed man standing over her with lust and hate in his eyes. It would take a lot of days like this day to erase that memory, but she was young and had a lot of days left.

The bus reached the castle. Akard and Zelda-Corrine toured the castle and the grounds.

"This is what I wanted to see, Akard. I love every moment of this. I wish we could stay here forever," Zelda-Corrine said.

"I wish we could, too. I want to spend the rest of my life making you happy. I want to grow old with you. When we are old, we can buy a Buick. In fact, I want you to marry me," Akard said.

Zelda-Corrine looked deeply into Akard's eyes. "Akard, I love you. I really do. I am not sure, in light of what I have been through, I can think clearly now. If there were a preacher here at this very moment, I would probably say yes. What I will say is not 'yes' or 'no.' but a very strong 'maybe.'"

"That is good enough for me. Enjoy this moment. Perhaps in time, that strong 'maybe' will turn into a 'yes,'" he said holding her close.

"Perhaps it will," she said losing herself in his arms. "But if we do ever get married, You can drive the Buick. I want a Mercedes."

# Epilogue

*William Arrington sat in his room with the window drapes drawn* shut. In the dim light of his apartment, he stared at the two wooden boxes sitting on the coffee table in front of his chair. The boxes contained the ashes of his best friends, Jacob and Bernie. It had been his idea to kill those people who had gone unpunished for their wrongs. It seemed like such a good idea at the time. As a result, eight people had lost their lives. Bernie and Jacob would have died anyway. Monroe and Goose would have probably been caught and executed. Helga and Armando might have lived out their lives. He never met and would never know of the tattooed man and Adolph.

The police would never connect the dots. He would never be linked with all these deaths. He would never know that Hentsch and his grandiose plans had failed. True, a lot of evil had been removed from the earth. On the other hand, four decent people had been put in harm's way. Akard, Zelda-Corrine and Dellifield escaped with their lives. Grueber would recover. Does vengeance belong solely to the Lord? That was a question between William Arrington and his maker. With his failing health, William Arrington would soon know. He would have to answer for his role in the cast of the Deadly Dying.

Printed in the United States
89767LV00004B/1-123/A